Dead Man Talking

by

Michelle Witvliet

Medium Rare

Dead Man Talking

Cover Art by *Diana Carlile*

The Wild Rose Press, Inc.
PO Box 708
Adams Basin, NY 14410-0708
Visit us at www.thewildrosepress.com

Publishing History
First Paranormal Mainstream Mystery Edition, 2013
Print ISBN 978-1-62830-131-1
Digital ISBN 978-1-62830-132-8

Medium Rare, Book 1
Published in the United States of America

Dedication

To Marv,
who walks on the other side
but lives in my heart forever

Chapter One

Close proximity to dead bodies made me nervous, and I tried to avoid them with the same aversion as I do men projecting serious intentions. So what the heck was I doing traipsing through Mount Pleasant Cemetery toting a bunch of carnations at dusk on a Friday in late November? Just the thought of what lay six feet beneath my cherry red Wellingtons left me craving a big ol' dose of caffeine to calm me down.

With each cautious step, a particularly mushy stretch of ground made sickening, sucky noises at the soles of my boots. Mount Pleasant indeed. This is northwest Indiana. The sand dunes are the closest thing to a mount of anything around these parts. As for the pleasant part, well, it's a cemetery, 'nuff said. But I suppose Mount Pleasant looked better over the entrance than Headstone Acres.

A gust of frigid air straight out of Canada whooshed up my trench coat like the unexpected blast from the funhouse at St. Sebastian's annual carnival. I raised the collar of my Burberry knockoff, regrettably sans zip-in fleece lining, and headed for, from what I could tell, the only fresh grave. I'm talking buried-just-this-morning fresh so there's no headstone, but I know who's down there without checking the little placard stuck in the ground to mark the man's final resting place. We're sort of friends.

I came to a stumbling halt when my boot toe butted against the pile of unadorned dirt. The lighting at Mount Pleasant left much to be desired. It was darker out there than a witch's heart, and I cast a glance at the supplied lighting located half a block away near the gated entrance, which wasn't much help from where I was standing. Why I didn't bring a flashlight is not a question I cared to address while standing there in the descending darkness.

Plus, I really hated this time of year. From October through March there's a nasty gray nothingness that settles over everything and doesn't lift until the first daffodils pop their pretty yellow heads in the spring. If it wasn't for the upcoming holidays, I could easily climb under the covers and not stick my not-always-so-pretty curly red head out until the lilacs were in full bloom.

"Well, here I am, Murray—just like I promised." I didn't expect an answer. Murray wasn't much of a talker when we were together, so I wasn't all that surprised he didn't have anything to say now. I tossed the cellophane-wrapped bouquet in the general direction of where I figured the headstone would eventually go. There wasn't much else for me to say. Like so many before him, I'd known Murray briefly, but when he'd begged me to check out his final resting place, I'd agreed because it's almost practically impossible for me to refuse any man's last request.

Another gust of wind slammed against my back and sent piles of leaves swirling across the ground. That's it. It was time to go.

As I turned to leave, I caught the shadowy flicker of movement out of the corner of my eye and whirled around to see who or what was there. Shivering where I stood, I stared into the intelligent beady black eyes of an abnormally large crow perched on the curved top of a granite headstone.

"Shit," I muttered as we cautiously considered one another.

The appearance of a solitary crow did not bode well. The only thing worse would be if he brought friends. The big bird cawed and bobbed his shiny black head with a sharp-eyed wink, as if confirming my ominous thoughts.

"You wouldn't happen to be here because of Murray, would you?"

He shook his shiny, black head at my foolish question.

"Yeah, didn't think so," I said as another expectant chill coursed through me. "You know, Wendell, I'm not in any mood to deal with you right now so I'd appreciate you coming back some other time." Then again, when I was ever ready to deal with Wendell or the message he carried? I accepted his regular appearances and the meaning behind them because I didn't have any control over his actions or what followed.

Having delivered his message, however ambiguous, Wendell spread his wings and took off straight toward me, veering at the last second to avoid collision with his usual spot-on accuracy. I ducked out of sheer self-preservation in spite of his stellar record and spun to follow his line of flight. He swooped and soared with Blue Angel precision before joining a neat row of carbon copies perched on the peak of a nearby rooftop, their silhouettes barely visible against the deepening sky.

Eight crows. Double shit. Here I was surrounded by death, and Wendell had to choose that moment to announce I could soon expect more of the same.

I counted the line of crows twice out of habit, the whole time wondering how and when this latest portent would manifest itself. Crow augury wasn't an exact science, but it was pretty darn close when it came to foretelling my immediate future.

I was halfway back to my car when I heard another noise behind me. This one sounded decidedly more human, or at least was once human. Is it any wonder why I detested cemeteries? Nobody dislikes the convergence of the living and the dead more than me.

"You bitch, I hate you. You ruined my father's life."

"Yeah, like I've never heard that before." I sighed dramatically, turning in the nick of time to find Murray Johnson's daughter charging toward me with a full head of steam and wielding a—Holy hell! Was that a sword? And who would have guessed a woman of her queen-sized proportions and age, in a dark cemetery, no less, could move with such amazing speed and agility? She was on me before I could think about dodging her attack.

The best I could do was duck and deflect the blow. When it made contact, I was surprised it didn't hurt like I'd anticipated. It didn't hurt at all, actually, which really caught me off-guard. The hollow *thwack* sounded a lot like an empty paper towel tube bouncing off my arm as an eerie green glow radiated up its shaft before collapsing section by section into itself.

Well hell, this pushing seventy, big-boned crazy woman had attacked me with nothing more than a toy light saber, and not even a quality one.

"Give me that…" I snatched it out of her hand and tossed it aside. It hit a hulking granite monument and busted into a dozen plus pieces. Yep, dollar store variety was my guess.

"What are you doing here, Sue? You told me you were going straight home after the funeral."

"My crystal ball told me there were bad spirits here."

Judging from the stench of cheap booze emanating from Sue, the only bad spirits around here were inside her, and I guessed her crystal ball was more in the shape of a long-necked fifth.

"My father will never rest in peace until I neutralize the spirits and vanquish them from this place."

"Have you tried a pot of strong black coffee?"

My suggestion went unnoticed. Sue was too busy picking up the pieces of her shattered spirit neutralizer, otherwise known as cheap light saber. "Now you've broken my only means of doing that. My father will never rest in peace now and I'm doomed to live with my failure." She buried her face in her hands and began to boo-hoo.

Yeah, well, good luck with that, Sue Johnson. I stopped letting tears sway me since I lived with two older sisters who turned on the waterworks for everything from a broken nail to a broken condom. "How does attacking me enter into this ritual of yours?" I really wanted to know.

"You brought them here in the first place. They follow you everywhere." She'd said it so matter-of-factly, I found myself looking around to see if I could spot one. It was time for me to get the heck out of there.

"Look, Sue, I want to reimburse you so you can get yourself another one of those spirit thingies." I dug into my purse, pulled out a twenty, and stuffed it into her coat pocket. That ought to be enough to replace the one I broke plus a couple spares. "I'll even drive you to the store and bring you back so you can finish your vanquishing ceremony."

She immediately dug the money out, her eyes lighting up when she saw the denomination. "You don't have to do that," she said, crushing the bill in her fist. "I know exactly where to go to get another one."

I'm sure she did. There was a liquor store in a strip mall around the corner and a Daily Dollar Deals two doors down—one stop shopping at its finest for Sue Johnson.

Leaving Sue to do whatever she had to do, I trudged back to my car and climbed in, knowing there was nothing I could do about Sue or Wendell and his friends, but there was something I could do to chase away this sense of foreboding gnawing at me like cramps. I dropped the gearshift into drive and pointed my car toward Nirvana, otherwise known as Starbucks.

****

With a cup of steaming, caffeinated bliss warming my hand and working its soothing magic, I turned my sights toward Briar Cliff Estates. For me, there's nothing like sucking on a super-charged pumpkin spiced latte while cruising past mega-buck mansions to exorcise my own brand of evil spirits.

The fact that the most exclusive neighborhood in the region was a gated community didn't stop me. It barely slowed me down. The thirty-something guard at the gatehouse took the large coffee with extra cream and two sugars I extended and waved me on through. It's good to have slow-pitch buddies in high places, or at least in the right ones.

"Thanks, Bill," I said as I raised my window and cruised into a world I knew only from the outside.

It was the big blue OPEN HOUSE sign that made me slam on the brakes and back up to make sure my eyes weren't playing tricks on me. Even staring me right in the face, I couldn't believe this stroke of unprecedented luck. Things like this just didn't happen. Folks in this snooty neighborhood weren't inclined to open their doors to people they knew, much less total strangers.

Then again, how many qualified buyers could there be for a house in this price bracket? One in a bazillion, maybe? That was accountant-speak for a lot. This open house was undoubtedly the homeowner's way of generating maximum exposure in a depressed market.

As sure as a shot of main-lined adrenaline, I felt my rationalization skills kicking into maximum overdrive. Danny's told me more than once I could rationalize my way into or out of anything if I wanted it badly enough. Guess he was right. Danny was right about a lot of things, and occasionally I was woman enough to admit it. One of these days I might even get around to telling him as much.

All that aside, regardless of the seller's reasons for the sign, since I didn't travel in the same social circles, my chances of ever seeing the inside of one of these mansions any other way were, in the words of my daddy, as likely as a fox getting welcomed into the henhouse. So, I asked myself, who was I to pass up this once in a lifetime opportunity to see how the other one-tenth of one-percent of the chickens lived?

I parked across the street and locked all the doors with the keyless remote, hitting the lock button a couple extra times to favor the side of caution. Vehicles without the Briar Cliff Estates medallion displayed on the windshield, or at the very least a visitor placard dangling from the rearview mirror, were rumored to vanish from these streets with more frequency than ships in the Bermuda Triangle. Just urban legends, I was sure, but I was willing to risk the slim chance that they weren't for a peek inside that fabulous house. Just in case, I pressed my keyless remote a couple of extra times as I boldly strolled up the curved driveway like I owned not only the place but the entire block.

My grandma taught me a long time ago the key to going places where you don't belong is act like you belong where you're going. As I tried the doorknob, in spite of Grandma's lesson, I kept an ear out for snarling Dobermans just the same.

Well what do you know, it wasn't locked. No guard dogs, no audible alarms, no S.W.A.T. team rappelling from the roof…That sure seemed like an all-systems-go to me. I did one last quick glance around before I reached the point of no return.

Oh, who was I kidding? I'd reached that point the second I spotted the sign.

"Hellooo," I called as I poked my head into the foyer. I heard scraping and a couple of muffled thumps, the hurried patter of footsteps, and then nothing but silence.

"Hello?" I said again. "I'm Jen Flagg. I saw the sign out front. I've come to look at the house." More silence.

The hairs on my neck prickled a little and sent a wary, though no less disappointed, shiver down my spine. "If this is a bad time, I can come back."

"No, no, please come in," a pleasant voice invited just as I was about to retreat. "Your timing is perfect."

He sounded friendly enough, and eager, of course. I would imagine I'd sound eager and friendly too if I was the Realtor selling this place. His cheery demeanor was all it took to chase away my earlier moment of apprehension.

"I'm in the kitchen, straight down the main hall."

That sounded promising. The kitchen probably meant there'd be coffee, and maybe even cookies. The enticement of refreshments propelled me forward.

Oh man, I was Alice seeing Wonderland for the first time. I stepped through the looking glass, also known as the front door, and stared at a sweeping staircase straight out of *Gone with the Wind*. I counted twenty-seven. That's how many steps there were.

I was all about the numbers, but what was Rhett thinking hauling Scarlett all the way up that huge flight of stairs just to have his way with her when he could have just as easily nailed her on the dining room table and be done with it? The age of chivalry might not have been dead way back then, but the men sure as hell had to be exhausted from toting their women around like that.

My gaze traveled upward and settled on the dazzling crystal chandelier high over my head. How did one clean something suspended twenty plus feet in the air? The process escaped me. Now that I thought about it, there were a lot of things I wasn't all that familiar with cleaning. Behind and under the stove and refrigerator back at my condo immediately came to mind.

"What in the hell is takin' you so long? Are you comin', or what?"

Whoa. That was so not the professional tone of an eager-to-please real estate agent itching to get his hands on the hefty commission this place was sure to bring. Not that I was the person to bring it.

"Are you talking to me?" I asked, heading for the sound of his voice. I had to at least consider the possibility the questions he posed weren't directed at me.

He cleared up any misconception when he replied, "Yeah, I'm talkin' to you. You see anybody else around I could be talkin' to?"

His tone was clipped, and his accent was unmistakably Brooklyn Italian. I know Brooklyn Italian when I hear it. My college roommate, Luciana Valentino, was a fifth generation Brooklynite.

A cold draft swept down the corridor, bringing with it a funky smell that reminded me of the Dumpster behind my condo the day before pickup in the middle of July.

I later realized a prudent person would have found the unfolding scene a little suspicious and left the premises. Not me. I moved forward with a combination of inborn caution and rampant curiosity, heavy on the latter.

I did, however, wind my purse strap around my

fingers and tightened my grip in preparation to roundhouse anyone stupid enough to catch me by surprise. Any woman with a decent-sized handbag loaded with life's everyday necessities was always armed and dangerous. I usually kept a few rolls of quarters and sometimes a .22 revolver in the bottom for additional heft, but I'd just used up my emergency ballast on a couple of weeks' worth of laundry and the gun, well, let's just say I didn't presently have it with me for extenuating circumstances I'd rather not go into right now.

The moment I passed through the doorway, I discovered the source of the smell. Horrified, I stumbled back, my knees buckled, and I slid slowly down the doorframe to the floor.

The Brooklyn Italian was dead.

I know dead when I hear it, too, because they sometimes talk to me.

Chapter Two

"What happened?" asked the first person to arrive on the scene, which in itself came as more of a surprise to me than finding the dead guy. I've known Andrew Ramos for more years than I cared to count, almost as far back as I can remember, and from what I've heard from a few of his co-workers, Andy wasn't known for being the quickest responder on the Briar Cliff Estates security staff.

Now that I thought about it, he wasn't known for being the quickest anything—on the job or anywhere else for that matter. Okay, in all fairness, he was always first to belly up to the buffet, which explained the way the buttons strained on his uniform shirt. I seriously doubted he could run if his butt was on fire, and he needed the extra momentum to put out the flames. Of course, I could be wrong. I was willing to test my theory by striking the first match.

All right, I admit it. I don't like Andy, never have, and it goes back long before my dad married the widow next door, also known as Andy's mother, when I was eight and Andy was twelve.

Over the years, the animosity has remained mutual. Thank God. I count on the fact he doesn't like me any more than I like him. I do what I can to stay out of his way, and he does likewise. But since he's my dad's stepson as well as a good friend of my brother Rob, it tends to complicate what should have been an easy thing to do under normal circumstances in a city the size of Lake Ridge. As anyone can imagine, it makes for interesting family get-togethers.

Andy flipped open a generic spiral-topped notepad and withdrew the cheap pen sticking out of his vest pocket. The cap was gnawed ragged and had bright orangey clumps of what I could only guess were either masticated carrots or cheese puffs clinging to the frayed end. That was just plain wrong. But knowing Andy like I did, my money was on the cheese puffs.

"You want to tell me what you were doing here, Flagg?"

"Well… I was driving by and saw the open house sign out front. The door was open so I—"

"Excuse me," he interrupted. "Sign? What sign? You couldn't have seen a sign. Not in this neighborhood. The homeowners' association doesn't allow yard signs." Ramos pushed aside the drape and glanced out the bay window to check anyway. More so to cover his own big butt, I imagined, since a sign in the yard would mean he and his crack team weren't doing their job.

"There was an open house sign on the front lawn," I stated, wondering if his blood sugar was dropping. Must be time for another donut, I decided as I jabbed the air with a finger in the direction of the yard. "It was big and blue with bright yellow and red graphics. Rothschild Realty, I think it said. You couldn't miss it."

Although judging from the blank look on his face he obviously had. "Sharp as ever," I said under my breath as the dead Italian moved through Ramos to peer out the window.

"There's no sign," the dead guy confirmed.

I knew enough to ignore him. What the hell did he know, anyway? I'd learned the hard way the recently deceased were not the most reliable sources of accurate information. A newly departed's sense of reality was more often than not a tad skewed.

"I don't know what you thought you saw, but there's no sign," Ramos insisted, echoing the dead guy's observation.

"Of course there's a sign," I snapped as I elbowed my way around him. "Why would I walk into a stranger's house otherwise?"

"That's what I'm trying to find out," Andy stated.

I waved my hand and pointed. "It's right there!"

Uh oh. I blinked and looked again. Where in the hell did it go?

"Huh. Well what do you know? No sign," the dead guy taunted.

This guy was riding a nerve, and with a great deal more attitude than any recently departed should possess, I might add.

"Shut up," I hissed under my breath.

"What did you say?" Ramos demanded as one hand moved to rest on the butt of his recently acquired holstered service revolver. Never let it be said the Briar Cliff Estates residents didn't take their security seriously. After a rash of break-ins clear on the other side of town, the homeowners elected to arm their security staff as an added precaution.

Oh yeah, wouldn't he love for me to give him a reason to use his new toy. "Nothing," I grumbled, glaring daggers at my deceased companion.

"So who's the dead guy?"

"I have no idea," I replied. "We were never formally introduced."

"The name's Antonio Barrera," the deceased whispered in my ear.

I was curious as to how a guy named Barrera came off sounding like a Brooklyn Italian in this part of Northwest Indiana.

"Antonio Barrera," I repeated, more to myself, at the same time wondering where I'd heard that name before. It sounded more familiar than I thought it should.

"Who?" Ramos questioned.

"The dead guy," I answered. "That's his name." The newspaper, I decided. I was sure it was something I'd read about a Barrera in the newspaper. Only what was it?

"I thought you said you didn't know him."

"I don't," I said. "Never saw him before today." That wasn't entirely true. I'd seen him someplace before, too. Again, the newspaper came to mind. There'd been an article and a photo, as I recalled. Aside from my occasional ability to talk to dead people, I have an uncanny memory for photographs and names. If I've seen it, I remember it in a vague, obscure kind of way. This peculiar ability is not to be confused with an eidetic or more commonly known photographic memory, which I do not have. I also know it serves no useful purpose other than driving me crazy, like now for example.

Andy's gaze narrowed. "What'd you do, go through his pockets?"

"Uh, that would be a big no." Touch a dead guy? I don't think so. All I've ever done was talk to them. Grandma Flagg never mentioned anything about touching when giving me the lowdown on dealing with the dead. Then again, I suddenly realized, I'd never had contact with the deceased's physical self before today, either. So, from the very beginning, this experience couldn't be classified as a typical contact for me.

"Then how'd you know his name?" Ramos questioned.

"He told me."

"He was still alive when you found him?"

"Uh, that would be an even bigger no. In case you didn't notice, the man's been fermenting for a while." How long exactly would be difficult to determine considering the open windows.

"Ugh," the dead guy groaned. "That's a visual I could have done without."

Andy stood there for a moment, looking at me with a…What exactly was that look? I was at a loss. With Andy it wasn't always easy to tell. I finally decided the expression was definitely bordering on perplexed, possibly combined with indigestion from his well-balanced cheese puff and/or carrot lunch.

"Oh no, no-no-no," he stammered, taking a couple of wary steps back to distance himself as he grasped the realization of what I was telling him. "Jesus, Flagg. You're doing that creepy thing you do, aren't you?"

I grinned at his apparent discomfort. If creeping out Andy Ramos was part of this deal, I was all over it. My grin turned into a full-blown smile.

"What can I tell you, Ramos? It's the gift that keeps on giving." A gift I would have gladly returned once upon a time. As if twelve-year-old girls didn't have enough to cope with in the puberty department without something like that dropped into the whole hormonally charged process of growing up.

"The detectives can finish taking your statement." Ramos shuddered, setting his belly to jiggle. "They don't pay me enough to deal with freaks like you." He turned his back on me and walked toward the entryway.

"Hey, they talk to me," I corrected as I hitched a thumb in the direction of the guy only I could see and hear. "I don't go looking for them if that's what you're thinking." If the truth be known, I couldn't find a dead guy with two hands and a spectral-detector. That's not how it worked for me.

Andy never acknowledged me and kept on walking. I was sorely tempted to start walking myself, right out the door and down the drive. I'd do it too, if I thought it would do me any good. The problem was, I was born and raised in this town. I could run but I couldn't hide. Half the police force knew where I lived. The other half could find out easily enough. All they had to do was ask my big brother, Eddie. He's the current chief of police.

"I'll be right here when the *real* cops show up," I said, loud enough for Ramos to hear me as I parked myself on one end of the massive sectional sofa in the living room. Antonio Barrera situated himself beside me. I could see the tone-on-tone pattern of the caramel-colored upholstery right through him.

"Who did this to you?" I asked, thinking how nice it would be if I had some useful information to give the detectives when they showed up. Boy, wouldn't the name of the murderer be a real good start?

He gave a shrug and shook his head. "I don't know. I was attacked from behind. I never saw who did it."

I took a long, hard look at him. He looked like a kid, not much older than my seventeen-year-old nephew. "How old are you, Antonio?"

"Call me Tony," he insisted.

"Okay, Tony. How old are you?"

"Twenty-nine," he answered. "Gonna be...I mean would have been thirty next month."

Wow. He was my age. And dead, I quickly added to the list of things I knew about this guy. Let's not forget dead. That was not a particularly comforting thought knowing someone my age wasn't going to get any older. I suppressed a shudder and moved on.

"You don't look it," I told him. Then again, that's what people often said about me. Don't get me wrong, I didn't look seventeen, not even on one of my really good hair days, but I didn't look like I was teetering on the precipice of a new decade, either.

"That's what all the ladies tell me," he said with a cocky grin. "They find this baby-face irresistible. They all want to *mother* me, if ya know what I mean."

Unfortunately, I did. Eeewww.

If his next words mentioned anything about diapers or breast-feeding I was going to heave my latte behind the credenza and leave it for the crime scene investigators to figure out.

Chapter Three

I studied Tony with an experienced eye. It's hard to explain how the dead present themselves to me. Everything about them is clearly defined and distinguishable, just not entirely solid.

Another important thing I should mention about the way my dead contacts look is however they were dressed at the time of their death is how I see them. I'm the first to admit I've been lucky so far. Nobody's slipped on a bar of soap and hit their head in the bathtub or had a massive coronary while doing the horizontal tango. Thank goodness for small favors is all I have to say about that.

Because the average age of all my other deceased contacts up until now was well past seventy-five, their manner of dress at the time of their demise had varied from putter pants and poly pantsuits to nylon nighties or hospital gowns. Until now, that is.

I did another quick assessment of my half-dressed translucent companion. Tony's hair was glossy black, wavy, and long enough to brush his collar if he'd been wearing one. One stubborn lock insisted on hanging across his forehead in spite of his attempts to shake it back. His full-lipped, expressive mouth pursed into a thoughtful pout as he watched me with eyes almost as dark as his raven hair. But it was the deep dimpled cheeks that gave him that youthful, boyish appearance. Tony Barrera was a Latin hottie, no doubt about it.

Okay, I understood the attraction. He was most definitely above average in the looks department, cute as a button in fact, and since he was naked from the waist up I couldn't help noticing his body wasn't half bad, either. From the way a pair of low-riding jeans sat on his lean hip bones, it wasn't difficult to imagine the rest of him.

But, in light of the fact I was the furthest thing from the *motherly* type, I was able to remain somewhat objective. I managed to keep my wandering thoughts to myself and my line of questioning focused. That he was dead, I suppose, also kept me from getting too interested. Nice pecs and abs, notwithstanding, the man was still a ghost for all practical purposes.

"Why do you think you were murdered?" I asked as I watched closely for his reaction. I learned a lot from visual cues, even those made by dead people. This guy, unfortunately, wasn't giving me much to go on.

"I got no idea," he said.

I wasn't buying it. "You want to try that again?"

"I'm telling you, I don't know. I don't remember."

"And I'm telling you I don't believe you," I returned. "You must remember something. Everybody remembers their last minutes." At least that's what I've been led to believe. What possible reason would there be for a dead man to lie about that?

"I can't tell you what I don't know," he insisted.

"Tony," I said, wishing I could shake some sense into him. "Have you taken a good look at yourself? You're dead. You have no substance. There's no coming back from that. You connected with me for a reason. I'm here to help."

He stared at the floor, quiet and pensive, before he spoke again. "How can you help me?"

His question caught me by surprise. No one had ever asked me that before. Odd as it seemed, it was an eye-opening realization, and I wondered why that was. Everyone else over the years had accepted me without question, as if instinctively knowing why we were brought together. Tony's question forced me to examine my reasons for being there, and I wasn't sure I could formulate an answer to satisfy either one of us. Nevertheless, I gave it a feeble shot.

"Well, for one, if there's nothing you need me to help you with, there would be no purpose in your appearing to me."

"It's too late to help me. There's nothing you can do for me now."

"There has to be something," I insisted. There was always something motivating a dearly departed's appearance. That was the one constant I counted on. Most knew right away what they wanted, a few needed prompting, but none were ever this reluctant to give it up. There had to be another reason for his reticence, and I thought I knew what it might be.

"Who are you protecting, Tony?" If I'd hoped my question would coax a reaction out of him, I was more than a teensy bit disappointed. There was nothing. His expression never wavered.

"Nobody," he answered with a little too much conviction to convince me he wasn't covering for someone. He knew his killer. I was sure of it. Now all I had to do was convince him I could be trusted with the information.

I persevered, but any further attempts to get Tony to open up and tell me something, anything, were met with the same closed-mouth resistance. He refused to cooperate and stonewalled every other question I threw at him, no matter how subtle or off topic I tried to make them.

About the same time I realized I wasn't getting anywhere with Tony, I picked out a familiar voice from the assembly of law enforcement crowding the foyer. I looked up and found my good buddy and occasional boyfriend Danny Prince with the newest and only female detective on the force, Jeri Novak. They were also part of the county's major crimes task force, and they were talking to one of the few uniformed officers I didn't recognize. Chickenshit Ramos was nowhere to be seen. Hah! Big shock there. He had an uncanny knack for avoiding anything resembling confrontational or controversial.

In this instance, that could be a good thing. It would be better if I told Danny about Tony in my own way and in my own time. Ramos possessed all the finesse of a bull moose on the loose in Crate and Barrel. His version of the events would undoubtedly be tainted by his narrow-minded opinion of that *creepy thing I do.*

Danny barely acknowledged me before heading toward the kitchen. He was in detective mode, and I knew better than to interfere. He'd get around to me sooner or later. He always did.

Danny and I have been friends forever. Well, since we were thirteen anyway, which was practically forever. It wasn't until we went away to college that we became friends with benefits. Although we'd never set boundaries or conditions on our relationship, we were always careful to never invade each other's space when we were away at school, but we always managed to hook up and hang out during breaks and summer vacation. We had what we called a No-Good relationship. *No* strings, *no* demands, *no* commitment— *good* friends, *good* times, *good* sex. Sounds simple, right? Hah. There was nothing more complex than my on-again off-again relationship with Dan Prince.

At the moment, we're just friends, sort of, I guess. Since I hadn't seen or heard from him since the Labor Day FOP picnic, I guess we're in one of our off phases. It's not always easy to keep track of these things. The lover thing didn't work out after graduation, not on a permanent basis anyway. We still get together and have dinner and a few drinks, usually around one holiday or another. We are friends after all, and that's what friends do. But if we spend too much time together, we always wind up in bed.

That in itself isn't such a bad thing because sex with Danny is nice, very nice, in fact. He's safe and comfortable, not to mention sexy as hell. He's got the most gorgeous blue eyes and sun-bleached blond hair he keeps short and spiky. The nicest thing about Danny is, aside from the occasional sex, of course, he's always there for me. I can't say that about too many people. I'd do the same for him. That's where the safe and comfortable part of our relationship comes in. What can I say? It's an arrangement that works for us, complexities notwithstanding.

Now that I thought about it, the sex between us was downright self-serving. Since we're not out to please or impress, we tend to work on our own needs first and foremost, which makes for some intense sexual activity in our race for the finish line.

Gee, when I put it that way, it sounded damn exciting, and it got me to thinking. Hmmm, his birthday was too far off. And Thanksgiving was still a week away. There had to be some holiday we could celebrate. I wondered if he had any plans for the coming weekend.

"I know that look," said Tony, sounding pretty cocksure, I might add. "You're thinking about getting laid."

"I am not," I lied.

Sheesh. What was it about Latin men? Even dead, this one's antenna for spotting a horny woman still worked like a fine-tuned Rolex. I was led to believe that hearing was the last sense to go after death. It gave me pause to wonder what else might still be working on this guy.

Revealing those adorable dimples, he asked, "So tell me, which one of them gets your panties wet?"

Chapter Four

"That's none of your business," I said as my hand sliced through the air to smack him in what could only be described as a knee-jerk reaction to his crude remark. The momentum pitched me forward and I landed against the couch cushions, grappling and flailing to right myself and looking, I'm sure, like I was in the throes of a seizure.

Now I've been interacting with dead folks for a heck of a lot of years. The rules of engagement were pretty clear cut. I can look all I want. I can talk 'til I'm blue in the face, but I can't ever initiate a touch. That's a real bummer in situations like this when all I want to do is smack the crap out of one of them.

"Is she all right?" Jeri Novak questioned as I struggled to right myself on the sofa.

"She's fine," Danny assured her. "She does that sometimes."

I scrambled to my feet, pushed a clump of loose curls from my face, and grinned like the fool I felt.

Oh my, Danny looked particularly hot today. I was pleased to see he was wearing the black lambskin jacket I gave him for Christmas last year, and there was something about a gun and handcuffs hanging from a man's belt that really turned me on. Oh yeah, it was definitely time for us to celebrate something.

I gave him one of my brightest smiles and was more than a little disappointed when he didn't return the greeting. He sent Novak an unspoken message and jerked his head toward the front door. She nodded in understanding and took her leave.

"You need to come with me, Jennifer," was all Danny said without ever making eye contact.

A disturbing chill ran down my spine. Uh oh. It was never a good sign when Danny called me by my full name, especially when he couldn't even look at me when he said it.

He took me by the arm, none too gently I noted, and steered me around the end of the sectional. I could only describe his treatment as manhandling, pure and simple. That's what it was all right, and I didn't like it one least little bit.

I managed to snatch my purse from the end table before he whisked me away. Good thing I was still wearing my coat because I wasn't sure he would have let me take the time to look for it let alone put it on.

"Where are we going?" I questioned as he hustled me toward the front door.

"Down to the station," he said.

"Can't you take my statement here? I need to get home and feed my cats."

Danny hesitated. "Not this time, Jennifer."

Again with the Jennifer. "I already told Ramos everything," I said. Well, practically almost everything. "Why should I have to repeat myself?"

"Andy doesn't think you told him half of what you know about this murder, and frankly neither do I."

That wasn't good. I rolled my eyes in his direction.

"You've already talked to Ramos?" Boy, wasn't that just like Ramos to sneak around and talk about me behind my back.

Danny stopped in his tracks and peered at me with those damnable, I know-what-you-look-like-naked blue eyes. "Briefly," he said, adding, "Outside, when I first arrived." Those piercing baby-blues narrowed. "Why?"

"Just wondering," I said with a casual shrug. I knew from Dan's tone and demeanor that Andy hadn't told him everything about our earlier conversation. Not the part about how I knew the victim's name, at least. Danny would have said something about it otherwise. If Ramos chose not to mention it, then I saw no reason to bring it up either.

"Let's go," he said, steering me toward the front door.

Then a ludicrous thought popped into my head. Where they come from, I have no idea.

"Are you arresting me?" I tried to wrench my arm out of his grip, but he held on tight. Another sign of foreboding. Like the crows weren't enough.

"Not yet," he said, keeping his grip firm and his direction focused.

"For what?" I demanded, dragging my feet to slow him down. Once I'd reached the conclusion his treatment of me was unacceptable, I doubled up my fist and socked him one hard in the arm. After the empty swing I'd taken at Tony earlier, it felt really good making contact with solid bone and hard muscle.

The smack of my knuckles against fine leather brought me back to reality and reinforced what I'd just done.

"Oooo," Tony winced. "I don't think you should

have oughta done that."

That's the first thing he'd said I couldn't dispute. It would appear that I'd forgotten one very important thing. This wasn't my friend Dan, and it definitely wasn't Danny my occasional lover. The guy standing here, at this moment, was Daniel Prince the police detective. And I'd just socked him. I wondered what the penalty was these days for assaulting an officer. I had a feeling I was going to find out.

He came to a sudden stop and turned on me. The look on his face confirmed my conclusions. "Now I'm ready to slap the cuffs on you."

My jaw went slack as my eyes widened at the very idea. No doubt about it, I was one sick, twisted individual.

Dan's eyes grew in direct proportion to mine when it appeared he caught the direction my mind wandered. "Jeez, Jen, this is a murder investigation. You want to try and focus?"

"Yeah," Tony interjected, clearly offended. "A little respect for the dead, if you don't mind."

I gave a dismissive toss of my head. "I don't know what you're talking about," I told them both.

Although I'd never admit it, he'd nailed it. His threat hadn't intimidated me nearly as much as it had turned me on. All my body fluids flowed southward, leaving my throat and mouth as dry as a toasted bagel without benefit of cream cheese. It didn't get much drier than that.

He leaned closer, his nearness bringing the familiar scent of his cologne tinged with a hint of peppermint. "You're sick, you know that," he said.

And twisted—let's not forget twisted. In my mind

the two always went together, sort of like chips and dip.

"It's not going to work this time, Jen," he said, taking me by the elbow. "You can't distract me from what I have to do."

"Wait a minute." I didn't like where this was leading. "You don't think…" I croaked as I tried to work up some spit. "You don't think I had anything to do with Tony's murder, do you?"

Danny came to another grinding halt and jerked me around to look me in the face. "Tony? You're on awfully familiar terms with a guy you claim you don't know."

"I don't know him." Not in a way that mattered to Danny, anyway. Why muddy the waters with unnecessary technicalities. "And I sure as hell didn't kill him," I added, pointing to a woman wearing a navy jacket identifying her as a member of the Lake County Crime Lab. "Have her do one of those tests on me."

"What test might that be?"

"You know, that GPS test that shows up gun powder…" Oh hell, I couldn't remember what the S stood for. My mind went blank. "…stuff," I finished. Close enough for me.

For the first time that evening, I spotted a twitch of a grin on Dan's handsome face, even if it was competing with the seriously throbbing vein in his forehead. Tony, on the other hand, didn't hold anything back. He was cracking up next to me. I didn't find anything funny about my situation and I resented that anyone did. Dead didn't give him the right to be rude.

"It's G-S-R, Jennifer," Danny explained with a forced tolerance he tended to use exclusively on criminals and me. At the moment, I guess I was one in the same. "And it stands for gunshot residue, not gun powder... *stuff*."

"Well pardon me for getting it wrong. I'm a CPA not a CSI."

There was the luxurious creak of leather as he crossed his arms and leveled a knowing glance in my direction. "As far as I know, you aren't either one."

I glared at him with every ounce of indignation I could gather. See, this was the problem with having long-term friends. They knew too much and didn't hesitate to use certain information when it suited them. A casual acquaintance wouldn't know enough to throw that little fact about not passing the CPA exam in my face. I wanted to smack that smug look right off him.

I settled for tossing my hands in the air. "Just do the damn test so I can prove I didn't shoot the guy!"

"Uh, Jennifer," Tony said between snorts and guffaws. "There's something—"

I hoisted my purse strap higher on my shoulder and turned my back on Tony to indicate I wasn't interested in whatever it was he was trying to tell me. I'd reached my fill of both men.

"I know you didn't shoot him." Without missing a beat, Danny started to work me toward the door again.

"You do?" I asked. Whew, that was a relief.

"Nobody shot him. The poor bastard was stabbed."

"That's what I was trying to tell you," Tony interjected.

"Stabbed?" I reiterated. "Are you sure?"

Instead of heading out the door when we reached the foyer, Dan directed me away from the flow of steady foot traffic and into an alcove under the stairs.

"Punctured, actually," Danny amended.

"How do you know this?"

"The penetrations are round and shallow, no more than two and a half to three inches deep, without any exit wounds," Danny said. "Two holes—one in the chest and one…" There was a distinct hitch in his voice when he finished. "…in the crotch."

Even I winced and groaned at that one. The implication of that blow was about as personal as it could get.

"You said it, doll," said Tony, shuddering.

The murderer had to be a woman, I concluded. No man, no matter how vicious or cold-blooded, would strike a blow like that. No, this was the work of a woman—a really vindictive, pissed off woman.

"That would certainly explain why I thought the wounds looked like gunshots."

"Did you move the body, touch it or roll it over?"

"Absolutely not." My one and only instinct had been to get the hell out of there. "I never went past the doorway." I'd collapsed and clung to the doorframe in fact until the nausea had passed. When my legs gained enough strength to hold me up, I tore ass out of there and never looked back.

"Then how did you see the wounds if you didn't roll him over? He was lying face down."

I jerked to a stop. "He was what?" I would have sworn Tony had been laying face up when I found him. I tried to visualize the scene in my head. Try as I might, I honestly couldn't remember the exact details. Which was it—heads or tails? Both seemed right—and wrong. Had I just imagined seeing the wounds? It all seemed pretty unclear to me at the moment. Never was there a better example of the difference between a memory for photos and a photographic memory.

Tony had said he hadn't seen his attacker. "If he was stabbed from the front, how could he have not seen his attacker?"

I searched around for Tony, hoping he could bring some sense and order to my mounting confusion, but he was nowhere to be found. Had I imagined him too?

Danny never gave me a chance to think through my musings. I barely took my next breath before he had me by the shoulders, looking me square in the eye. "Have you made contact with the victim?"

"Sort of," I said. Danny accepted my ability to converse with the dead as much as he accepted my green eyes and curly red hair. But like my hair and eyes, it wasn't a subject we discussed too often.

"He was waiting for me when I got here," I finally admitted.

"And you didn't think that might be an important thing to mention?"

"I would have gotten around to it," I told him. Eventually. Maybe. "What difference does it make?"

"Did you hear or see anything before you found the body?"

I nodded. "There was thumping and what sounded like footsteps when I first arrived. Oh, and a door slammed somewhere in the house."

Without another word he dragged me outside, pushed me through the gathering crowd, hustled me past flashing cameras and outstretched microphones, and shoved me into the backseat of his unmarked Crown Vic as he shouted instructions to one of the uniforms to move the crowd back.

Then he crawled in behind me and pulled the door

in, but didn't shut it all the way. We both knew what a mistake that would be if he did.

He turned to me and said, "Listen to me, Jennifer. It makes a difference because whoever killed him could come after you next."

Chapter Five

An icy fist slammed into my empty stomach. "Wh-what?" I stammered. "Why would you say a thing like that?" I stared over Danny's shoulder and spotted Tony standing among the milling crowd watching his bagged body wheeled out by the coroner. He looked so sad and miserable. I guess the reality of his situation was finally sinking in. Grief apparently wasn't only for the living.

"I can pretty much guarantee you there're going to be a lot more questions as to why you were in Franklin Roth's house in the first place than about the dead body you happened to find there."

"Franklin Roth, the real estate mogul?"

Danny confirmed my question with a tight nod.

Oh, man, I'd walked into the home of one of the wealthiest, most influential men in Northwest Indiana, quite possibly the whole state. The governor might have the title, but everyone knew Roth had the power. Yikes. No wonder the place was crawling with reporters and camera crews. This was big news.

"What do you suppose Tony Barrera was doing there?" I wondered aloud.

"*He* had every right to be there. He and Roth's daughter, Angela, were engaged. What I still want to know is what *you* were doing there?"

"I already told Ramos why I was there."

"That open house story isn't going to fly, Jen. The evidence recovery team has been all over the house and yard. There's no sign of a sign, open house or otherwise."

"Damn it, Danny, I'm not making this up! Why won't you believe me?"

"I want to believe you, Jen. Really, I do. But the evidence, or lack of it in this case, proves differently. And it doesn't help that your obsessive fascination with these Briar Cliff houses is common knowledge with anyone who knows you. I'm doing everything I can to keep you from being charged with breaking and entering, but it may not be enough."

"Yes, I entered. I'm not denying that. But I won't admit to breaking into anything because I didn't. The door was unlocked."

"You didn't help unlock it by any chance, did you?"

"I can't believe you asked me that."

"It's a fair enough question. You can, after all, pick a lock better than anyone I know."

That was true enough. I'd mastered the skill during my teens, having learned how much easier it was to sneak into the house after curfew when locked doors were no longer a deterrent. Danny knew that better than anyone, since it was usually him I was out with past curfew. But if Danny didn't believe me, what chance did I have in convincing anyone else? "Do you really think I'd waltz into a total stranger's house without some kind of invitation?"

Again, knowing what he knew about me and my past, he cocked his head and stared at me.

Note to self: Find some new, clueless friends.

"All right," I said. "There was that one other time, but I'm stone cold sober now." There were some things some people wouldn't ever let other people forget. This particular time was a night a couple summers ago when I'd had one too many margaritas at a block party and walked into a neighbor's house thinking it was my uncle's. They found me passed out in their bathtub. "It's not my fault all those tract ranches look alike."

"Anyway," I insisted. "There *was* a sign." I know what I saw. There was nothing he or anyone else could say that would make me say otherwise.

He expelled a weary sigh. "Whether there was a sign or not is the least of your problems."

"What's that supposed to mean?" I was practically positive I wasn't going to like his answer.

"It seems you've been pegged by the press as the other woman."

"Whose?" I gasped.

"What difference does that make?" Danny exclaimed, looking at me like I'd lost what was left of my mind. On some abstract level, I think I had.

"None, I guess, except if I'm going to be labeled as somebody's mistress, I'd like to think it'd be the rich guy's." Was that wrong?

Danny rubbed the throbbing pulse on his forehead before speaking. "The point I'm trying to make here is," he said with a deadly evenness. "That once the press starts delving into your past, and they will, they're going to find out about this thing you do with dead people. And when that happens, every nutcase with a dead relative is going to be knocking at your door."

"Look, Danny, I've been doing this for a long

time," I said, hoping to waylay his fears. "That's never happened before. I've always managed to stay under the media radar. Once the press discovers my ability isn't one I can control, they won't find me all that newsworthy."

I fell silent and stared out the side window, thinking maybe I was trying to waylay a few of my own fears. I did what I did because I didn't have any choice. I didn't want what I did made common knowledge in the press or anywhere else any more than Danny did.

"If it comes out you've been chatting with the victim, let's hope the murderer doesn't find you all that interesting, either."

He said it so quietly, I wasn't sure if I'd really heard him or if it was just my own thoughts creeping into my consciousness. Either way, I couldn't ignore the fact my connection with Tony had become a serious liability.

"What makes you say that?" I was interested in hearing his spin on the whole situation. He was the professional.

His face was a shadowy mask of indecision. "There's evidence that suggests the body was moved after you called it in."

"What kind of evidence?"

"I can't give you specifics right now, but it could prove you weren't alone in the house when you found the body. Somebody might have seen you."

"Somebody like the murderer, you mean?"

"Or somebody helping dispose of the body after the fact."

My empty stomach took a decidedly downward spiral.

A black limo splattered with crusty road grime turned the corner. It cruised slowly past and finally stopped in the middle of the cul-de-sac. A tall, distinguished looking gentleman, dressed in formal attire and black overcoat, stepped out of the back and surveyed the commotion like a general overseeing his troops. Franklin Roth had arrived.

Danny climbed out of the car. "Stay here," he ordered as he slammed the door in my face.

Yeah right, like I had a choice. Police cars were equipped with back doors that didn't open from the inside to keep criminals from escaping. I was stuck there until someone realized I wasn't being charged with anything and let me out.

I slouched low in the seat and crossed my arms. Danny could forget about celebrating anything with me this weekend or any other for a long, long time. What a pity he wasn't around so I could tell him.

I sensed Tony's presence before I saw him. His translucent body sort of blended with the squad's dark interior, but I knew he was there. He never said a word. He just stared at a young woman standing apart from the crowd near a row of leafless hedges bordering the neighbor's lawn. Dressed as she was, she appeared lost and out of place. When she hugged the folds of the ill-fitting overcoat around her, it was all too apparent there was a great deal more coat than woman as she rocked from one foot to the other in an obvious attempt to keep warm. The voluminous folds of the coat looked like they were all that kept her anchored to the ground.

When the moon came out from behind the clouds and the shadows lifted, I made out sad, delicate features and huge, searching eyes.

"Pretty girl," I commented, leaving out she'd be a lot prettier with a little more meat on her bones. "Who is she?"

Without taking his eyes off her, he answered without hesitation. "The love of my life."

I didn't expect that. "That's Angela Roth?" She sure didn't look like the pampered, well-heeled daughter of a wealthy man. Maybe she was one of those wealthy girls who dressed down to prove they were just an average Jane among the masses.

"That's not Angie. That's the neighbor's domestic, Mia Ruiz."

An icky feeling churned inside me. I've always developed a close affinity with my deceased friends, never the sickening aversion I experienced now. I was at a loss as to how to deal with these foreign feelings.

Whenever a dead person appeared to me, there was always some unfinished business they wanted me to take care of for them. It looked like Tony had lots of unfinished business. It made me wonder where I fit into his plans.

"Don't you beat all?" I drawled, unable or even wanting to hide my disillusionment. "Not even married yet, and you're already fooling around with the neighbor's hired help."

I'd always hoped there was a special place reserved for two-timers like Antonio Barrera. Once a man made a commitment like the one Tony'd made to Angela, was faithfulness too much expect? Second-hand experience had taught me for some the concept of fidelity was beyond their comprehension. Tony was apparently one of those people.

"It's not like that," he said, never taking his eyes

off the sad, young woman.

"Why don't you explain it to me then?"

"It's complicated."

It always is. "I'm not going anywhere," I told him as I glanced around the dark, confines of the squad.

"But I am," he told me as he started to fade.

"Tony wait," I said as I instinctively reached to stop him. My knuckles smacked against the seat. The street lights shimmered through his movements like heat waves off hot pavement. "She can't hear you," I told him as his image rematerialized.

He turned to me with the saddest brown eyes I've ever seen in an individual, dead or alive. "I can still be with her," he said as he disappeared.

A moment later, he stood behind the young woman. He leaned in, his lips near her ear. I couldn't hear him, but I wanted to think he whispered words of love and solace. She sure looked like she could use a massive dose of both.

Then something quite amazing happened. I'd swear I detected a significant change in her solemn expression. I'd never known it to happen before, but I wanted to believe he had connected with her on some level. Maybe Tony wasn't such a bad guy after all. In order for me to help him, I needed to believe that.

This whole business with Tony had me scratching my head. Was Mia his unfinished business? Or was it Angela?

Then again, it could be something totally unrelated to the two women. The only thing I knew for certain was I couldn't keep guessing. I needed to hear it from him. And soon. His time in this form was finite.

Chapter Six

According to my watch, fifty-seven minutes passed before Danny remembered he had me trapped in the backseat of his squad. By the time he released me, my annoyance with him had evolved into a fiery wrath worthy of my red-headed temperament. I was spitting mad with a full head of steam and ready to go for his jewels or jugular. My objective was whichever I could grab first.

As he swung open the car door, I exploded out of the vehicle with all the force of a champagne cork. He avoided a collision by doing a quick sidestep. With nothing to stop me, I landed in a flat out belly-flop. The air rushed from my lungs as I hit the frosty ground. *Oooomph!*

Breathless and stunned, I lay there gasping and sputtering in a misty cloud.

"Does she have these fits often?" I heard Novak question.

"Often enough," said Danny. He hooked his hands under my arms and hoisted me to my feet. "What can I tell you, Jeri? She's Eddie Flagg's kid sister."

"Say no more," replied Novak, waving off any further explanation as she walked around the front of the Ford to the driver's side.

I did not imagine Danny giving my left breast a little squeeze before he released me. He was so dead, and I shot him a look that told him it wouldn't be quick or painless. He grinned and winked. It wasn't easy staying mad at that face, but I was going to try.

"Come on," he said. "I'll walk you to your car." He turned to his partner. "Give me a minute." Jeri gave a terse nod and climbed into the sedan.

"So you're not taking me in after all, eh, copper?" I asked in a pretty decent James Cagney voice, even I did say so myself.

"I was never going to arrest you, although I should cite you right now for that dreadful impersonation of Uncle Arthur."

"It was Jimmy Cagney!"

"In that case maybe I will arrest you."

I waved to push our topic of conversation aside. He was changing the subject, and doing a fine job of it I might add, but I wasn't that easily distracted. Not tonight, anyway.

"If you never had any intention of arresting me, why the big pretense back there?"

He was slow to answer, but when he did it took me by surprise. "I was trying to protect you."

"How sweet," I gushed as I proceeded to sock him in the arm again.

"Hey! What was that for?"

"Just to let you know I didn't appreciate your bullying tactics."

"Point taken," he said as he took me by the elbow. "I still need to take your statement, but you can come in tomorrow to do that."

He continued to be awfully pushy and grabby. I

wondered what that was all about. I'd learned a long time ago to pick my battles with Danny, and this one wasn't worth wasting my breath. There were more important things currently on my mind than Danny's sudden caveman impersonations.

"What did Franklin Roth have to say?"

"He agreed not to press charges against you," he said. "Let's get you out of here before the press gets wind of his generosity and starts asking why."

"That's it? That's all you're going to tell me?"

"That's all you need to know."

There were dozens of questions flying around in my head, but the only one I spoke aloud was, "Did he say anything about the neighbor's maid, Mia Ruiz?"

"How did you—" He stopped himself and looked at me with that expression he always got when I said something he couldn't explain, which I happened to do quite often now that I thought about it. I swear I saw the light bulb go off when it dawned on him. "*He* told you, didn't he?"

"He might have mentioned it," I said.

"What else did he tell you?" The second the words were out of his mouth, his face scrunched, and his gloved fingers balled into fists at his side. "I can't believe I asked you what the victim—the *dead* victim—said to you." He tossed his hands in the air. "*After* he was dead!"

I smiled at that. "This is kind of nice that we're going to be working this case together," I said. This was a first for both of us. He'd discussed cases with me in the past, and I'd offered my perspective, but never had his victim been my dead man talking. We'd reached a new plateau in our relationship. I was tickled pink at the prospect.

"This is not nice, Jennifer. This is a high profile murder investigation. And we are *not,* I repeat, *not* working this case together," he stated. "I expect you to keep this thing you do with dead people separate from my investigation."

Well, that pink feeling didn't last long. "How would you suggest I do that?" I queried. "This *thing I do* has landed me smack dab in the middle of your investigation. So like it or not, Detective Dan, I'm already involved."

"Don't I know it," he answered with a begrudging frown. "But I refuse to like it," he added.

"I can't believe you don't see the advantages of having me work this case with you." I had an inside track to the victim. Why couldn't he see what a good thing that was?

"Stay out of this, Jennifer," he told me in a tone I didn't need translated.

"Fine," I said, feeling a little hurt by his whole attitude. Agreeing with him was easier than arguing, at least for the moment. I'd try again later when he was hopefully in a better mood.

"So," he said, running his gloved fingertips down the front of my coat. "What did Barrera tell you about this Mia person?"

"You're unbelievable, you know that?" I plucked a wind-blown lock of hair from my cheek and shoved it behind my ear. It didn't stay there for long, and soon it was back to whipping around my face.

"I have my moments," he said as he tugged off his glove to try his hand at taming the wild curl. His fingers, warm and gentle, tucked the ringlet around the curve of my ear and lingered there to hold it in place.

"Why should I tell you anything?" I questioned, jerking my head out from under his touch. "You just told me to stay out of it."

He flashed me one of his charming I-can-get-Jennifer-to-do-anything grins and took a step closer. "Because I know you're dying to tell me," he replied with that damnable grin.

I was, too. But he didn't have to be so doggone smug about knowing it. "All he said was he knew who she was," I told him. Danny was not going to hear about Tony's wandering eye from me, at least not yet. He was the detective. Let him *detect* it first. "What did Roth tell you about her?"

"Just that he thought his future son-in-law was paying a little too much attention to the neighbor's maid," he answered, but his attention appeared to be wandering.

"Did he name Mia Ruiz specifically?" I prodded, needing him to refocus on me and our conversation. I figured anything I discovered about Tony and those connected to him could only help me down the road. With what precisely, I wasn't sure, but any information was better than nothing.

"Wait here a sec," Danny told me as he walked away, leaving me alone under the street light. He ducked under the perimeter crime scene tape and loped across the frozen lawn toward the uniformed officer posted near the Roth's front door.

An eerie feeling crept through me, like I was being watched, so I moved out from under the arc of light and into the night's shadows. I watched Dan, studied the way he moved, with strong male grace and an authoritative posture that never seemed pushy or overbearing. He was tall, but not too tall at six-one, and well proportioned. That *celebration* feeling was starting to return.

"Why didn't you tell him about me and Mia?" Tony questioned.

"I'm not sure," I answered. "It's not like he won't find out. Franklin Roth has already pointed him in the right direction."

I couldn't shake that feeling of eyes following my every move. I glanced around and caught a glimpse of a slender silhouette in one of the next-door neighbor's upstairs windows. The curtain dropped and the window went dark. Could be just a nosy neighbor. There were plenty of those hanging around, but I didn't think so. I trusted my instincts even when there was nothing to base it on.

I pointed to the house on the left. "Who lives there?"

"Why do you want to know?" There was an expected wariness in his tone.

"Isn't that where Mia works?"

"Mia's got nothing to do with this."

"Is that a statement of fact or just a gut feeling you've got?"

"I *know* she's not responsible."

"Meaning you know who is," I practically shouted. From out of the corner of my eye, I caught Danny turning to the sound of my raised voice. Even in the dark, I knew he was frowning. I adjusted my volume and turned my back to Danny's scrutiny.

"Tell me, Tony," I whispered. "Who killed you?"

"I can't do that, Jennifer."

"You can't or you won't?"

"It's all the same to me. Nothing I tell you will change what's happened."

"Don't you want to see your murderer brought to justice?"

"It's not that simple," he said. His voice trailed off as his image vanished.

"Shit," I muttered. I hated when they did that. Of course, it was worse when they popped in on me when I wasn't expecting them. Most of them respected my privacy, or gave me a little warning before they showed up, but there have been a few I would have gladly strangled if I'd been able. One in particular jumped to mind. There was one old man a few years ago who thought it was great sport to join me in the shower every morning. Now I'm all for an occasional coed shower, but it's unnerving to find an uninvited man in my bathroom even when he's an old harmless dead one.

"Okay, let's get you out of here," said Danny as he rejoined me. "So, where's your car?"

"It's right over there," I told him, pointing to where I knew I'd parked the Malibu. "Where the hell's my car?"

Danny started to laugh. "I thought that car on the end of Smitty's wrecker looked familiar when I saw it going down the street earlier."

"I knew it!" I screeched, stomping my feet and raising my fists to the heavens. "I knew this was going to happen. Chevys aren't safe in this neighborhood."

Chapter Seven

It took Danny another hour to locate my car and have it returned from the impound lot.

By the time I pulled into the parking lot of the building where I lived in, I was tired, grumpy, and hungry. Make that exhausted, cantankerous, and starving, just as I knew my cats were going to be when I opened the door. They weren't accustomed to being kept waiting.

I lived on the second floor of a three-story, twenty-four unit building that had been converted from rentals to condos three years ago. The biggest problem about buying an apartment in a building that turned condo is the previous renters who bought their units during the conversion. Some of them can't seem to shake their renter's mentality and make the transition to homeowner. It hasn't been easy for the board, of which I am a member, to enforce the rules and regulations they're expected to adhere to now.

Tonight was a perfect example. I entered the building and found one of the first floor tenants getting ready to paint his front door. He was a nice enough elderly man with a wife in the early stages of Alzheimer's, but he was one of those who couldn't quite grasp the concept of condo ownership or understand the difference between what was his to do with as he pleased and what were untouchable common areas.

"You can't do that, Mr. Clarke," I said, trying not to sound like the Enforcer, which was one of the nicer names I'd been called when I've stopped certain tenants from doing something they shouldn't be doing. Since I didn't have any problem understanding the rules, I couldn't figure out why they all couldn't.

"Why not," he questioned. "It's my door, isn't it?"

"Well, yes, technically. And you have the right to paint the other side of that door any color you want. But this side has to remain like all the rest of the doors in the building. Any changes to the building or common areas need permission from the board. And I'm pretty sure nobody's going to give you the okay to paint your door…" I peered into the open paint can. "…purple." A hideous, anemic shade of purple, no less.

"It's called Lilac Lace. Millie picked it out."

"It's lovely," I said.

"We thought it might be easier for her to find our apartment," he sighed as he tucked the paintbrush into his back pocket and slapped the lid onto the can. "She gets so confused with all these doors that look alike."

I could relate to that. Case in point: The incident with my uncle's house looking like the neighbor's and most every other house on the block. "I understand," I commiserated. "But it's still not allowed. I'm sorry."

"I guess we'll have to think of something else," he said.

"I'll give it some thought, too," I told him as I headed up the stairs.

"Reowww!" Fred scolded the second I slipped the

key in the lock.

"Eeeat!" Ethel chimed in.

Anyone unfamiliar with this particular breed needed to understand that Siamese cries are loud and demanding, and often sound like human speech. When they speak, I understand and obey. Simple enough from my perspective.

Added to the mix of nagging pets came a deep "Woof, woof!" from Buddy, my dearly departed dog.

He wasn't my dog before he died. I found him on the side of the road one night, obviously the victim of a reckless, uncaring driver. He'd been still alive but wounded beyond help. He died in my arms before I could get him to a vet.

The weird thing is, unlike his human equivalent, he's never left from that day forward. I figured he didn't have any place better to go.

Buddy had been a huge dog in life—my closest guess was somewhere between a Saint Bernard and a Budweiser Clydesdale—and the best kind of big dog to have in death. I never had to feed him, or walk him, or scoop his poop. Anyone who owns a big dog in real life knows what I'm talking about with that last one. He was there when I needed company, but it was just as easy to ignore him if I wanted to be alone. Not something I could do with my demanding pair of Siamese cats who pretty much treated me the way I treated Buddy.

"I know mommy's late," I said to them as they rubbed and weaved around and through my legs. "You must be starving!" I know I was.

Buddy was already waiting for us when we got there. It didn't appear to bother him that he couldn't partake in the pleasure of eating anymore, but he seemed to enjoy watching others do it.

I popped opened two cans of Fancy Feast and dumped them into matching paw print ceramic bowls. They were chowing down before I could set their dishes on the floor. I gave them both a pat on their furry tan backs and wished my dinner was as easy to solve. I could open up the human equivalent, I suppose, but one look in my narrow, little pantry told me there wasn't a can of people tuna to be found.

"What to fix, what to fix," I chanted, standing in front of the open fridge like I expected something to magically appear if I looked long and hard enough. I sure could use a little help in the kitchen tonight. Well, any night, actually. Cooking wasn't a favorite pastime of mine. It wasn't even in the top twenty. Most people I know have to clean the grease off their stove. I'm required by the fire marshal to dust mine on a regular basis. My kitchen was used more like a walk-in pantry.

I stared into the cavern of my refrigerator and did a quick inventory. In addition to the ever-present staples of catsup, mustard, mayo, butter and jelly, there was a quarter jug of two-percent milk amazingly still in code, a carton of O.J. with at best two swallows, one lowly Heineken Light, two cans of Coke Zero, a cardboard takeout carton from Wok Inn I was afraid to touch let alone open since I couldn't remember the last time I'd ordered from Woks, and three stacked plastic containers holding what had to be classified as toxic waste by now. There was fuzzy grayish-green stuff pushing up the lid on the top two containers and something reduced to sloshy black slime in the other.

I dragged the garbage can to the open fridge and

scooped every UFO—that's unidentifiable food object—into the trash. There was even less from which to choose when I was finished.

What I really wanted was a large, gooey, double cheese and sausage pizza, but delivery on a Friday night would take another hour or more, and I couldn't wait that long. I needed immediate sustenance.

The freezer was my next place to hunt and hopefully gather. I found a bag of frozen waffles, half a carton of Ben and Jerry's Chunky Monkey, and two crystallized hotdogs that had long ago fallen out of their plastic wrapper. Sheesh! If I got snowed in before I went to the store, I'd be in serious trouble. I'd starve to death long before my cats because somehow I knew they wouldn't think twice about looking at me as their next meal.

The phone rang just as I was rationalizing how a couple scoops of Chunky Monkey smushed between two toasted waffles constituted a nutritious meal.

"Hello," I said as I sucked the ice off a frozen hot dog.

Pant. Pant. Moan. Whispered, "Fuck me, baby." Longer moan. Grunt. Click. Dial tone.

I checked the caller ID in case the guy was too busy with his own hot dog to remember to block his number. Lucky me, I got an ambidextrous heavy breather.

I stuffed the hot dog down the garbage disposal in a symbolic gesture of retribution and reached for my all time last resort—the corn flakes. Only two bites into the bowl and the door buzzer went off.

"Now what?" I grumbled as I pressed the intercom. "Who is it?"

"Pizza Palace."

"I didn't order a pizza," I told him, although I was sorely tempted to buzz him in and claim it for my own. Pizza Palace wouldn't have been my first choice, but it'd do in a pinch.

"That's what the guy who ordered it said you'd say. You're Flagg in number 12, aren't you?"

"Does this guy have a name?"

"He said you'd know who ordered it."

"What's on it?"

"Sausage, mushrooms, and...uh, *green* olives."

Only one guy I knew liked green olives on his pizza. Not my most favorite combination, but again, beggars can't be choosers, I decided as I pressed the buzzer and reached for my purse. Danny could be so thoughtful when he wanted to be. I wondered what else he had on his agenda for tonight, and if he planned on having me for dessert. My evening was looking up. Pizza *and* sex? How much better could it get?

I answered on the first knock and asked, "How much?"

"It's paid for," he told me as he slipped the pizza box out of the red insulated carrier.

My neighbor from across the hall came out of his unit with a stained brown paper grocery bag as I was swapping the delivery guy a tip for the flat, white box.

He *tsk-tsked* and shook his head at what I knew he thought was a total lack of self-restraint on my part. "Pizza again, Jennifer?" he questioned.

Ben Walters was a middle-aged body builder and health food fanatic. If it wasn't organic, no-fat, whole-grain, or low glycemic, he didn't put it into his body. He was also an eco-friendly soul who always requested paper over plastic, thus explaining the nasty, soggy garbage bag he hauled to the Dumpster.

I shrugged and gave him an I'm-never-going-to-change grimace as I scurried into my place before the man started his *your body is your temple* speech on me for the umpteenth time. Maybe *his* body was a temple. Mine, I'd come to realize a long time ago, was more like the food court at the mall.

The spicy aromas escaping from the box triggered every salivary gland I possessed into overdrive, but if Danny thought this large pizza would make up for threatening to arrest me and keeping me prisoner in his squad for over an hour, well, he was absolutely right. I was a pizza junkie, and he knew it. I was nothing if not a creature of easy persuasion when it came to food, particularly, but not exclusively, food I had no hand in preparing.

I plopped the pizza box on the coffee table and went to get myself the last beer from the fridge. I was about to take my first bite, after carefully picking off most of the olive slices, when I heard the key in the door. Danny's had his own key to my place for as long as I've lived there. It was easier that way. Besides, I mean really, who better to trust with a spare key than a cop?

After giving the matter some thought, I realized he hadn't used his key even once in the last few months, which of course meant he hadn't used me, either. This led me to the conclusion that there must be a new woman in his life. I couldn't help wondering who she was and how long it would last. Since he was using his key, my guess was she was already history. Neither one of us were known for longevity in relationships. In spite of its on-again off-again cycles, ours was the longest relationship either of us had ever had.

"Hi," he said, swinging a six-pack in his hand. "I thought we could order a pizza."

One of those really creepy feelings slithered down my spine. "What do you mean you *thought* we could order a pizza?" I gave the slice in my hand a sickening glance.

He eyed the contents on the table. "Hey, that's great," he said. "You already had one delivered."

"No," I said, tossing the piece onto the box lid. "I didn't order this. I thought you did."

He gave me one of those puzzled glances I'd seen on his face a thousand times before whenever I said something he didn't understand. "Why would you think that?"

I jumped to my feet and pointed. "It's got green olives. Who else but you likes green olives?" I glanced at the pile of chopped olive slivers I'd picked off, and my stomach lurched. "It was paid for and everything."

Danny reached for the phone. "What'd the delivery guy look like?" he wanted to know.

"Dark hair," I stammered, trying to think. I'd been raised around cops. I knew well enough how I was expected to answer a question like that. Give them the facts, just the facts. "Early twenties, my height, husky build," I said.

"What was he wearing?"

"Baggy jeans, black I think, maybe dark denim, and a green hoodie. He stuffed his tip into the front pocket."

"Was the hood up or down?"

"Up," I said.

"How did you see the color of his hair if the hood was up?"

"It was hanging in his eyes. I remember thinking he could use a haircut." Not to mention a good washing.

Danny dialed before I'd finished my last sentence. "This is detective Daniel Prince, shield number two-four-zero-eight. I'm at one-three-one Forest Park Lane, unit twelve. I need you to send a tech out here to pick up a pizza for tox analysis." There was a brief pause before he added, "Yes, that's right, I said a pizza."

Chapter Eight

Danny stood in the middle of my living room with his head down, slowly shaking his head as he rubbed the back of his neck like I've seen him do hundreds of times. "What I don't understand," he said. "Is why you'd accept a pizza from a total stranger?"

Danny's logic escaped me, so I used some of my own. "Isn't that what anyone does when they order food and have it delivered?"

"But you didn't order it."

I really didn't want to think I answered my door to a fake delivery man. "I thought you ordered it, and the guy had one of those insulated carriers," I told him. "You've got to be in the business to get your hands on one of those, don't you?"

"There must be a dozen other ways to get one," he said. "Maybe he used to deliver pizzas, maybe he stole one out of a delivery car, maybe he bought the damn thing on eBay! You can get everything but a kidney for granny on that site!"

That was true enough. I knew because I'd checked when my Grandma Flagg's kidneys started failing. "Why are you yelling at me?" I'd never seen Danny behave quite like this before. I was usually the one who takes the express lane into the land of irrationality and hysteria, and he was my calm and rational influence.

"I'm yelling because I don't have the first clue as to what this is about. I don't like that you're involved. And I really don't like that somebody knows I like green olives on my pizza and used it to get to you!"

Dan's reaction to the mystery pizza started me thinking. Some months ago there had been a guy gaining entry into single women's apartments with the delivery man ploy. If I remembered correctly, it wasn't always pizza he delivered. Sometimes he used Chinese or Mexican to get his victims to open their doors. It was obvious he'd studied their habits and preferences before making his move.

Once inside, however, his modus operandi had always been the same. He raped them, robbed them, and escaped without leaving a clue. The police had been stymied. After six attacks in as many weeks, they'd stopped as suddenly as they'd started, and the case had gone cold. Danny's theory was the guy stopped because he'd been arrested and jailed for another crime. If that was the case, it looked like he could be out and picking up right where he left off.

The reality of the situation slammed into me and made me wonder what would have happened if Ben hadn't come out of his apartment when he had? Blood pulsed in my ears and my knees turned to over-cooked elbow macaroni.

"You don't think he could be the…the…" I couldn't catch my breath. Panicked, I glanced around, hoping to find something, anything, to anchor my attention away from my conclusion.

"You're not going to do something girly on me, like faint, are you?"

"Of course not," I answered. Fainting is for siss—Thank goodness I wasn't standing too far from Danny or the couch. Between the two I made a soft enough landing as everything went from fuzzy gray to blacker than black.

I slowly emerged from the dark void to find two paramedics, three patrolmen, and Danny gathered around me like pallbearers waiting to cart the body away.

Somebody stuck something under my nose that burned clear into my sinuses and made me cough. I pushed it away and tried to sit, but none of my parts seemed to cooperate.

I groaned, clutched my head, and flopped back against the cushions.

"She's coming around," one of them said, although I couldn't be certain who. I knew most of the guys on the force, but I didn't recognize that one.

"What happened?" I asked.

"You fainted," said a different voice. I was pretty certain that one was Danny's. It was the I-told-you-so tone that gave it away.

I tried to sit up again and succeeded this time. "What the hell?"

My blouse was hanging wide open and my skirt was bunched up my thighs just short of the Promised Land—in a room full of men, no less. Most of them were grinning without so much as one of them having the decency to look away. I'd had dreams like this, only I was wearing much prettier underwear.

Speaking of underwear... My very next thought tried to recall what panties I'd put on that morning. I had underwear for all occasions, from the skimpiest thong to full granny panties for those days when a girl needed a little something extra. I sincerely hoped I was wearing something in the middle coverage category for this unexpected occasion.

"Don't worry, Jen," said one of the cops. "Dan made sure we only groped what we absolutely had to under the circumstances."

I shot Dan a look that told him he'd better have done a lot more than that as I clutched my blouse together with one hand and shooed them toward the door with the other.

"Peep show is over, boys," I told them. "Now get the hell out."

"My work is done here. She's back to her old charming self," said the paramedic kneeling next to me as he ripped the blood pressure cuff off my arm. Him I recognized as a guy my sister Lani dated in high school. He was an insensitive jerk twenty years ago, and it didn't seem he'd improved any with age.

Everyone shuffled out except for Danny.

One of the cops, Ross Von Something-or-other, just couldn't resist a parting shot, "By the way, Flagg, nice rack. You doing anything Saturday night?"

"He's going to pay for that," I grumbled as I concentrated on getting the right button through the right hole.

"You don't have to do that on my account," Danny said the minute we were alone. He eyed me with a lascivious grin as he sat next to me and unfastened the button I'd just done. Slipping his thumb under the lacy cup of my bra, he dipped it deeper until he grazed the tip of my budding nipple. "Nope, you don't have to get dressed for me."

I smacked his hand away. "Isn't there something else you could be doing? Aside from groping me, that is."

"Like what, for instance," he asked as he slipped his hand around my waist and pulled me nearer. His gaze turned soft and endearing. Those darn blue eyes would be my total undoing one of these days. More likely any minute now.

"Oh, I don't know—maybe tracking down the delivery man, for starters?" It was all I managed to get out as he pressed me into the sofa cushions.

"Everything we can do at the moment is already being done." He nuzzled my neck and planted playful little kisses along my collar bone. His tactics were distracting, which I suspected was his intention. Although I wasn't entirely compliant to his overtures, I wasn't complaining, either. Since I didn't get the pizza, maybe I could salvage what was left of my evening. Sex was the only substitution I was willing to swap for sustenance.

"And for the record," he breathed against my exposed breastbone. "We don't think it's the same guy, Jen. Your description doesn't come close to that of his earlier victims."

His head dipped lower, and his playful kisses took a serious turn. Concentrating on anything else but his next move was beyond my present capabilities.

His cell phone twittered. A bucket of cold water couldn't have shattered the moment or pulled us apart any more effectively.

With a murmured curse, he snatched the offensive interruption from his belt clip, and moved to the kitchen to answer it.

He could have saved himself the trip. For one, my place wasn't that big. I could still hear him. And two, there was nothing remotely interesting or informative about his one word responses. And believe me, if there had been anything worth hearing, I would have heard it. Eavesdropping was an ability I developed from a very early age.

Besides, on top of everything else, I couldn't concentrate because my stomach was starting to hurt something fierce. I was so past the point of hungry I think it was trying to devour itself. That in itself wasn't such a bad thing if I could redirect its attention to my hips and butt.

He snapped his phone shut and reached for his jacket. "I have to go."

"What?" How could he leave me unfed *and* unloved?

"I said I have to go."

"Why?"

"Because it's my job," he answered as he stuffed his arms into his coat.

"Did they pick up a suspect?"

"No, they haven't," he answered, heading for the door.

"But what if he comes back?"

"Don't open the door and call the police."

"What should I do if he calls again?"

He did one of those slow motion turns and stared at me with eyes that had lost all their tenderness. "Call? You got a call? You never said anything about a call."

I nodded and told him about the obscene call I received right before the delivery guy buzzed. I hadn't made the connection until that very minute. Maybe there wasn't a connection at all—there more than likely wasn't—but I figured it could be worth checking out. Danny agreed and said he'd have my incoming calls investigated. After a promise to call if he had any news, he was gone.

I was amazed by how quiet, eerily so, my place was once Danny was gone. The only sounds were the steady ticking of the cuckoo clock in the four-by-four square entry hall and the rumbling of my empty belly.

The painful gnawing propelled me toward the kitchen.

Chapter Nine

All things considered, my choices were every bit as limited as before. On the positive side, there was a six-pack taking up some of the empty space in the fridge, but still nothing to go with it.

I really should go to the store, I told myself, but I couldn't muster enough energy to put on shoes let alone get into my car and drive all the way to the nearest supermarket. Recent events had taken their toll and left me running on empty. I did the next best thing and decided to bring the food to me. I broke down and ordered from Pizza Pete's, which happened to be my all-time personal favorite. Hold the olives, please.

I changed into sweats and then, just to take the edge off while I waited for the pizza, I ate a generous helping of cereal. As I tipped the cereal bowl to my lips and slurped the milk dregs from the bottom, Fred and Ethel mewled on the counter behind me, pawing at my back to let me know those dregs belonged to them.

"Sorry guys," I said, as I loaded the bowl and spoon into the dishwasher. "Maybe next time."

Ethel gave an indignant yowl and stalked from the room, swishing her tail in what I'd learned was her way of flipping me off. Maybe I forgot to mention Siamese cats were nothing but attitudes upholstered in brown and tan fur.

Then it was Fred's turn to express his displeasure. The fur on his back rose up as he arched and hissed. I knew in an instant it wasn't just me he was showing his irritation at, it was Tony, too.

Whether my cats can see or only sense my dead visitors, I'll never know, but they act like an early detection warning system, so I'm hardly ever caught unaware when they're around. I say *hardly ever* because they've been caught napping once or twice. Not that it really mattered one way or the other, I continually reminded myself. Except for startling the crap out of me once in a while, my dead guests were harmless—annoying, frustrating, and bothersome, no argument there, but harmless nevertheless.

"I was wondering how long it'd take you to find me," I said, reaching for my favorite mug to fix a cup of tea. I needed something to wash down the sleeve of Ritz crackers I'd discovered at the back of my pantry. The pizza would make a great main course when it arrived.

"So how'd I do?" he asked. His expression reminded me of my five-year-old nephew waiting for his mother's approval.

I gave a little hand wobble. "Not bad," I told him. The microwave dinged. "Everyone's needs are different and everyone adjusts their behavior to suit those needs."

He practically oozed skepticism. "And that means what exactly?"

Buddy nudged his hand until Tony took the hint and started scratching him behind the ears. Because of my inability to initiate contact with the dead, poor

Buddy only received affection when I entertained a dearly departed. If there was a doggy heaven, this was it for Buddy.

"There are some who won't leave my side. I call them Cling-ons. Then there are others, like yourself, who prefer to roam where no dead men roamed before. I call them Trekkers. For a Trekker, I'd have to say you're a little above average."

His smile was inspired. "Ah, I get it—Death: The Final Frontier. You're a Star Trek fan."

I pursed my lips and shook my head against his assumption. "Not really. I like all kinds of movies, so it stands to reason that my points of reference come from the films I watch. I could use *Night of the Living Dead* or *The Ghost and Mrs. Muir*, if you prefer the classics."

"How long have you been doing this?"

"Talking to dead people, you mean?" I asked.

"No, makin' tea in your microwave. Of course I mean talkin' to dead people."

"I talked to my first dead person when I was twelve." I gave the tea bag one last good dunk and tossed it into the sink. "Lucky me," I murmured. "Some girls only get cramps and pimples when they reach puberty."

"That must have been scary, being so young and all." His tone carried the right mixture of sympathy and curiosity. Buddy leaned against Tony's leg and rolled his eyes like he was in love.

"More for my family than me," I told him as I sank the corner of a cracker into my tea. I brought it to my lips and filled my mouth with the hot, soggy mush. Dunking can turn pretty much anything into an eatable treat.

"Why's that?"

I licked my fingers and reached for a paper towel. "For whatever the reason, it wasn't that big a deal for me. I grew up listening to my grandma's tales about her communicating with the dead. I always knew there was a chance it'd happen to me. When my sisters saw me talking to nobody at our Uncle Marty's wake, they knew I'd inherited the curse."

"The curse?"

I tried not to grin at his reaction. "That's pretty much the family's take on it. What would *you* call it?"

"How about public service?" Tony followed me into the living room.

"That works too," I said as I curled on the couch.

Tony parked himself across from me on the recliner. This time I did grin. That chair had a natural gravitational pull with the male species, dead or alive. It was Danny's favorite seat in the house, too.

"So what have you been doing since I left you at the scene of the crime?"

"Just trying to get my head around this dead thing," he answered as he tried to pick up the TV remote. He came up empty-handed.

"You can do better than that," I told him. "Concentrate. Imagine the feel of the remote in your hand."

"Imagine it?" he reiterated. "Concentrate?"

I smiled at Tony's expression, wondering what it was about those words that made people squint and scrunch their faces like they were constipated. I've yet to meet a person, living or dead, who didn't. I found myself making a similar face explaining it to him.

"That's right," I told him. "You've got to

remember you're not solid any more, while everything around you still is. Imagine the weight of the remote in your hand, remember what it felt like."

"So what you're saying is, in my case it really is mind over matter."

He wrapped his fingers around the remote. I could see him feel it. His reaction was one of pure elation. "Wow," he said, looking amazed by his simple accomplishment. He lifted it higher, raising it a good six inches before it slipped through his fingers and clattered to the table.

"You'll get the hang of it," I told him. What I didn't add was I hoped it was before he moved on. His days left on this earth, in this form at least, were limited. No sense in depressing him needlessly for something neither of us could control. That was probably the most frustrating part about all of this. I couldn't control their arrivals and I had no say in their departures.

"What's with the dog?" Tony finally asked as he stroked Buddy's shaggy head. I wondered when he'd get around to mentioning a dog only me and my dead visitors could see.

"I found him lying on the side of the road a few months ago. He was barely alive and died on the way to the vet's. A dog mustn't have any options after death because he's been with me ever since."

"Are you saying *I* do—have options, I mean?"

"Uh, not exactly." I hadn't planned on broaching this part of the deal with him yet, but it looked like I didn't have any choice. "Tony, you've got to understand this current state you're in is only temporary. You'll be moving on soon enough. What happens after that is anybody's guess."

He appeared thoughtful, as if he wasn't sure what to make of what I'd just told him. "How much time do I have?"

"It varies by individual."

"Why can't you ever give a straight answer?" He appeared angry, and frustrated, neither of which surprised me. I'd been expecting this reaction, actually.

"Because there's nothing straightforward about death or what happens after. I wish I had a manual for you—one that would answer all your questions and make this easier for both of us—but I don't. I'm sorry."

Never taking their eyes off Tony, Fred and Ethel leaped on the couch and positioned themselves next to me, one on each side. It was time to put the rest of my cards on the table, so to speak. I hoped he was ready and willing to show his hand in return.

"You know, Tony," I started as I rubbed Fred under the chin. His powerful purr vibrated through my fingers. "This ability of mine has limitations. The only time I've ever been approached by a deceased is because they need my help to finish something they started before they died. What's your unfinished business?"

He stared long and hard at me, as if trying to determine if I was on the level. It was pretty obvious this guy had some major trust issues, not necessarily with me, but with the human race in general. I suppose dying so young and all, murdered no less, could turn a person distrustful and wary.

"Give it some thought," I said. "And get back to me." Pushy and demanding never worked with these people. Patience and understanding made all the difference when dealing with folks who didn't have much else going for them anymore.

"I need you to get something from my apartment," he blurted.

See what I mean? Patience and understanding—worked every time. "What is it?"

"I'll show you when you get there."

Okay, so trust still wasn't the major motivator for this guy. "What do you want me to do with this something after I get it?"

"I'll tell you afterward," he said as he started to fade. In an effort to avoid more probing questions out of me would be my guess. And it was working, for him anyway. His actions were frustrating the hell out of me.

"Wait!" I jumped to my feet, startling my cats and banging my knee on the coffee table in the process.

"I really gotta go now," he said as he vanished.

I've never had this much trouble holding a guy's attention.

"Woof!" Buddy interjected. He didn't like Tony leaving so abruptly either.

I rubbed the throbbing knot on my knee and told myself I should be grateful he wasn't a Cling-on. A dead soul sticking to me like cat hair on a black wool sweater can put a serious crimp in a girl's social life.

Then again, the problem with Trekkers was they were so unpredictable. I never knew when they'd pop in. They also can get so wrapped up in wandering they sometimes lose their way and forget their purpose for being "left behind," so to speak. The explanation for this phenomenon is what I like to call the Swiss-cheese effect. Since I wasn't a part of their living existence, the holes in their memory can easily forget about me. When that happened, these folks move on before they had a chance to tell me what they needed me to do for them, which in turn leaves me with the unfinished business. I hated when that happened.

It made me wonder what it was that kept taking Tony away.

One thing for certain—Tony was my most difficult encounter to date. I sure hoped I was up for the challenge.

Chapter Ten

I was dozing when the pizza arrived. I jumped off the couch, buzzed in the delivery man, and checked the peephole. I was relieved to see it was Pizza Pete's older brother and partner, Calvin. For the last twenty years, Pete was the sauce and dough genius in the back of the house. Calvin was the front man and picked up the slack on weekend deliveries.

"Hi, Jennifer," he said as he handed me the hot cardboard box with the most heavenly smells coming from under its red and white checkerboard lid.

Before I could speak, I swallowed the excess saliva pooling in my mouth. "Hey, Cal, how's it going?"

"Sorry it took so long. We've been crazy busy tonight."

"Pete's Friday night special is worth the extra wait."

A door opened across the hall just as Cal turned to leave. Ben came out with another bag of garbage, dry this time and looked to be all newspapers. He stared at me like I was holding a severed head instead of a pizza box. Maybe it wasn't my health he was concerned about as much as the trees I was single-handedly destroying from all these delivery boxes.

The best I could do was a sheepish grin. "It's not

what it looks like," I said.

A single brow arched. "So that's not another pizza you've got there?"

"Oh, it's another pizza, all right, but it's still not how it looks. There were, uh, extenuating circumstances with the first one. I didn't eat it..." I closed my eyes and prayed for somebody to shoot me and stop the blathering.

Cal stopped at the top of the stairs and looked over his shoulder. I swear he was looking for the knife I'd just twisted in his back. "You had pizza delivered from someone else?"

Two pairs of accusing eyes bore into me. "No, I didn't—not technically. It just showed up at my door, but I didn't order it, and I didn't eat it. You've got to believe me!"

Clutching his bag of recyclables, Ben shook his head. "You really should think about cutting back, Jennifer."

"I'll give it some thought," I mumbled as I backed into my unit and slammed the door.

Stuffed after eating only a quarter of the pie— probably shouldn't have had that second bowl of cereal—I dozed fitfully on the couch still waiting for Danny's call. I woke up a couple of hours later to find Fred and Ethel nibbling at the sausage chunks and lapping at the grease puddles. So much for my breakfast plans.

An infomercial touting the amazing results of the greatest weight loss supplement to come around in decades blared from the television. I reached for the remote and wondered if anyone would rush to their phonc to order a weight loss program that claimed surprising benefits from a sensible diet and regular exercise.

As soon as I swung my feet to the floor, my cats hopped off the coffee table in tandem, each giving a perturbed yowl, and headed for the kitchen.

"Eeeaat," Ethel demanded.

"Nowww," Fred added.

My waking up, whenever and wherever, triggered their thinking it was time to be fed. The pizza had only been an appetizer. Knowing I wouldn't get a moment's peace until I fed them, I pushed off the couch and stumbled to the kitchen to do their bidding.

The clock on the stove said it was close to three. As I portioned dry food into clean bowls and filled their water dish, I couldn't help wondering what'd happened to Danny. He'd promised to call.

No sooner did I think it when the phone rang. I hurried to answer it. It was always like that with us. I answered without bothering to check the caller ID. I knew it was him.

"Hi," I said.

"You answered on the second ring. I hope you haven't been waiting up for my call."

I yawned as I turned off the lights and headed for the bedroom. "Fred and Ethel wanted to eat. So what did you find out about the delivery guy?"

"He's legit. So was the pizza. We've got nothing."

"Were you able to track down who ordered it or how it was paid for? Since the order was paid for in advance, it had to be a debit or credit card, right?"

I'd been giving this process some thought. It seemed only right that I share my thoughts with Danny. As if he needed my help. When it came to things like this, he was light years ahead of me.

"It was paid for with a pre-paid gift card, which every Pizza Palace franchise in the country sells. It'll be Monday before we can contact the home office and find out where the card was purchased. But I don't expect it to lead us anywhere."

"Then what's this all about?"

"Have you had any other anonymous gifts or calls recently?"

I tried to think back. Then something came to me. "There was a bag of candy hanging on my doorknob Halloween eve. I figured it came from one of the neighbors." Don't ask me why, but many of the residents, especially the elderly ones, were always leaving me little gifts, usually food. I guess Ben wasn't the only one who'd noticed my dreadful eating habits.

"Did you eat it?"

"It was chocolate." And since I hadn't seen him since Labor Day, I needed something to compensate.

"Enough said," I heard him mumble. Having scored me many a late night candy bar fix, he understood my addiction better than anyone. "Pizza and chocolate," he said. "Sounds like whoever it is knows your weaknesses."

"You think I've got a stalker?" I tried to keep the rising alarm from my voice.

"Don't panic," Danny told me.

I guess I didn't do a very good job at hiding it.

Whoever sent me the pizza had gone through some trouble to cover his tracks. Or hers. With equal opportunity being what it was these days I couldn't discount the possibility of a same sex stalker. Now I was really starting to freak out. I didn't have a clue. It could be anyone.

"It's probably just a secret admirer," Danny offered.

"Which is just a nice way of saying a stalker whose behavior hasn't escalated," I countered. I knew what he was doing, and it wasn't working. Changing the word didn't change the fact that there was somebody out there watching my comings and goings and sending me anonymous presents.

I'd feel a whole lot better if Danny was here with me. "Where are you?" I asked, hoping he'd tell me he was pulling into my parking lot as we spoke.

"Almost home," he answered on a stifled yawn. "I'm beat."

"Oh." I'd really hoped he'd come back here. I needed the company. It was more than that, I needed *his* company. But we'd never imposed on each other's privacy in the past, I wasn't about to start now. I couldn't. That type of behavior simply wasn't what we were about.

"I'll talk to you tomorrow then," I said, hanging up before I broke our unspoken rule and begged him to turn his car around and come back.

The phone rang again before I climbed into bed. This time I checked the caller ID. It was Danny. I knew it would be. I let it ring and pulled the covers over my head.

I pretended to be asleep when I heard him let himself into the apartment.

Guilt from my most recent behavior niggled at me. I knew hanging up the way I did would prompt him to follow up. I hated what I'd done, but I hated myself more for doing it.

The mattress dipped as he sat on the edge of the bed. "Jen," he said, stroking my shoulder. "What's going on?"

I scooted away and tucked the blankets under my chin. Damn, damn, damn. I couldn't believe it. I was crying. Now I really hated myself. This was so not like me.

"Are you crying?" he questioned, sounding... *What?* Appalled? Disgusted? He had every right to feel that way. He knew I didn't cry easily. It took a lot to make me cry—a lot more than this, at least. From the time we were teenagers he'd always told me that it was one of the things he liked best about me. Weepy, overly emotional females drove him crazy.

I sniffled and shook my head, sobbing louder the harder I tried to stop. "Go home, Danny," I wailed. "I'll be f-f-fine."

"I'm not going anywhere," he said as he kicked off his shoes and crawled in next to me. "Let it out, Jen."

"I was s-s-scared and I tricked you," I sobbed.

"I know," he said as he settled next to me.

I stopped crying and sniffled. "And you came anyway?" This was followed by a loud gulp and a hiccup.

"Of course," he answered. "What kind of friend would I be if I didn't?"

His simple response made me smile, followed again by another hiccup. "Thanks for that," I told him as I wiped away my tears with a corner of the sheet and relaxed against him. "This has been such a weird, awful day," I said, hoping it was explanation enough for my weird and awful behavior.

"Next time you want company, just ask, okay?"

Danny whispered.

"But we've never made demands like that on each other."

"Yeah, I know, but it doesn't mean we can't. There's nothing I wouldn't do for you, Jen. You know that, don't you?"

I wasn't ready to go where that statement was leading, so I said, "How do you suppose the guy knew about the green olives?" He gave a weary sigh, strong enough for me to feel it against my neck.

"Your garbage, most likely," he said as he rolled to his back. "I'm really exhausted. I hope you don't mind if I catch a few hours of shuteye here?"

I obviously wasn't the only one who could change the subject, so I scooted over to give him room. "You know you're always welcome in my bed, Danny. Not that I can remember the last time you've been in it."

"There's a good reason for that."

"What color was your reason this time—blonde, brunette, or redhead?"

As a friend, I had every right to ask that question. As a sometimes girlfriend, I was teetering dangerously to crossing the line. Then again, that line in our relationship was constantly shifting. Is it any wonder I have trouble knowing when I was close to crossing the sucker?

"It wasn't like that this time, Jen," was all he said in a manner I clearly recognized as his desire to drop the subject and end our discussion. "I'm back. Let's leave it at that for now, okay?"

"Okay, Danny," I said, scooting over a little more to give him the space he obviously needed.

Chapter Eleven

"Jennifer, wake up!"

"Huh? What's going on?" I opened my eyes and found Tony standing at the end of my bed wildly waving his arms to get my attention like his life depended on it. Okay, bad analogy. Let's just say he looked pretty desperate and leave it at that.

I studied him with newfound curiosity. Tony was turning into one big inconsistency. I'd never seen a dead person act like that before. There was normally an aura of serenity around them that I envied. I'd often wished I could bottle it to take out and sprinkle over me like fairy dust whenever my own life went berserk.

"You've got to get up." He poked me in the ribs, and I felt it.

"Nice touch," I said. "I guess I don't need to ask what you've been doing since I last saw you."

"Never mind that now," he said. "I need you to go to my apartment and get that stuff."

I sat up and pushed a tangle of curls out of my sleepy face. "How much stuff are we talking about? Am I going to need a truck?"

"No, nothing like that," he said. Scrunching his face, he grabbed for my covers. The blanket crept slowly down my legs. I was impressed. None of my previous contacts had ever developed their ability to this amazing point, which got me to thinking.

All the others had been sick and elderly when they died. Every one of natural causes, I should emphasize. Tony had been a young, healthy man at the time of his murder. Maybe that explained the disparity in their capabilities. It was something to consider. I made a mental note to ask my mentor about it the next time I saw her.

The removal of the blankets found me still in my sweats. I loved sweats. When I was home I lived in sweats. I had sweats in every style and color imaginable. If I thought I could get away with wearing them to work, I would, but I can't, so I don't. In the summer I switch to cutoff sweatpants and tee shirts. Sweats were my all-time comfy clothes. If it's made in fleece, in all likelihood I owned it. Flannel ran a close second in my wardrobe department.

This morning I wore a pair of fuchsia pink sweatpants and matching sweatshirt. I had socks on my feet, but I wasn't wearing underwear. That's another reason why I liked sweats so much. The fabric was heavy enough to get away without wearing a bra and panties, at least around the house. I never went out in public without underwear—always clean and pristine. The women in my family—generations of them—were sticklers about that. I'd rebelled against a lot of things growing up, but I'd never felt right breaking with tradition on that particular issue.

"You've got to hurry," said Tony as his gaze fixated where my unbound breasts jiggled beneath the pink fleece.

A warm flush crept up my neck. "Stop that," I said,

crossing my arms against his scrutiny.

"Sorry," he said, glancing away.

This was the part about being dead I found the most dispiriting. All earthly pleasures were a thing of the past. Not one of my other deceased friends ever looked at me like they wanted to ravage me on the spot. Here again, Tony was the anomaly. All my past clients had been in their seventies and beyond. Although they remembered sex fondly, they weren't obsessed with the opposite sex or the act itself anymore. More is the pity.

"What's the rush?" I questioned, stretching. I hardly ever motivated before noon on a Saturday. A glance at my alarm clock told me it was only a few minutes past eight. Eight! I'd only been in bed a couple of hours.

"I heard your boyfriend on the phone this morning. They're working on getting a warrant to search my place."

I scooted to end of the bed and dangled my legs over the side. My mattress was a new extreme pillow top, and I was still learning the best way to climb off. "Danny's not my boyfriend," I said as I took the leap.

Okay, so climbing into bed with me last night might lead some people to reach that conclusion. That and the fact he had his own key, I suppose. But I didn't consider him a boyfriend, per se. And neither should anyone else. Not in the strictest sense of the word, anyway. "We're just good friends," I added, feeling the need to explain and straighten out any misconception.

"Yeah, okay," Tony drawled, giving me a look that said he didn't believe me for a second. "Whatever you say, Jennifer."

"It's true," I said. What was it about my

relationship with Danny that nobody understood but us? "We have a mutual understanding," I further explained.

"Your *understanding good friend* left you a note," said Tony.

I found Danny's note folded and stuck to the refrigerator with a hunk of duct tape. Two dozen of the cutest clips and magnets cluttered the front of my fridge and he still found it necessary to dig through the junk drawer for the tape. I guess butterflies and kittens weren't manly enough for Danny.

The note was brief and to the point: *Dinner tonight? See you later. Love, Dan.*

Love, Dan. When did he start signing his notes *Love, Dan*? A better question was when did he start leaving me notes? Had he ever left me one? I couldn't remember. I didn't think so, but I couldn't say for positive. We'd known each other for a lot of years. There must have been a note or two in there somewhere. At least during our school days—before cell phones, text messaging, and email changed the face of communication forever.

I stuffed the note in the drawer with the duct tape and headed for the shower. Tony might be in a hurry but no way was I going anywhere without first showering and doing my hair.

I did it all in record time, though, especially for a Saturday morning. Tony prodded me every step of the way, urging me to hurry up and get moving.

I dressed in jeans and layered an oversized fisherman's sweater over a form-fitting turtleneck, and grabbed my hooded parka and matching knit scarf and gloves from the hall closet. My purse and keys were the last things I snatched off the kitchen table on my way out the door.

Tony was right on my heels. I caught myself from telling him he needed to put on a coat before we left. These little nuances, like not needing a coat or clothes, never eating or having to use the bathroom, never sank in. These people were real to me in every way, and I couldn't help treating them as such.

Chapter Twelve

Before heading anywhere, I pulled into the nearest Dunkin' Donuts drive-thru and ordered my usual Saturday fare—two glazed and a large coffee with skim milk and two Splendas. Hey, life was nothing if not a series of trade-offs and compromises.

I snagged one of the donuts from the bag on my lap and took a big, sweet, luscious bite.

Tony growled.

I cast him a sideward glance. Omigod. How could I have been so careless? I was one donut bite away from dealing with a raging dead man. Which, considering his highly developed ability to move stuff, could cause some serious problems if provoked.

"I'm sorry," I said, dropping the donut into the bag and brushing the glaze crumbs from my lips and the front of my jacket. "I forgot all about the sugar thing."

"Sugar thing?"

I pitched the bakery bag over my shoulder into the back seat. "I've never figured out why exactly, and nobody's been able to explain it, but anything with visible amounts of sugar acts like a red flag on dead people."

"It does?"

"It does," I said, pulling into traffic. "The sight of

sugar can turn a perfectly normal dearly departed into a raving lunatic." As if being dead wasn't enough.

"I did feel a little annoyed when you pulled out the donut."

Just annoyed? Hmmm, that was interesting. All the others had described the feeling as an intense sensation to the point of unbearable. Here again, Tony was contrariwise from what I learned in the past. I should be taking notes.

"All I can tell you is, stay away from it, don't look at it, don't even think about it. I promise to be more careful in the future."

"Damn," he breathed. "There's a lot to learn about being dead."

"Yep, you got that right," I agreed as I glanced into the rearview mirror and signaled to change lanes. I followed Ridge to Armada and headed north.

Tony's apartment was located in a huge complex in Griffith not too far from I-94. The Gables—named more for the clubhouse's design then the buildings themselves—spanned both sides of Ridge Road and encompassed hundreds of basic one and two bedroom apartments.

My Grandma Flagg lived there until the day she died, as had other family members and friends over the years, so I was familiar with the complex's sprawling layout. I didn't have any problem maneuvering through the maze of narrow side streets connecting the various parking lots situated around three or four building clusters. Tony motioned toward a building at the far end of the complex near the river, and I slipped into a slot near the front entrance.

"Okay, so where do you hide your extra key?"

Eager to get this done, I released my seatbelt and reached for the door handle. Sneaking into a dead man's apartment and taking his stuff made me nervous. Posthumous permission wasn't an arguable defense, except for maybe getting myself committed to the nearest mental health facility for long-term observation.

I turned to him expecting an answer, what I got was an expression that conveyed all the frustrated helplessness he was experiencing as he patted his front pockets for a key that was useless to me. The real key, the only one that would do me any good, was in all likelihood sitting in the coroner's office in an envelope marked *Personal Effects*.

"You don't have an extra key, do you?" I said, stating the all too obvious.

"No problem. I'll fade into the apartment and open the door from the inside."

I hated these moments, but it was my responsibility to give him all the *facts of life on the other side*. "I don't think you're strong enough to do that. Pulling off blankets and poking me in the ribs isn't the same as finding the energy to turn a lock."

"I can do it," he said as he faded. "I've got to do it."

I gave a long sigh and reached through the seats for the donut bag in the back. There's nothing worse than a cocky dead guy, except for maybe a mediocre medium in desperate need of a donut.

My cell rang just as I stuffed the last of the second donut into my mouth. "Helrow," I mumbled, sounding remarkably like Scooby Doo, as I swallowed the lump of dough and reached for my coffee.

"Where are you?" Danny asked, sounding none too

happy in his query. "You were supposed to come in and give your statement."

"I was?" That was news to me.

"How could you forget something like that? It was the last thing I said to you before I left this morning. You promised."

That explained it. A promise made under those conditions didn't count. "Oh, like you don't know better than to tell me something important, much less expect me to remember, when I'm half asleep." The man was not going to pin this one on me. I glanced at my watch. "I can be there in about an hour." It was all the concession I was willing to make.

"I've got more important things to do than wait around for you." His annoyance crackled through the phone.

I crushed the bakery bag against my leg in a futile show of defiance. There wasn't much good with being defiant when there wasn't anyone to see me be it, but it still made me feel better. So there.

"What are you doing?" Danny asked in that inquisitive way that told me he wanted me to spill my guts.

I wasn't above telling a fib to keep myself out of trouble, it's a natural defense for most people, and I'd told a few whoppers in my day, but lying to Danny always made my heart race and my stomach cramp. He's got a remarkable sixth sense about lies and the people who tell them. I'm sure it's one of the reasons why he's such a good cop, but the trait scared the crap out of me. Always did and probably always would. He was a lot like my father in that respect.

"Eating a donut," I said.

"Where are you eating it?" Danny asked in his official interrogator voice that left me shaking in my sneakers.

"In my car," I told him.

"And where, precisely, are you and your car?" From the grating edge in his voice I could tell he was losing patience. Or was it his temper? Since I've been the source of his losing both, I sometimes get the two confused.

"Are you sure you want to know?" I always asked him that when I didn't want to tell him what I knew he didn't want to know. No surprise that I heard him breathe the mother of all bad words. I could take him to that point faster than any other human on the planet, and in a weird, warped way I was pleased by that accomplishment. As I've said before—I was a sick, twisted individual. I can't help the way my mind works.

"No," he said. "Just tell me this. Are you doing anything, even remotely, connected with the Barrera case?"

"Sort of," I answered.

There was that word again.

"Are you going to tell me where you are, or not?"

"Not," I said.

"So help me, Jennifer, if you're caught someplace doing something you're not supposed to be, I'm going to let them arrest you, and then I'm going to help them throw away the key."

Then I did what I do even better than skirt an issue. I changed the subject. "Are we still on for dinner tonight?"

"Yeah," he grunted. "As long as you're not behind bars, I'll try to pick you up around seven-thirty."

"Okay, see you then." He'd already hung up. I hoped his day was going better than mine. But not by too much, of course, because I needed to get in and out of Tony's place before they showed up with the warrant.

Chapter Thirteen

Donuts gone and phone call over, I couldn't delay the inevitable. It was time for me to go into the place I wasn't supposed to be in and do the thing I wasn't supposed to be doing. I climbed out of the car and entered Tony's building. After checking the mailboxes lining the entry wall, I found his apartment number and took the steps to the lower level.

His place was what rental agencies called a garden apartment, which was, in my opinion, just a fancy name for a unit half submerged below ground level. It wasn't as bad as a basement apartment, but it was darn close. From my experience, they were usually dark and dreary, more often than not damp, and always harder to heat.

They were also the cheapest apartments to rent, which in itself didn't make any sense to me why Tony was living in one. He'd been engaged to the daughter of a very wealthy man. These apartments were okay for Mr. and Mrs. Joe Average. Like I mentioned before, my grandma lived here for nine years and loved it, but she'd been on a fixed income. They were priced right, well-maintained, and conveniently located, but hardly where the future son-in-law of Franklin Roth would be expected to live. Something wasn't adding up.

So many questions about Tony's relationship with Angela Roth were bouncing around in my head—the biggest one being why she hooked up with a guy like him in the first place. Okay, sure, he was good-looking and had a great body, and he possessed a certain rough-around-the-edges charm, but that alone wasn't enough to base a long-term relationship on, was it? I didn't think so. Marriage was a big, make that huge, commitment. Tony didn't seem to fit the mold of what I'd come to categorize as Briar Cliff people.

I know that sounded like reverse snobbery on my part, but like it or not, it was a fact of life—the kind of rich who lived in Briar Cliff Estates were a breed onto themselves, and they almost always stuck to their own kind.

All these added thoughts were making it difficult to concentrate on my main objective. I had to force myself to redirect my attention to the task at hand.

I tried the door and smiled. Tony's diligence had obviously paid off. Good for him, I thought. I liked an indomitable spirit in a man, even more so in a dead one. They had so little else going for them, after all.

"Tony?" I whispered, peering into the dim interior.

I pushed the door open farther and shuffled forward, sweeping one foot in front of the other as I groped along the wall for a light switch. The toe of my shoe met with something hard at the same moment I flipped the switch and flooded the room with light.

I wanted to scream. I stopped breathing instead. The desk clock lying near my foot ticked off the seconds one by one as I forced myself to breathe and focus on the chaotic surroundings.

The room was in shambles, tossed and searched in

a manner I found alarming in its thoroughness. Nothing had been left untouched.

Tony came out of what I assumed was the bedroom, walking straight through the toppled furniture instead of around it as only an apparition could. His lack of concern for the condition of his place helped calm my anxiety.

"So who's your decorator?" I asked, giving the place another dubious scan.

"They call themselves the Smith Brothers," he answered as he surveyed what was left of his worldly possessions. "See there?" He pointed to a black and red business card lying on the floor. "They left their calling card."

I picked it up and read, "Smith Brothers— Acquisition Experts Extraordinaire. No job too big— No job too small—If you want it—We'll get it."

"Catchy," I said as I tucked the card into my back pocket. My money was betting the phone number on the bottom was attached to an untraceable pre-paid cell. It didn't take a detective to figure out that one. Ah, the beauty and anonymity of modern technology.

"Who did this isn't nearly as important as they didn't find what they were after," he said. "It's in here." He motioned for me to follow him into the bathroom.

The bathroom? There weren't a whole lot of hiding places in there. At least not stuff that couldn't be found by anyone as experienced at the Smith Brothers boasted.

It was a typical apartment-style bathroom. Not much different than the one in my converted condo— basic, functional, and nothing else. There was a molded white tub/shower surround, white toilet, and small, laminated wood vanity with a recessed mirrored medicine cabinet hanging above the white sink. The cabinet door was hanging open, displaying a bottle of generic pain reliever, toothpaste and toothbrush, stick deodorant, condoms, a can of shaving gel, and a package of disposable razors—none of which, not even the box of condoms, looked like they'd ever been opened much less used. Now I was no expert, but to me, it looked like a neatly arranged display set up to appear as if somebody lived there. My curiosity meter jumped a couple of healthy notches.

Whatever those Smith guys had been looking for must be too big to fit in there because they didn't waste their efforts rifling through it, but the lid from the toilet tank was off and leaning against the tub, telling me whatever it was had to be either waterproof or easily placed in a protective wrapper. The room was otherwise pretty much untouched. I guess even acquisition experts can't upend a bathtub or toilet, which carried me back to why Tony had brought me there in the first place.

"They're good," Tony said as he placed his hands on either side of the medicine cabinet. "But I'm better." He closed his eyes, screwed his face into a mask of concentration, and pulled. The cabinet barely shifted. I could see how the exertion had drained him. He was never going to get it out on his own.

"Let me have a go," I said.

Tony stepped aside, purely out of habit than actual need, and let me have at it. I braced open the mirrored door with an elbow, grasped the inside lip edges, and gave it one good yank. The recessed cabinet broke loose, the weight of it throwing me off balance. I lost my grip and the whole thing crashed into the sink. The mirror cracked against the faucet and splintered into a million reflective reminders of what I'd caused. Just what I needed, seven years bad luck on top of everything else. *Could life get any better?*

"Reach inside the hole," Tony told me. "You'll find a small canvas bag hanging from a nail. It should be easy to lift out by the drawstrings."

I looked at him like he was out of his freaking mind. I'd dated a few construction workers. I knew firsthand what kind of disgusting things they were inclined to leave inside walls and between ceiling rafters. And construction debris was just the tip of the iceberg. That didn't include the things that took up residence after the fact. Eeewww.

"I'm not sticking my hand in there," I said. No way, no how. Not gonna do it.

"Jennifer, please," he begged. "I'd do it myself, but I don't seem to have the strength right now."

"Guess I forgot to mention that one little side effect about overexerting yourself," I said as I wedged myself between the sink and toilet, gritted my teeth, and plunged my hand into the abyss.

Lucky for me I'd never taken off my one-size-fits-all stretchy knit gloves. For more reasons than one, I realized. None of that yucky stuff getting on my skin was certainly a big one on the plus side, but not leaving fingerprints behind was right up there, too. How did the Smith Brothers do it?

"First the sugar thing and now this. Anything else you've failed to share?"

"Nothing that can't wait," I said as I groped around and found the thin straps on the nail exactly where Tony had said it would be. I tugged. Nothing. A little harder. Still nothing. The bag itself seemed to be caught on something between the studs and it took some twisting and jerking to wiggle it loose and maneuver it out.

As I wrangled the bag out of the wall, whatever was in it rattled, sounding like rocks inside a hard plastic or maybe metal container. I know this because my nephew Zak had a favorite noisemaker made out of a plastic mayonnaise jar filled with dried great northern beans. The sounds coming out of Tony's bag and Zak's homemade maraca was similarly annoying.

Once retrieved, I discovered the small cloth drawstring sack covered with thick cobwebs, crumbled drywall dust, and flecks of debris I refused to think about let alone try to identify. It was better not to know.

I hacked and wheezed against a billowing cloud of unidentified flying crud. There had to be a vaccination for exposure to crap like this, didn't there? "How long has this been in there?"

"Couple of weeks maybe."

Looked more like a couple of decades. "Let's get out of here."

"There's something else. It's in the bedroom."

I gave him that look again. But I could tell from the stubborn set of his jaw I wasn't going to get him out of there until I did what he wanted. It would appear men didn't get any less demanding post mortem.

"What?" I asked, winding the drawstrings around my fingers.

It was then I noticed the inside of my wrist. It was scraped and bleeding just above the glove cuff. I gave it a cursory inspection and decided there wasn't enough blood to be concerned, and since adhesive bandages weren't in Tony's medicine cabinet inventory, it would have to wait until I got home. I could feel my white corpuscles rushing to defend my open wound against invading microscopic invaders. Maybe stopping at an emergency care clinic on the way home for a tetanus booster might not be a bad idea, either.

"There," he said. Tony pointed to a smaller drawstring pouch half hidden under a leather-bound copy of *Sonnets from the Portuguese.* Love Poems? Tony didn't seem like a love poem kind of guy. Bawdy limericks, maybe.

I picked up the pouch and dropped it into my jacket pocket. "Got it. Let's go."

"Not that," he said like I was the dumbest female on the face of the planet. "The book."

"The book?" I repeated, dumbfounded. I didn't have the heart to tell him he wasn't going to be around long enough to read one sonnet, let alone the entire collection.

"Just pick it up," he snapped.

"You're getting kind of bossy for somebody who needs all this help," I told him as I scooped up the book. "Now can we get out of here?"

"There's one other thing," he said.

Lucky for him he was already dead because the next thing I knew he had me on my knees peeling back a corner of the living room carpet.

"You are so not going to get your security deposit back," I grumbled as more disgusting crud flew up and lodged in my throat and nasal passages. I was no doubt breathing that nasty asbestos garbage that caused mesothelioma. Okay, I admit it. I was one of those people who actually paid attention to late night class action commercials.

"What exactly am I looking for?" All I saw was some of the nastiest padding I'd ever seen. Not that I was an expert on carpet padding or anything like that. My own could look just as bad for all I knew, but I didn't think it was supposed to be stained the muddy colors I was seeing here. It didn't smell very good, either. I wondered if dried urine was toxic. I was teetering on the brink of losing my donuts.

"There," he said, pointing to what looked like the corner of an envelope. I caught a gloved fingertip under the edge and worked it out from between the carpet and pad. Another cloud of filthy crap swirled around my face. I coughed and hacked some more, sounding like one of my cats with a stubborn hairball, and crammed the envelope into the back pocket of my jeans as I pushed off the floor and stood.

I heard Tony's mumbled, "Fuck," a millisecond before I heard something rattled off in hasty Spanish from a guy who wasn't Tony.

This other person stood in the doorway and looked around. His gaze finally settled on me. I recognized that accusatory look. I should. I'd been on the receiving end of it enough times. He thought I was responsible for this mess, or I was going to accuse him of making it. Either way, I wasn't prepared for a confrontation.

"I don't suppose that bulge in his pocket means he's just happy to see me," I said under my breath. I felt like I was about to add to the carpet contributions.

"It's a gun," Tony stated like I really needed confirmation.

The guy said something else to me in Spanish. I couldn't say for certain, but my guess was he wasn't trying to sell me a subscription to *Better Haciendas and Garden.*

"Try telling him you're a friend of mine," Tony suggested.

"I'm a friend of Tony's," I said.

"In Spanish," Tony said, clearly annoyed.

"Uh... me and Tony be amigos," I stammered. The guy just looked at me, but the words *Tony* and *amigo* seemed to strike a familiar note.

"I said in Spanish," Tony snapped.

"I don't speak Spanish," I shot back.

"I thought you spoke Spanish."

"Whatever gave you that idea?" Then I remembered the brief exchange I'd had with one of my neighbors that morning. "One *Buenos Dias, Senor Gonzalez*, doesn't make me bilingual."

The guy in the doorway looked confused as he rattled off, "*Mi nombre no es Gonzalez.*"

"He just told you his name isn't Gonzales," Tony translated.

"No shit, Sherlock," I said. "That much I understood."

"*Mi nombre no es Sherlock, tampoco,*" the other guy interjected.

"Says his name isn't Sherlock, either," Tony supplied.

"That's good to know," I said. "When he shoots me I'll be able to tell the police what his name isn't."

"It's Ramon," Tony said. "Ramon Morales. He lives down the hall with six other illegals."

"Ramon?" I repeated.

Wide-eyed, Ramon nodded vigorously. "*Si, si,*" he said. "*Mi nombre es Ramon.*"

"He said—"

"Mi nombre no es idiot," I snapped. "How about telling me what to say to get rid of him."

I repeated word for word what Tony told me to say.

Whatever Tony had me say worked like a charm. Ramon jumped back and was gone like a shot. Two seconds later a door slammed, followed briefly by muffled shouts, then the eerie sound of total silence.

"Now might be a good time to get the hell out of here," I suggested as I headed for the door.

"Right behind ya, doll," Tony said.

His Brooklyn accent, I noticed, was more pronounced than it had been all morning—from Brooklynese to fluent Español and back again without so much as a single slip of the tongue. Who the hell was this guy?

"Just out of curiosity, what did I just tell your buddy Ramon?" I asked as I climbed behind the wheel and started the engine.

"That you were from the Board of Health and you were doing door to door genitalia inspections with the intention of reporting any foreign foreskins as required by international law."

"Sorry I asked."

Chapter Fourteen

After extracting a cross-my-heart-and-hope-to-die promise out of me not to look at the stuff I'd shoved into a flip-top shoebox and hid at the back of my closet, Tony left me alone for the rest of the afternoon, which probably wasn't the wisest move on his part since I was a notorious snoop.

I was dying to find out what it was that had people turning his apartment upside down to find. But once I made a promise to someone, I never reneged. Well, hardly ever, and not recently that I could recall. It's better not to keep track of those things.

I wandered into my bedroom three times in less than half an hour on the pretense of looking through my closet to find something to wear to dinner with Danny. The shoebox tucked in the corner on the floor behind a Rubbermaid tote filled with old purses and belts kept drawing my attention away from the task at hand.

Surely one little peek wouldn't hurt. I scooted the tote to the other side of the closet and gave the shoebox a little nudge with my toe. If it fell open and the contents spilled out, I'd have to check for damage, right?

The lid never budged.

I kicked it a little harder. It shifted but the lid held

tight. Another kick proved more of the same unsatisfactory results. Once more with feeling, I decided, as I swung my foot and sent it sailing. The box bounced off the back closet wall, rolled a couple of times top over bottom and, after a series of rattles and thumps, landed inches from where it had originally started—with the cover still snuggly seated.

That was it for me. I conceded defeat. Like so many Flagg women before me, I believed in signs, and this was not a good one. Not for me anyway. For shoe manufacturers everywhere, however, this was the box for them.

I rifled through my clothes to channel my thoughts in a direction I could control and, after careful deliberation, decided on a short brown distressed leather skirt and deep V-neck ivory cashmere sweater with little pearl buttons running down the front. Danny loved those little pearl buttons. He considered them a worthy challenge.

Danny liked it when I wore skirts, too—more specifically short ones. He was an admitted leg man and told me more than once how great he thought mine were. Of course, on most of those occasions we were naked and my legs were wrapped around some part of his body, but a compliment is still a compliment in my book even when there wasn't an ounce of blood left in his brain when he delivered it.

In my humble opinion, my legs are okay, a little longer than average in proportion to the rest of my five-foot-eight frame, but nothing out of the ordinary as far as I'm concerned. But if showing some cleavage and a little leg kept the detective part of the man from giving me the third degree about what I did today, then that's what I'd do. Okay, I admit it—I'm shameless when it came to using whatever assets I possessed, physical or otherwise, to keep the ball in my court and me out of hot water.

I dug out a perfect pair of medium-heeled, mid-calf boots just in case the skirt and sweater weren't enough. Yep, shameless from the top of my curly copper head to the tip of my copper rose-lacquered toes.

I showered and dressed and was finishing the final touches on my hair when I heard the key in the door.

"Hi," I said as I leaned against a hallway wall in order to finish zipping up the left boot.

Without saying a word, he gave me the once over. His silent perusal was making me nervous.

"It's not going to work, Jennifer."

Sheesh. Again with the Jennifer? "What? You don't like the boots?" I struck a pose that showed the boot and a lot of the calf inside it. "I thought they looked good with the skirt."

"I meant the skirt. Inasmuch as I appreciate the gesture, it's not going to work this time."

Rats. I tugged on the hem of my sweater to reveal a tad more cleavage. Victoria's pushup bras were designed for moments like these.

"That goes for the sweater, too."

Double rats. "I'll go change then," I said as I turned with a flourish. No sense in wasting a perfectly good short skirt and low cut top if it wasn't going to work to my advantage.

"Don't even think about it," he responded. "You're going to need all the help you can get."

I didn't like the sound of that. "What exactly do you mean?"

"This afternoon we found Barrera's apartment tossed and trashed. You wouldn't happen to know anything about that, would you?"

I shook my head. "No," I told him. I really didn't know anything about it, except for maybe the Smith Brothers part. The briefer the answer the less chance there was in incriminating myself. The Smith Boys were on their own. The skirt ploy had already been shot down, and that had been my ace card. It looked like I was reduced to bluffing and punting, neither of which had ever been whopping strengths in my arsenal of distractions.

"The place has been dusted for fingerprints. They aren't going to find any that belong to you, are they? I ask because a car matching yours was seen leaving the Lake Shore Apartments shortly before I called you this morning."

"That's what you're basing this third degree on? My car? Do you have any idea how many white Malibus there are on the streets of Lake County? There are two at this building alone." I'd lost count on how many times I'd tried to get into the wrong one first thing in the morning.

Then it hit me. "Did you say Lake Shore Apartments?" They weren't anywhere close to The Gables complex, in location or price range. "Is that where Tony Barrera lived?" I didn't have to fake my interest. I was genuinely surprised by that bit of information.

Hmmm—two apartments, a girlfriend and a fiancée—looks like my dead man Tony was leading at the very least a double life. That stuff he had me retrieve from his other apartment was screaming from the closet as I wondered what else he was hiding.

"He's never mentioned to you where he lived?"

"He never said a word to me about an apartment in Lake Shore." There, that wasn't too bad. I could get used to telling truths like this, and as long as Danny kept asking me questions like that, I'd be okay.

Danny stared at me, his gaze narrowing in such a way I felt like he was trying to see what color underwear I was wearing.

A sudden breath exploded from his chest. "Jesus, Jen. I can't tell if you're lying or not this time."

I inwardly smiled at that. Was I getting good or what? "Maybe because I'm not," I offered.

"Then again, maybe I'm not asking the right questions."

Yeah, there was that, too.

"Are we going out to eat or what? I'm starving." I marched to the front closet and reached for my long wool camel dress coat. I'm no fool. Danny's car had leather seats.

Chapter Fifteen

When Danny pulled into the parking lot of his favorite steak house, I asked, "Kelso's? What's the occasion?"

We'd eaten there before, I loved the place, but it wasn't one of our usual, no-special-occasion dinner hangouts. We had one list for our everyday favorite restaurants, and another for our favorite special occasion restaurants. Kelso's was at the top of the special occasion list. The food was fabulous, the steaks were phenomenal, but it was a tad pricier than either of us wanted to spend on a regular basis. Yeah, I picked up a check now and then. I hoped he didn't expect this to be one of those times.

"I had a hankering for prime red meat."

When Danny said red meat, he meant it with a passion. While I enjoyed a few sautéed mushrooms or onions accompanying my main course, he liked his steaks rare and bare.

Danny gave his name to the hostess who suggested we wait for our table in the cocktail lounge. We found two seats at the bar and placed our drink order with the bartender—beer for him, Jack and Coke for me.

I always found it fascinating to watch the reactions of other women when Danny entered a room. I tend to forget what a total hottie he is, and it takes other women's eyeballs popping out of their sockets to remind me.

He carried himself with a casual air of self-assuredness, like he wasn't afraid of anything but he didn't have to prove it to anyone. The fact that he never went anywhere without a gun somewhere on his person could have something to do with that attitude, but I knew there was more to it. That he wasn't the least bit aware of his good looks seemed to make him that much more attractive to the opposite sex.

I was so busy watching other women trying to get his attention, I didn't hear him speaking to me. His voice finally penetrated my concentration. "Huh? I'm sorry, Dan, what were you saying?"

"I asked if you'd like me to leave." He sounded a little too serious to be teasing.

"Why would I want you to do that? You invited me, remember?"

He faked an amused laugh. I knew his real laugh as well as I knew my own. And that wasn't it.

"You've been staring at that guy across the bar since we sat down. I'd hate to think I was coming between you and true lust."

I started to laugh for real. "Don't be silly," I said, scoffing at his observation. "If you must know, I was watching the woman sitting next to him. Who, by the way, has been staring at *you* since we sat down."

Danny couldn't resist looking. The second he turned his attention in her direction, the attractive brunette did a well-practiced hair flip and a dandy little maneuver I liked to call a bust thrust. I'd done it once or twice myself, but this chick had a lot more bust to thrust than I possessed, pushup bra notwithstanding. Yowee. It must be a lot colder on the other side of the room.

Danny looked away quicker than I could say, well, there wasn't much else for me to say. He was, for lack of a better description, a man of contradictions. In his cop persona, Danny could stare a criminal down until the guy cracked and confessed, but put a pretty girl in front of him who's showing him undue interest and he wasn't the same man. That's one of the reasons I think he keeps me around. We're past all that sexual game nonsense.

There came a sheepish grin this time and a chuckle as he reached for his beer. For a man so comfortable in his own skin, there was something equally endearing about this current, on-the-brink-of-blushing behavior. I couldn't help myself. I had to try and ease his discomfort. What are good friends for, after all?

I gave his hand a reassuring pat and said in my most soothing tone, "Don't worry, Danny, I'll protect you." Then I added, laughing, "Unless, of course, you'd rather I left the two of you alone?" I started to slide off the barstool.

He clamped a hand across my wrist, pinning my arm to the bar top. His unwavering gaze nailed me to my seat as his thumb rubbed lazy circles over my pulse point. He suddenly gripped my wrist and turned it over.

"How'd you do this?" he asked, running his finger across the barely scabbed-over scratch as if its origin could be discovered by reading it like Braille. It was pretty obvious that it was a fresh injury. He had to know it wasn't there last night.

I shrugged and laughed as I tugged my arm out

from under his touchy-feely scrutiny. "I must have scratched it on something."

"I can see that," he said. "What I asked is how you did it?"

"I have no idea," I replied. "Haven't you ever gotten a scratch and not known how it happened?" I tugged at my sweater sleeve to cover the wound.

"No," he drawled. "Never." Oh, those damn blue eyes. They never blinked. They never wavered. When he leveled them on me in that scrutinizing way of his, I knew I was going down. But not without a fight if I could help it.

"Well I have, all the time." I crossed my arms across my chest. "And this is one of them."

"How about another drink?" Danny motioned to the bartender with his empty.

My stomach rumbled in response to his question. More alcohol would only hasten my journey down that path I feared to travel. I looked around for the hostess, for one because I didn't want to look at Danny, and two because we needed to get seated and served. Pronto. I needed to eat before I cracked.

I wouldn't make a very good prisoner of war. When I'm hungry, I get cranky. When that happens I blurt incriminating stuff, mostly about myself although I've managed to take a family member down with me on more than one occasion. Actually, it was me who spilled the beans about my mother carrying on with one of the mechanics at my father's garage. It was an innocent slip of the tongue. I was only six at the time, for crying out loud. How was I supposed to know those greasy fingerprints on the inside of her thigh weren't supposed to be there? To this day, I know, in my heart, she still holds it against me. I am, however, Daddy's favorite child. He knows how easily I can be manipulated. And apparently, so did Danny.

Now I knew why Danny brought me here. Hankering for red meat, my freckled butt! He's counting on me spilling my guts by dangling a fillet mignon under my nose. And if he got a few alcoholic beverages down my throat before feeding me, I'd be singing like my Aunt Rosie's canary by the second course.

Who did he think he was using a sneaky, underhanded, lowdown trick like that on? Me?

Chapter Sixteen

I survived dinner without incriminating myself, or anyone else, for that matter. I considered it a personal victory. Danny, however, appeared somewhat disappointed.

After feeding me, very well I might add, Danny personally escorted me to the police station to take my statement. He wasn't taking any chances of me forgetting again. I didn't tell him anything different from what I'd told Ramos, but I guess this time made it official.

"So you're sticking with the open house story you handed Andy?" He sat behind his desk, rocking a pen between his fingers, and did that thing he did with his eyes. If he kept that up I'd be ready to confess to being the second shooter on the grassy knoll if he'd stop looking at me that way.

"It isn't going to change because it's the truth. If I was making this up, don't you think I would have come up with something more plausible by now?" That Andy Ramos didn't believe me didn't bother me one bit, but it hurt that Danny wasn't buying it. "I don't know what else you want me to say."

"I guess I was hoping you'd remember something, anything, to help me with this case." He tossed down his pen, pushed out of his chair, and reached for his jacket. "Let's get out of here."

He took my hand and walked me down the back hallway to the rear exit. Our footsteps echoed down the empty corridor. It was thirty minutes before shift change and all the patrol officers were still on the street. The only other people around were the pair of swing shift dispatchers waiting for their graveyard replacement.

I was always amazed at the quiet that settled over the department at night when the offices were empty. It felt like the whole world, at least this little corner of it, was holding its breath, waiting for something to happen.

There was an unnatural calmness about the place that was never there during the day, which I always found kind of weird since the majority of crimes took place after normal business hours. That it was Saturday night made the event even more of an oddity. There should be at least one DUI or wife beater sitting in the holding cell by this time of night. Then again, as any cop would agree, the night wasn't anywhere near over.

Danny's grip was a little tighter than I thought necessary, but I didn't say anything because I could see he was frustrated to the point of distraction. I let him get away with leading me around because I didn't want to add to his current state of mind. See there, I could be thoughtful and considerate if I wanted to be. If for nothing else, I was proud of myself for that much.

"There's very little to go on in this case, isn't there?" I asked him as we pulled out of the parking lot. My loyalties to Danny were beginning to supersede those I felt for Tony. If those things in my closet could help Danny, then I should hand them over, right?

"I've got no motive, no weapon, and no suspects, so *very little* would be an improvement at this point. That you showed up when you did is nothing more than an unfortunate coincidence for both of us."

I needed clarification. "Meaning what?"

"The lowered temperatures from the open windows compromised the time of death. From the coroner's best estimate, Barrera had been dead between twelve to twenty-four hours before you found his body."

"If that's true, there's something I don't understand. Where were Franklin Roth and his daughter during all that time?"

"They were in Indy on business and to attend a gubernatorial fundraiser. They have hundreds of the governor's nearest and dearest to alibi their whereabouts for the timeframe in question."

"If they were in Indy, how'd they get back so fast?"

"Private jet," Danny answered.

"What about the staff? That house doesn't clean itself. Where were they?"

"Roth doesn't have any live-in staff. He values his privacy and protects it by using only day help. Since he and his daughter were going to be out of town, he gave the staff the rest of the week off. They were due back Sunday night, the staff not until the next morning."

"That's convenient," I said. "Tony's murdered during the same time nobody's home. Don't you find that a bit too well planned?"

"That depends from whose perspective you're looking at it. The murderer saw the Roths' absence as a means of opportunity."

"Other than telling you he thought his future son-in-law was fooling around with the neighbor's maid, what else did he have to say about his only child's fiancé?"

"Except for that, not much else at all."

I whirled in my seat so fast I nearly choked myself on the shoulder harness. "I don't get it. Franklin Roth doesn't have any problem volunteering information that could devastate his daughter if it became public knowledge, and you don't find that peculiar coming from a man who *values his privacy*?"

"Of course I do," he answered straight away, never taking his eyes off the road. "But it's not enough for me to conclude he had Barrera killed for cheating on his daughter, not in his own home, anyway."

"So you don't suspect Roth of any wrongdoing?"

"I didn't say that. There just isn't any evidence to connect Roth or Angela to the murder. Although I seriously doubt he had anything to do with the murder. If Roth had wanted Barrera dead, there wouldn't have been a body for you or anybody else to find."

"Aren't stabbings considered personal?"

He shot me a curious glance before returning his attention to the road. "I'm not sure we should be discussing the specifics of this case. I've probably said too much already."

"Hypothetically, then," I amended. "Aren't stabbings usually a more personal form of homicide?"

"Hypothetically, yes," he drawled. "That's what the experts tell me."

"So do you believe Tony, I mean the hypothetical victim, knew his, or her, attacker?"

"It would be a distinct probability, and one we've

considered."

I nodded in agreement. "That's what I think too, but what's the probability the victim didn't see who stabbed him?"

"It's possible he didn't," Danny said. "Not if he was drugged prior to the stabbing. There were no defensive wounds to indicate he fought off his attacker."

"Are you saying they found drugs in Tony's—I mean the victim's, system?"

"The hypothetical toxicology report isn't back yet," said Danny.

"Has it been determined whether it was ingested or injected?"

He stopped for a red light and cast me an amused glance. "You know, Jen, I think you're watching way too many crime shows. You're asking some pretty explicit hypothetical questions."

"And you're trying to change the subject," I told him as I crossed my legs. The flaps of my coat fell open and exposed a generous length of leg above the knee. I gave Dan a quick eyeful before I shifted in my seat and tucked the soft wool around my thighs. It never hurt to throw in an occasional distraction of my own.

When the light turned green, he returned his attention to the road and chuckled without further comment.

We both knew I wasn't discouraged that easily. "Did the crime scene techs find the source of the drug or how it might have been administered?"

"You're not going to stop hounding me until I satisfy your curiosity, are you?

"Not likely," I answered.

"They found a half empty wine bottle on the nightstand that's been tested for residual toxins. Before you ask, that report isn't back yet either. These things take time. They aren't solved as expediently as they are on TV."

"He couldn't fight back..." I murmured. "What kind of person does that? Who poisons a man just to stab him to death?"

"I think you already answered that question when you said it was personal."

"What about the puncture wounds? Have they determined how they were made?"

"Andi Robanski, the assistant M.E. figured that one out. It was a stiletto heel."

"I knew it!" exclaimed. "I knew the murder had to be a woman!"

"And how exactly did you reach that conclusion?"

"Aside from the fact the murder weapon was a fuck-me pump, you mean?"

"Yeah," he said. "Aside from that."

"Only a woman would strike below the belt like that, but it wasn't the killing blow, was it?"

"No, it wasn't," he answered.

"That one was just a parting gift. It was the chest wound that killed him."

"That pretty much sums it up. He was drugged then whacked with the shoe once he was subdued."

"So he was telling me the truth. He really didn't see it coming."

"You know, I'm not used to hearing the victim referred to in the present tense."

"I know. It's not always an easy concept to grasp, is it? You have to remember I'm still talking to him in the present," I explained. "I'd be happy to relay any questions you might want to ask him. I can't guarantee his cooperation, but I can ask."

He shook his head and chuckled, as if he couldn't quite believe he was having this conversation at all. "The problem here is if Tony tells you something I can use in the investigation, it's still inadmissible in court."

"What?" I exclaimed. "Why?"

"If he tells you and you tell me, its hearsay. Even if it comes straight from the victim's mouth. There's no precedent for testimony given from the hereafter. There's certainly no law governing it."

"You mean if Tony came right out and told you, I mean me, who his murderer is, you couldn't arrest that person?"

"That about sums it up. We'd still need evidence from this world to corroborate it."

"Well, that sucks," I declared. "Then what good is my telling you anything I know if you can't use it to solve this case?"

"Not much, I'm afraid."

My desire to admit my earlier day's activities was diminishing by leaps and bounds. There wasn't any sense in putting myself in hot water if I couldn't come clean in the process.

Chapter Seventeen

Danny came to a rolling stop in front of my building.

"You want to come up for a while?" I asked.

I really wanted the company, but after the fool I'd made of myself the night before, I wasn't about to act like the clinging, conniving female again. Short skirts and low-cut tops to get what I wanted were one thing. It was a conscious choice. I hadn't cried and carried on the night before by choice. One night of that kind of behavior was one night too many, and it wasn't what our relationship was about. The funny thing is, although I'm certain I know what our relationship isn't about, it was a lot harder to define what it was about.

"Yeah, sure," he said. "I can come up for a while."

"You have to work tomorrow?" I asked, practically certain of what his answer was going to be. Because criminals didn't commit crimes from nine-to-five, detectives' schedules weren't governed by the hour of the day, any more than the days of the week. He worked when he was needed. Many a date night had been cut short or canceled because he was called into work. Here again, I think he keeps me around because as an unofficial girlfriend, I'm not allowed the luxury of complaining or pouting if our plans get ruined. But on the flipside, he can't say a word if I happen to cancel at the last minute, either.

And one of these days I might do it just to let him know how it felt. Except for a few monthly group activities, I have a stagnant social life outside of the one Danny provided, which, now that I think about it, makes me pretty pathetic for someone not even thirty. I definitely needed to get out more and meet new people, preferably the alive and breathing variety.

He used his key to unlock the outside entrance door. That's another reason I gave him a key to my place. It's so much easier to let him use the keys he already had in his hand because he always drives whenever we go anywhere together. It's one of his macho demands to which I gladly concede. With the price of gas these days, I'd be crazy not to let him use his car.

In the quiet contentment that blossomed out of familiarity, we walked side-by-side up the stairs and down the central hall to my unit.

I noticed something sticking out from under my door. It looked like the corner of an envelope. "I wonder which one of my crazy neighbors has a complaint this time," I muttered as I crouched to retrieve the note. All I managed to do was push it farther under the door.

I wasn't the president or even the vice-president of the condo association. Actually, I was only the board member at large, which wasn't nearly as exciting as it sounded. All I did was round out the board to an uneven number so there'd never be a tie during a vote—that and take on any odd jobs none of the other members wanted. But it seemed the majority of the residents preferred to come to me with their complaints, even though I've never cut them any slack when it came to abiding by the rules.

I understood their reasons for not wanting to go to the president—he was a fucking idiot. As it turned out, the *business experience* he boasted about as his qualifications for the position was nothing more than running a two-bit junk booth at weekend flea markets. But the rest of the board members, myself included, were perfectly normal, capable people, which was fortunate because we had the controlling say over what went on around here. On the unfortunate side of the same coin, we were in the minority. The oddballs, eccentrics, and whackos living in this building outnumbered the normal by five to one. That I'm considered one of the normal ones pretty much said it all.

Once Danny had the door open and I had the envelope in my hand, I decided not to deal with whatever it was until tomorrow and tossed in on the table. If it was really urgent, they wouldn't hesitate to call or come a knocking.

"Aren't you going to open it?" Danny asked as he took off his jacket. He tossed it over the back of a kitchen chair and stripped off his tie. I took it as a good sign, and hoped he was planning to strip off more than that before the night was through.

"Nope," I said, shaking my head. "Whatever it is can wait. I don't feel like dealing with anything condo related tonight." I pulled off my boots and headed for the kitchen.

Coffee?" I asked, knowing there wasn't much else to offer.

"It could be important," he stated in a way that told me he wasn't going to let it go until I opened the darn thing. "Or something that needs a timely response."

"If you're that curious, then open it."

"I can't do that. It's addressed to you."

"Fine," I said as I snatched the envelope off the table and tore back the flap. Out fell two twenty-five dollar gift cards—one for Starbucks and one for Dunkin' Donuts. No note, no clues as to the giver, just the cards. I stared at them lying on the table like I expected them to jump up and do a little jig. Reciting a clever limerick with rhyming hints as to the benefactor would also be a big help.

The strangest part about it was I didn't feel the least bit threatened this time like I had the night before with the pizza. It was just another harmless anonymous gift as far as I was concerned. It wasn't going to rule my life. It sure as hell wasn't about to ruin the rest of my evening.

"First chocolate and pizza, now the enticement of free coffee products—looks like your secret admirer just parlayed a daily double into a winning trifecta."

"That's what it looks like all right," I agreed as I calmly scooped up the cards and set them aside with the rest of my mail. I'd figure out what to do with them later.

"You're not seriously thinking about using them?"

"I haven't decided what I'm going to do yet." Although my first inclination had been to spend them, I gave the cards further consideration and still reached the same conclusion.

"Yes you have," he countered. "You've already made up your mind. You're going to use them the first chance you get."

"I don't see what the big deal is."

"At least check them out first. Make sure they're legit. For all we know they could be stolen or counterfeit."

"All right, you win." When Danny climbed onto his moral horse like this I'd learned it was easier to agree. "I'll call the number on the back of the card before I use them. Happy now?" I walked away, hoping that would be the end of the great gift card debate.

Fred and Ethel followed me into the kitchen and sat by their dishes watching every move I made.

"I fed you before I left," I told them. "Look, there's still food in your dishes. You're not getting anything else until morning."

Ethel gave me the tail and stalked out. Fred was much more subtle about showing his true feelings. He rubbed against my legs, arching and purring, then proceeded to wrap his paws around my ankle and sink his fangs into my arch, not hard enough to break the skin but enough to let me know he was one pissed pussy cat.

"You little shit," I yelped, shaking him off. He bounded from the room before I could retaliate. Smart cat. I knew what this was really about. He's never forgiven me for having his nuts lopped off when he was kitten. Elephants aren't the only mammals that never forget.

I found Danny kicked back in the recliner. It had to be a chromosomal thing. There must be a magnet in the seat cushion that attracts only Y butts. I hate the thing, and so did my sister Maddie, which is why she pawned it off on me in spite of her husband's protests when she redecorated. It's big and cumbersome, and when it's in the laid-back, footrest-up position, it takes up half of my living room. If it weren't for the men, dead or alive, who come and go in my life, that chair would be history.

I handed him the coffee and curled up with mine on one end of the *lofa*. I call it that because it was smaller than what I considered a full-size sofa but it was slightly larger than a two-seater love seat. It was sort of a hybrid—a love-sofa, or lofa for short. Not that it'd seen much loving on it lately, which reminded me…

"So tell me, Danny Boy, if it hasn't been a woman keeping you away these last couple of months, what exactly has it been?" I'd always assumed it was another woman occupying his free time when he wasn't coming around here. Danny was a virile, healthy male. Have I mentioned he was sexy as hell? If he wasn't coming around me, the only other logical conclusion I could reach was he had to be coming around somebody else.

He lifted his gaze, and stared at me from over the rim of his mug. Those damn baby blues studied me. The expression, *undressing me with his eyes*, took on a whole new meaning. He was doing a lot more than undressing me. He was doing a full body CAT scan.

My nipples responded to the intensity of his perusal and the feeling crept southward. I sure hoped he planned on spending the night. I'm sure we could find something to celebrate. I'd invent a holiday if there wasn't anything on my calendar.

"I was trying to see how long I could stay away from you," he finally answered.

I straightened in surprise, spilling my coffee in the

process. It wasn't much, a little splash over the side of the mug, but it was hot as it spread down the inside of my thigh.

"What's that supposed to mean?" I inquired as I scurried to the kitchen for a paper towel.

"I needed time to re-evaluate our relationship, that's all," he said, coming behind me. He filled the doorway, blocking the only exit.

My kitchen was a narrow galley with cabinets, dishwasher, and sink on one side and more cabinets, stove, and fridge on the other. It wasn't meant to accommodate two adults. It was barely adequate for one. But since I didn't practice the joys of cooking—I rarely practiced the joys of defrosting—it was the one part of the condo I hadn't been too concerned with when I'd bought it. I'd been more impressed with the decent sized master bedroom, walk-in closet, and adjoining bath, for starters, all of which I used way more than the kitchen.

With Danny taking up a good part of the narrow space, I felt a smidgen claustrophobic. Trapped, I was feeling downright trapped. Danny knew better than to corner me like this.

"That took you almost three months?" I asked. "What's to think about? It's not all that complicated. Good friends, good sex, good times. That's what we agreed on, isn't it?"

"That's not enough for me anymore," he said.

Chapter Eighteen

I did not want to be having this conversation. I glanced around to see if there was any way I could slip around him, and I resisted the childish urge to cover my ears and start chanting, *la la la la la*, to keep from hearing anything else he had to say on the subject.

Danny knew how I felt about him, about us. He had to know. I didn't think it was necessary to say it all the time. I thought I knew how he felt in return. I've based my whole life—past, present, and future—on the way I thought he felt. I needed to know how this happened.

"Just what part of the relationship did you decide needed evaluating? The friendship? Or the sex?"

He retreated, snatched his jacket off the chair, and headed for the door. "I can see you're not ready to have this discussion."

Maybe his leaving tonight was for the best I told myself as I followed to see him out. If we didn't finish this discussion then it didn't count, right? He wouldn't leave and never come back, would he? No, he wouldn't do that. I depended on him not doing that.

With his jacket bunched in his fist, Danny stepped into the hall and turned to face me. He leaned a shoulder against the doorframe as that wonderful blue gaze settled on me. "Good night, Bunny Fur."

The tension between us shattered and I breathed a little laugh. "You haven't called me that in a long time," I told him. The endearment developed from a teenage obsession I'd had to stylize my signature. Danny'd insisted it looked like Bunnifur when I showed him.

"I haven't felt this way about you in a long time." He cupped my chin and ran his thumb across my lips.

My stomach did a funny lurch. It was the same feeling I got when I rode a roller coaster. Exhilaration mixed with a knot of trepidation tumbled through my body. Danny scared me when he said stuff like that. It made me feel like he wanted me to say something equally mushy in return.

I leaned into him and breathed his familiar scent. He smelled so good, spicy and enticing, and yes, sexy as hell. There was something about his own distinctive scent combined with the lingering remnants of his aftershave that made the words pop into my head and out my mouth. "Do you want to stay?"

I swear to God that wasn't what I'd intended. Those darn pheromones sure could make a person act all weird and goofy sometimes, like now for instance. I held my breath and waited for his reply. I really did want him to stay.

"You sure about that?" Danny asked, sounding more than a little surprised. "I got the impression you didn't want my company tonight." He kneaded the small of my back, making certain his thumb and forefinger settled in the dimples at the base of my spine. I reacted just as he knew I would. It wasn't fair. The man knew every erogenous zone I possessed.

"Oh," I sighed, feeling his breath on my neck as he dipped his head to nibble on my collarbone. "I'm more than sure." I yanked him out of the hall and into my apartment, kicking the door closed as I went for the buttons on his shirt. He had me pinned against the wall and my skirt zipper down before I had the third button popped on his oxford.

"Wait a minute," I said as my skirt dropped around my ankles along with my panties. The man had the hands of Houdini. "What..." I said between heated kisses. "...are we..." More eager kisses. "...celebrating?" Oh, man. He was Houdini with great lips.

"Jeez, Jen," he wheezed around licks and nibbles against my shoulder as his hand crept under my sweater. His pants were already open and hanging halfway down his thighs. "Can't we check the damn calendar later?" Danny queried, bracing my thigh to rest against his hipbone.

"You know the rules," I gasped, feeling his erection press hard against my stomach. "It'll only take a second." I was as eager as he was, but I was also superstitious about following protocol. This worked for us. Why screw up a good thing? "Please," I begged.

He glanced over his shoulder at the holiday-for-everything calendar I kept hanging near the door. I'd never been a scout, but I knew how to be prepared just the same.

"Okay, got it. National Moms and Dads Day."

We caught the implication at the same moment because he looked at me with that deer in the headlights look as I vigorously shook my head. I was on birth control, but why take chances celebrating anything that had to do with parenthood?

"Anything else?" I gasped.

He looked again and shook his head. "St. Margaret's Day, the patron of Scotland."

"That's no good," I said. "It should be American, don't you think?"

"Come on, Jennifer," he exasperated. "There's nothing else for today. How about cutting me a little slack?"

Just then, the hall clock started its midnight toll.

Danny gave me a sly smile and eyed the calendar once more. "National Baklava Day?"

"Baklava isn't American, either," I pointed out, stroking him repeatedly to let him know I wasn't trying to be too difficult.

He ripped the calendar off the wall and waved it like he was ready to smack me with it. "It's National Raisin Bread *Month*. Is that American enough for you?"

"Works for me," I said.

"Damn good thing, too," he growled as he adjusted my leg and entered me without further foreplay. "The only thing left was Take a Hike Day, which would have been my next move." He braced one hand on the wall behind me and thrust. "Happy Raisin Bread Month, Bunny Fur," he said on a breathless note.

I smiled the smile of a happy woman and held on tight. "Happy Raisin Bread Month to you, too, Danny."

Oh, yeah. Some traditions were worth keeping. Glorious O's were had by all. There's nothing like a partner-induced orgasm after a personal best dry spell. That alone was enough to celebrate.

Chapter Nineteen

We finished celebrating, gathered our scattered clothes, and headed down the hall for the bedroom. I went first because I knew how much he liked watching my bare bootie. I swear I heard him smiling behind me and cast a furtive over-the-shoulder glance to verify my suspicion. Yep, he wore a big-ass grin all right. Then again, show me a guy who'd just had balls-against-the-wall sex who wasn't smiling, and I'll show you a guy who missed the "wet paint" sign. Next time, though, I called dibs on the rear view. His bootie was grin-worthy, too.

"I'll be there in a few minutes," Danny told me as he ducked into the bathroom off the hall. I heard the shower as I headed for the bath off the bedroom to wash up and get ready for bed.

Curled on my side facing the door and quickly sinking into a post-coital coma, I was almost asleep when Danny entered the bedroom. I peeked at him through one sleepy eye and watched him duck into the closet to hang up his clothes. His skin looked dark against the glowing whiteness of the towel wrapped around his lean hips.

The pungent combination of soap, shaving cream, and toothpaste drifted to my nostrils as he walked past, and I felt my body gearing up for an encore.

I grinned into my pillow. The man was so obvious. There was only one reason why a man brushed his teeth, showered, *and* shaved before going to bed, and it had nothing to do with personal hygiene.

So he was expecting a repeat performance, huh? That was doable by me. After all, he was already naked and so was I for all practical purposes. What real barrier did my mid-thigh fleece nightshirt pose against a man determined to have his way with me? Looks like all systems were a go.

He tugged off the towel and crawled under the covers. His arm snaked around my waist as he scooted toward me and snuggled me into the bend of his legs.

"Have you ever wondered why we've never made this a permanent arrangement?" he whispered as he pressed a kiss to my ear.

Those were so not the words I expected. I swallowed hard and glanced over my shoulder. His eyes glittered in the darkness.

"You mean like live together?"

"Don't look so surprised," he said with a husky chuckle. "I already have a key."

"But wouldn't that mean making a commitment? I mean, are you ready to do that?" I knew where I stood on the matter. I needed to hear what he had to say on the subject. I never expected him to drop this on me, not out of blue like this anyway. A little warning would have been nice.

We'd made a vow seven, closer to eight, New Year's Eves ago that we'd marry each other if we hadn't found anyone else by the time we turned thirty-two. It's an odd number, I know, but at the time thirty seemed a little too soon and thirty-five seemed ancient to a couple of kids who just graduated from college. At the time ten years sounded like a lifetime, now it was only a couple years away and Danny was already starting to make noises to up the deadline.

"I've been giving it some thought," he said, rolling to his back and taking his warmth with him. "If living together is a problem, I'm willing to make you an honest woman."

"Marriage?" I squeaked.

"You say that like it's a bad thing."

"It is in my family."

"Not all marriages turn out like your parents'. Why can't you use your dad's current marriage as an example of a successful one?"

I stared into the darkness, wondering how I was going to talk my way out of this without changing our status quo. I liked things the way they were. Why'd he have to go and do something like this? This was his fault. It had to be. Otherwise it would mean it was mine, and I wasn't ready to take the blame.

Danny was right about one thing—I did use my parents' marriage as the yardstick on which I measured my own miserable relationship track record. I cared too much about Danny to add him to the rank and file of boyfriends past. He'd always been content with fallback position. It made me wonder what had changed.

I rolled toward him, bracing myself on my elbow. "We've always been on the same page about this, Dan. If something's changed for you, don't you think we ought to talk about it? It sounds like you want to up our deadline?"

He studied me. I mean really studied me, as if

searching for something he hoped to find. I felt really bad that he wasn't going to find what he was looking for—not yet anyway—and I couldn't fake the response he wanted because he knew me too well, so I didn't even try.

I cared about Danny, I really did, but I wasn't ready to settle down with anyone. If I was, well, Danny would be at the top of a very short list. There was still plenty of time before I needed to make this decision. If push came to shove, I honestly didn't know how I'd respond.

"Not necessarily," he answered, sounding like he wasn't sure at all. "I thought I'd mention it, you know, let you know you had options."

"Okay," I said. "I appreciate that." I really did appreciate his thoughtfulness. What I didn't appreciate was him trying to change the rules coming into the backstretch of our ten year plan.

"Okay then," he said. "We'll leave things the way they are for now. As long as you're sure."

"I'm sure," I told him, almost practically positive I was sure. I was as sure about this as I was about anything else at this point in my life.

"Then it's settled. So we've got what, three more years?" He sounded like a man who'd just been turned down for parole.

"It's closer to two," I said. "We both turn thirty this March." Mine was first and a week before Danny's. For seven fun-filled days he called me his cougar and I considered him my boy-toy. I'd hoped that reminding him of those decade-turning milestones might soften my reluctance to push our relationship to the next level.

It seemed to work until I couldn't leave well

enough alone and added, "If one of us hasn't found someone else by then." He tensed beneath my hand. I think he might have even stopped breathing for a second—or five.

"Of course," he said eventually. "That was always the stipulation."

I planted a kiss on his smooth cheek. "Then we're good?" I really wanted this resolved between us.

"Absolutely," he answered with a sigh that sounded more like capitulation than resolution.

He turned his back to me and flipped on the little portable television I'd put on the dresser a couple of months ago. Hey, he hadn't been around for a while. I needed something to occupy my solitary nights, didn't I? After weighing my options, I'd decided the television was the cheapest way for me to go. I would have gone broke buying batteries for the other electronic devices I'd considered.

His action ceased any further conversation—which was fine and dandy with me since I didn't want to have this discussion in the first place.

Unable to turn off my thoughts, I waited until Danny fell asleep. When I heard his slow, even breathing, I turned off the TV, stuffed my feet into fuzzy Garfield slippers and shuffled down the dark hall to the living room.

The only light I used when I moved around my place at night was the one I left on over the kitchen sink for my kitties. I know cats are supposed to have great night vision and all, but I'd also read somewhere that it wasn't really their eyesight but their whiskers that worked like curb feelers to help them move in the dark without bumping into walls and furniture. So I figured why take chances. My babies deserved the benefit of the doubt.

After pulling back the vertical blinds from the sliding balcony door, I stood there in my nightshirt and gazed across the frozen tundra, also known as the parking lot, and wondered how I could slow Danny down without totally pushing him away?

I'm not going to lie. I've given into an occasional daydream about what my life would be like married to Danny, but I've also had plenty of moments wondering what it would be like living without him.

The *with Danny* fantasies were always clearer than the *without*, but I figured that was because I hadn't been without him in one way or another since I was thirteen. We'd been friends for over half my life, on and off lovers for the last ten. The thought of not having him around scared the hell out of me, but then again, so did settling down.

I loved Danny. I've known that for years. He was my best friend, my soul mate in so many ways. I just wasn't sure if he loved me enough not to leave if things got rocky. If my own mother didn't have any problem taking a hike, what made me think I could keep a man from doing the same thing?

I pressed my forehead against the glass and peered into the desolate darkness. I knew I couldn't commit to anyone until I was able to figure out the answer to that.

A monster SUV turned off the side road and cruised through the parking lot. I knew it didn't belong here. Odd as it seemed, I knew every make and model of every tenant's vehicle in the building.

I watched the vehicle for a couple of reasons. For one, it was past midnight. Our building sat at the end of a quiet street in a residential area with no main thoroughfares running near it. There was only one way in and one way out. An unfamiliar vehicle practically crawling through a private lot in the middle of the night was plain old suspicious.

When the car rolled to a stop directly across from me and turned off its lights, I decided it was time to make a call to the cops and request a cruiser to check it out. I scanned the dimly lit living room for my cordless phone. Why was it never where it was supposed to be? Because I seldom remembered to return to its home base, that's why.

"Jennifer!" Tony screamed. "Get down!"

I dropped to the floor as the booming report of gunfire split the night. The sliding door exploded behind me. Beads of tempered glass rained down, peppering the back of my bare calves, as I ducked and covered.

Chapter Twenty

"Jen!" Danny screamed from the bedroom.

He was going to have to come to me because I couldn't move. He called my name again as he neared.

"Don't come any closer unless you're wearing shoes," I warned. "There's glass all over."

"What the hell happened?" Danny asked as he stopped short of the scattered glass.

"Somebody shot out my balcony door." I rose to my knees and shook the glass from my hair. A blast of freezing air hit my back as it swept through the living room, turning the space into an arctic wind tunnel.

"Jesus, Jen. Are you all right?" He turned on a lamp and surveyed the damage. Wearing nothing but a worried frown, he wasn't in any better position to help me than my dead pal Tony.

"I think so," I said as I climbed to my feet. The glass crunched beneath the rubber soles of my Garfields. I looked around for Fred and Ethel. I discovered them, wide-eyed and ears perked, crouched side-by-side under the table in the dining alcove looking like another pair of frightened, fuzzy cat slippers.

Persistent pounding on my front door forced me to move. One glance at Danny had me smiling in spite of the situation. Except for the gun dangling in his hand, he stood naked as the day he was born. "Maybe you ought to put that thing away before I answer the door," I suggested. "Wouldn't want to scare anyone."

"Good idea," he said, backing down the hall to the bedroom. "I should probably put the gun away, too," he added.

"Were you carrying a gun?" I queried. "I hadn't noticed."

When I peered through the peephole, I discovered what appeared to be the building's entire population clustered outside my door. When I pulled it open they all started talking at once, making it impossible to understand a single word coming at me.

I held up a hand to cease the uproar. My bodybuilder neighbor from across the hall stepped forward, taking on the role of official spokesperson. "We heard an explosion, Jennifer. Is everything okay? What happened?"

"My balcony door shattered."

"I thought I heard gunfire," said Mrs. Johansen from the third floor. Half a dozen more tenants concurred with her observation, and there wasn't a thing I could say to calm their speculations as to what went down.

"I'm not exactly sure what happened," I told them. I heard sirens and figured that Danny had called the police. "Hear that? The police are on their way. I'm sure they'll figure it out." I didn't want to stand there fielding questions, especially ones I couldn't answer. "I promise to give you all the details as soon as I know something."

"You call me if there's anything you need,

Jennifer," Ben said as he squeezed my shoulder.

I appreciated his calming gesture. "Thank you, Ben," I said, retreating into my unit.

I heard him add, "Anything at all," as I shut the door.

I found Danny dressed and inspecting the room with the eye of a professional. I tried to look at the mess through his eyes, but all I saw was the gaping hole where my glass door used to be and a handful of misshapen vertical blind slats flapping in the stiff breeze. It was all a little too personal for me to be objective.

I shivered and shook my head in disbelief. "Who would do something like this?" I wondered aloud.

"You tell me," he said, sounding anything but sympathetic. "What have you done to make people want to send you this kind of message?" He crouched and rooted through the debris with the eraser end of a mechanical pencil.

The only reason I could think of was sitting at the bottom of my closet in a virtually indestructible shoebox. But how was that possible? No one knew that stuff was there except for Tony. And who could he tell but another dead guy?

"My guess is someone's found out about this thing you do with dead people," he said. "More specifically with Tony Barrera."

I huffed an annoyed sigh. "I really wish you'd stop referring to my ability as *this thing I do with dead people*. I'm not doing anything immoral or illegal. All I do is talk to them."

"Semantics aside, whatever it is you do, it's still with dead people, and there are some who find that distinction hard to accept."

I was shocked by his reply. "Are you one of those people?"

He couldn't look at me. "Maybe I am," he said, stepping around the glass.

"Well," I breathed. "It's nice to know your real feelings on the subject."

"Jen," he said, taking a cautious step toward me. "You know what I mean."

I put out my hand to stop him from coming any closer. I did not want to discuss this with him. "I'll get the vacuum," I said, focusing my attention on something I could control.

"Don't touch anything," he stated.

"Oh, right." I knew better.

"I already called the board-up service. They should be here within the hour. But you'll need to call your insurance company."

"Oh, right," I said again, reaching the conclusion that I must be in shock or something because why else would I be having trouble remembering the carrier of my homeowner's policy. "Should I do that now?" I asked, trying to remember where I kept my agent's number.

"It can wait until morning."

I looked around and saw Tony standing in the middle of the mess. I didn't think it was possible, but he looked pale.

I glanced at Danny, who was busy ushering in the uniforms.

"I'm going to get dressed," I said, motioning to Tony to join me. Dan acknowledged me with a cursory wave and a nod. I hastened into the bedroom and closed the door.

"Okay, mister, start talking. How'd you know that was going to happen?"

If he hadn't been there to warn me— I couldn't finish the thought. My knees buckled and I collapsed on the bed.

There was nothing more sobering than the realization of how close to personal injury I'd come. In spite of the heated flush that washed over me, I shivered as if ice water had replaced the blood in my veins. I suppose the big hole in my living room where a sliding glass door used to be could have something to do with the drop in temperature, but I was pretty sure it wasn't the only reason for the unnatural cold that touched me to the core.

"I just knew."

"You just knew?" I screeched, jumping to my feet in a blind snit that at the very least got my blood pumping. "This has to do with that stuff from your apartment, doesn't it?"

Well, double duh on me. As if it could be anything else.

"You know, Tony, this is where you're supposed to jump in and deny that assumption. I'd even settle for some deceptive posturing right about now, but this, if you'll pardon the expression, dead silence isn't doing either of us any good."

I was teetering on hysteria. I knew it. Tony had to have a clue and, in all likelihood, so did all the persons congregating in my living room. I have never been a silent sufferer and wasn't about to start now.

Tony paced and rubbed the back of his neck and shoulders like a man who was trying to ease the tension building there. He wasn't fooling me. The dead didn't get tension. They didn't get headaches, or cramps, or constipation, sneeze, burp, fart, or hiccup, either. They existed on a plane of consciousness we, the living, would never understand no matter how hard we tried. I'd been dealing with these people going on twenty years, and I'd barely scratched the surface of understanding.

Tony's final days on this earth shouldn't be like this. Neither should my time helping him make the transition, damn it.

"Whatever you do, wherever you go, don't let that stuff out of your sight. Promise me, Jennifer. Please."

There came a knock on the door. "Jen, you okay?" Danny asked.

"Yeah, I'm fine," I told him as I hurried into my closet to get dressed. Now that was a lie, pure and simple. I wasn't anywhere near the definition of fine, but I couldn't very well tell him my dead friend was driving me crazy.

"Are you going to be much longer?" Dan asked, sounding more than curious. "There are some questions we have for you."

"I'll be right out," I said, tossing an angry glance in Tony's direction.

"I'm not through with you," I said to him as I stuffed my freezing feet into thick wool socks. I felt better, but it was going to take a lot more than socks and a sweat suit to give me the warmth and comfort I needed.

"If you're not ready to start talking when I get back, I'm turning that stuff of yours over to the police and let them deal with it."

Then I stormed out. I didn't wait for a response because I didn't want one. I've learned it's better to give a guy a little time to mull over an ultimatum. The outcome is often more favorable that way. Dead or alive, that's something that never changed.

Chapter Twenty-One

When I returned to the living room, I was accosted by my big brother. He swept me into his burly arms and crushed me into an encompassing bear hug. Eddie is a bear of a man—six foot three and two hundred and thirty pounds of rock solid muscle. It was only fitting, I suppose, that his hugs matched his size.

Eddie's seventeen years older than me and tends to be a mite overprotective, which is just a nice way of saying he's been driving me crazy with his quasi-parental hovering from the day I was born.

At first, I assumed he was here because he heard the call on his home scanner. But after giving it further thought, I realized it wasn't likely he heard it in the middle of the night. As chief of police, Eddie was Danny's superior. He learned about this from another source.

"Did Danny call you?" I asked. Except with my face smashed against his jacket, the words came out sounding more like, "Dud Dammy caw woo?"

"Of course," Eddie stated. "He would have been in serious shit if he hadn't."

Ah, how could I forget about the sacred code of the F.O.B.—that's Fraternal Order of Blabbermouths. I couldn't sneeze in my car without a police officer pulling me over to say, "Gesundheit."

I shot Danny a look that told him I didn't appreciate him expressing his loyalty to the brotherhood over respecting my privacy. He gave me one of those helpless looks that told me he did what he had to do. In other words, better me than him.

"Go pack a bag, Jenny," said Eddie. "You're coming home with me."

Now that suggestion frightened me a whole lot more than having my window shot out. Eddie had four kids, ages eleven through seventeen, two Labrador retrievers who looked like they were on anabolic steroids, and a mid-sized wife who considered me a bad influence on their teenage daughters. I suspected this was in part because I was pushing hard on thirty and unmarried was pushing back.

Although I could never be certain if her snide, off-handed comments were because she resented my state of singleness or envied it. She has one of those perpetually nasally voices that made it hard to tell.

Nope. I wasn't going anywhere near Eddie's house under these circumstances. Edie—yeah, Eddie and Edie, cute, huh?—would never let me hear the end of this latest fiasco. Her first observation would be this happened because I didn't have a man in my life. Hah! Fat little she knows. A man in my life? Hell, this happened to me when I had a detective in my bed.

"Inasmuch as I appreciate the offer, Eddie, you and I both know that'll never work," I said. "I'll go to Dad's house."

"You're not going to find any more room there," he told me. "Maddy and her family arrived late this afternoon. Uncle Carl and Aunt Bea are also in."

I forgot my sister was coming early for the holiday, but I didn't know about my dad's brother and his wife. That meant Dad and Lena already had a house busting at the seams. My options were dwindling.

"How about Rob's?" My other brother had only two kids, a wife who actually liked me, and a lovely guest room.

"No good," said Eddie, shaking his head. "Jan's parents are in from Florida."

"Doesn't anyone stay home for the holidays anymore?" I wondered aloud. This was downright frustrating.

"You could try Roger's," Eddie suggested.

My step-brother was a nice enough sort and wouldn't hesitate to open his door to me. "They're in the middle of a major remodel," I said as I shook my head with visions of myself sleeping on a stack of sheetrock.

Eddie didn't dare mention the last available family member living in the area. He and I both knew Andy wasn't an option. Andy's wife, Judy, would welcome me with open arms, but the thought of sharing quarters with her lesser half made me shudder.

"This is crazy," I said. It looked like I was going to have to go to a motel, which really sucked since I had enough relatives to fill a small township, and I couldn't find one who could put me up, or I could put up with, for a few days.

The obvious solution was right in front of me in the form of a six-foot-one blond detective. But after the conversation we'd just had, I hesitated to suggest it. He looked at me, as if waiting for me to do the asking. I turned away, refusing to be the one to relent. There was the matter of pride and principle involved.

"Oh, for chrissake," he mumbled. "Jen, you're coming home with me. I have plenty of room."

"Then it's settled," Eddie proclaimed as he patted me on the head. "I feel a whole lot better knowing Dan will be keeping an eye on you."

No doubt about that. At the moment, he was staring me down with both eyes and a tight-lipped frown.

I forced a smile. "I'll go pack."

Tony was nowhere to be found when I returned to the bedroom. No big surprise there. He had the disappearing part of this dead thing down pat.

"Woof," Buddy interjected. He jumped on the bed and eyed the suitcase I pulled from the closet.

"Sorry, fella. You're going to have to fend for yourself for a while. Keep an eye on the place for me. I'm leaving you in charge."

He gave pitiful whine and rested his jowls on his enormous paws. His liquid brown eyes shifted from the suitcase to me as furry brows waggled in contemplation of his forthcoming situation.

I cast him a regretful glance. There was nothing else I could do. I'd take him with if I could. That was the other big difference between Buddy appearance and the others. All my human contacts were free to move around from place to place, but Buddy refused to step foot outside my condo.

It didn't take me long to gather what I'd need for a couple of days. It's not like I couldn't come back if I needed anything else, which in all likelihood is what I'd have to do since the coming week was a short work week. The chance of getting anyone out to fix the sliding door before the holiday was doubtful.

I packed sweats, of course, and jeans, tees, sweaters, socks, and underwear. The sneakers I had on were the only shoes I planned on taking. I stuffed a small zippered makeup bag with the essentials and grabbed shampoo, conditioner, and moisturizer because I couldn't count on Danny having any of those things. As long as I've known him he was strictly a bar soap and water kind of guy.

At least, I didn't need to pack work clothes because I had the coming week off. For as long as I'd worked at Donaldson's Distributing, I always took off the week following the end of year audit. This year it just happened to fall the same week as Thanksgiving. Good thing, too. If I had to deal with going to work Monday morning on top of everything else, I'd have to hurt someone.

The last thing I crammed into the suitcase was the shoebox with Tony's stuff. I still hadn't decided whether I was going to tell Danny about the Griffith apartment or the things I'd taken. But if Tony didn't materialize with some answers for me soon, all promises were off, and it was every dead man for himself.

Chapter Twenty-Two

Fred and Ethel yowled at me from the cat carrier sitting on the passenger seat. Two pair of frightened blue eyes stared at me through the grated hatch.

"Poor babies," I cooed as I stuck my fingers through the grate and scratched Fred's ear. "You think you're going to Dr. Lou's, don't you?" They had every reason to think that since they never left the condo unless I was taking them to the vet.

The instant they saw me haul out the carrier, they'd scampered for cover. It took Danny and me twenty minutes to catch them, and another ten to stuff them into the carrier. We both bore bloody puncture marks on our hands from my feisty felines' attempts to evade capture.

"I've got a surprise for you," I trilled in my best kitty-soothing voice. "We're going to stay at Danny's for a few days."

Danny was kind enough not to insist I board them during my stay at his house, and for that I was going to owe him. Although I must admit the thought of taking them to a kennel had briefly crossed my mind when Fred sank his fangs into the fleshy part of my thumb for the second time in as many minutes. It still throbbed inside my glove.

"Won't that be fun?" I asked, not sounding the least bit convincing. Sharing a roof and a bathroom with a guy I'd just told I wasn't ready to live with was not my definition of fun. Far from it, any way I tried to look at it.

If Danny's strained behavior when we loaded my car was any indication of his feelings, he wasn't any more thrilled than I was at the prospect of sharing living quarters under these circumstances.

I kept telling myself he didn't have to do it, but the more I tried to convince myself otherwise, there was that annoying little voice that told me differently. He'd been backed into a corner, and he did the only decent thing he could do under the circumstance because he was a decent, caring man. I'm sure I was going to owe him for that, too.

At a red light I thought was taking an inordinate amount of time to turn, I glanced in my side view mirrors. Even dulled under a layer of region road grime, Danny's fire engine red Mustang was hard to miss a couple of cars behind me. He was intentionally hanging back, watching for anyone who might be following me. I know this because I overheard Eddie tell him to watch for any suspicious vehicles. Hey, I'm a medium and an eavesdropper, not a mind reader.

My cell twittered and I checked the screen like a good little girl who happened to have a maniac taking middle-of-the-night pot shots at her. I was surprised to see it was Danny. When he was a patrolman, he'd handled far too many accidents involving distracted drivers yakking or texting on their phones. He hardly ever used his cell while driving and constantly chewed me out for using mine, so I knew this had to be important.

He'd even bought me a Bluetooth headset, but of course I wasn't wearing it at the time. I answered in the only way I could and braced myself for the inevitable lecture.

"What's up?"

"Can you get a look at the guy driving the gray sedan behind you? He's been staying with you since we left your place."

"You think he's tailing me?" I cast a quick glance in my rear and side view mirrors. "I can't get a good look at the driver because he's got the visor down. It's hiding most of his face."

"I'm waiting for dispatch to get back to me on the plate," he told me.

"You want me to try and shake him?"

"No!"

"What should I do?"

"What you've been doing."

"I haven't been doing anything."

"Exactly," he replied. "But whatever you do, *don't* act like he's following you," he said as he disconnected.

I stuck out my tongue. A childish reaction, I know, but nevertheless gratifying. There was something so annoying about being told *not* to do something, I couldn't help myself.

Six blocks from Danny's house I slipped through the intersection as the light turned yellow. The gray sedan ran the light on full red and stuck to my bumper like we were magnetized.

Danny didn't waste any time in flipping on his dashboard lights and going after the violator. Familiar with the drill, I slowed to a rolling crawl and pulled to the curb.

The sedan whipped around, barely clearing my rear bumper, and zoomed past me with Danny in pursuit. When a marked squad joined the chase, I waited for Danny to return to where my car sat parked on the street near a mini-mart strip mall.

From the corner coffee shop I sipped a mocha latte and watched him park his Mustang nose to nose with my Malibu. It didn't take him long to realize I wasn't in it.

With his fists on his hips, he glanced around wearing a scowl I knew included gnashing teeth. When he finally spotted me, I smiled and raised my cup in a mock salute to his brilliant detective work.

He rubbed his knuckles across his jaw and marched across the street to where I sat waiting at a charming little bistro table for two. I had a large coffee with two sugars no cream waiting for his imminent arrival.

"You did that on purpose," he said as he slid into the chair.

"Guilty as charged," I said. "But while you only *thought* he was following me, I proved it, didn't I?"

"What exactly did you think busting this guy for a traffic violation was going to prove?" He thumbed the lid off his cup and took a swallow. "If he doesn't have an outstanding warrant we can hold him on, we're screwed."

"You'll get a look at his driver's license, at least, and then you can question him about tailgating me."

"Oh, that's right, how could I forget Jennifer's rules of interrogation? Just ask the suspect why he did something and he'll come clean and tell us everything. Case solved."

"Now you're being sarcastic," I said.

"That's one you've got right," he said, taking another long swallow of his coffee as he stood. The cell clipped to his belt twittered. He flipped it open and barked, "Prince."

Now I'd been around cops most of my life. I understood procedure and probable cause better than the average civilian. I can't put into words what was going through my head when I ran that yellow light, so there wasn't any sense in my attempting to explain to Danny why I did what I did when I didn't understand myself. He was angry with me and the situation I created. Keeping quiet was my best line of defense, I decided.

Danny closed his phone.

"Well?" I prompted. "Did they catch him?"

"They lost him," said Danny.

"They—lost—him?" I couldn't believe it. "How in the hell did that happen?"

"They backed off the second the guy turned into The Meadows."

I knew what that meant. Department directive prohibited high-speed chases into residential areas. It was better to let the pursued escape than risk involving an innocent bystander.

"I understand," I sighed. "Anything come back on the plate?"

"You're going to love this. The car was stolen from an alley garage two blocks from your condo."

"You're kidding!"

"The owner didn't even know it was missing until we informed him."

He gulped what was left of his coffee and pitched

the cup into the nearby trash receptacle. "I'm starving. You want to go for breakfast?"

I smiled and nodded, realizing the crisis between us had passed. It was always like that with us. He could never stay mad at me, which was a very good thing for me to keep in mind since I managed to piss him off on a regular basis.

Chapter Twenty-Three

The adrenaline rush of the last seven hours was ebbing fast, and in its place there settled unequivocal exhaustion. Even the Cozy Café's bottomless cup o' java couldn't stop my lids from drooping. Grateful I didn't have far to go, I finished the short drive from the restaurant to Danny's house on autopilot.

Danny still lived in the beige brick, Chicago-style bungalow where he was born and raised. He'd had his own apartment for a while, but when his elderly parents' health failed, the dutiful son and only child had moved back home to help.

He'd shown up when his parents gave up all hope of ever having a family. His mom had been forty-three and his dad only months shy of fifty when they learned they were going to be parents for the first time, and they doted on their late-in-life miracle.

Spending time at his house had been like going on vacation for me, and the Princes treated me like a princess. When they died within months of each other a little over a year ago, I felt their loss profoundly. Even now, thinking about them, made me hurt deep inside.

I smiled when I turned onto Danny's street. Some of my best teenage memories were made in the house that sat in an older section of town where the trees were mature, the sidewalks were a little worse for wear, and the blacktop streets were patched and faded to a dull, battleship gray. I grew up in a similar neighborhood on the opposite side of town, which explained why we'd never met until our opposing grade schools funneled into the one central junior high.

I pulled into the narrow side drive and hit the garage door opener Danny'd handed me when we left the restaurant. He didn't want my car sitting on the street, and I couldn't think of one good reason not to follow his cop instincts.

Per his instructions, I parked on the right side of the detached garage. I sat there for a moment, struck by how neat and organized the space had gotten since the last time I'd seen it. We'd hung around out there when we were teenagers, but the older and more mobile we got the less time we spent there or anywhere else parents might be lurking and waiting to catch us doing something we shouldn't.

Danny pulled in next to me as I cut my engine and popped the trunk.

"You really cleaned up," I commented as I hoisted my complaining felines from the front seat as Danny lifted my suitcase, a litter box, and a new bag of litter from the trunk.

"Dad was the prince of packrats, that's for sure. You wouldn't believe the crap I hauled to the dump after he died."

"You didn't pitch Blaze the Wonder Horse, did you?" I chuckled, remembering the three-legged rocking horse his father had rescued from a neighbor's garbage. "Gonna fix it up good as new for the grandkids," I'd overheard Alan Prince say to his wife.

Poor Danny took a lot of ribbing from me that summer. We were only fifteen at the time and the absurdity of Danny being a dad was too funny not to be turned into a running joke.

"Uh, no," Danny murmured. "It wasn't out here. It's probably still buried in the basement somewhere. I haven't gotten around to cleaning that out yet."

"I can give you a hand with that," I offered. "I'm free all week."

"Don't do that!" he blurted.

His response startled me, and I looked to him for further clarification. I would have thought he'd be jumping for joy at the chance of free labor.

"It's too dangerous, that's all," he explained, sounding much calmer. "There's stuff stacked to the rafters down there. I don't want to come home and find you at the bottom of a toppled pile."

I followed him up the porch steps and nudged him in the back with my elbow as he searched his ring for the house key. "Gee, Dan, I'm touched by your concern for my safety."

"I was thinking more about the awful mess you'd leave for me to clean up," he grumbled as he jabbed the key into the deadbolt. "Not to mention all the paperwork involved."

"You rat," I hissed as I poked him in the ribs. "Just for that I'm going to train my cats to pee on your pillow and poop in your shoes."

"Yeah, okay," he laughed, adding, "Like you could train those fur balls to do anything."

"True enough," I agreed. "It'd be simpler if I peed on your pillow."

He laughed at that too.

"You painted," I remarked as I stroked the creamy taupe door trim. I had trouble picturing Danny as a grass-mowing, snow-shoveling, window-washing homeowner even though I knew he'd been doing all of those things and more even before he'd moved back. In my mind, he would forever be the fun-loving high school point guard who spent more time trying to get out of chores than helping with them.

"Back in September," he replied as the door swung open. He wiped his feet on the rug inside the threshold before continuing. I wondered when he'd become so domesticated.

"Hmmm," I purred as I followed his example and swiped my sneakers across the bristly WELCOME mat. That's about the same time he stopped coming around my door. Coincidence? I think not.

I stepped only as far as the enclosed back porch before opening the cat carrier. My babies had been cooped up long enough. They needed to stretch and investigate their new surroundings.

While they sniffed and snooped, I set up their litter box and scooted it into a corner to give them a little privacy. The second I showed them where I'd put their potty, Ethel climbed in and started digging. Fred sat nearby, patiently waiting for his turn.

When I entered the next room, I realized I needed to do a little investigating of my own. Over the years, I'd logged a lot of hours in the Prince kitchen. I knew every inch of the circa 70s room by heart, and this wasn't it.

Where were the harvest gold appliances and dark walnut cabinets? And there was supposed to be grid-patterned brown and yellow linoleum under my feet, not this gleaming wood laminate.

It was gone, all gone. Instead of the comforting, familiar kitchen I remembered from my teens, I found myself standing in the middle of a beautifully appointed kitchen straight out of one of those home makeover shows. I wanted to cry, and had I been prone to that emotion I would have. As it was, I gave a little sniff.

I fingered a place on the tan granite countertop where there used to be a scorch mark on the old speckled Formica. I knew exactly where it'd been because I'd put it there with a hot cookie sheet. I could still feel Virginia Prince's arms around me as she told me my feelings meant more to her than a silly old countertop.

That woman more than likely saved me from a one-way ticket to the Indiana State Women's Correctional Facility. She'd recognized my rebellious streak as a cry for the love and attention I'd never received at home and gave it to me even when I didn't know I wanted or deserved it. I'm sure she also figured keeping me out of trouble was in turn saving her son from a similar life of crime.

"Were these home improvements how you passed the time while you were re-evaluating our relationship?" I asked. It felt more as if he was eliminating the things that reminded him of me.

"Something like that," he answered as he busied himself with carrying my suitcase toward the bedrooms. I followed on his heels because I was exhausted and needed to know where I would be sleeping. I was also dying to see what he'd done to the rest of the house.

He hesitated in the hallway, looking like he wasn't sure which direction he wanted to go.

"What's wrong? Is there a problem?"

"Yes," he answered. "There's a big problem."

"What? You didn't make your bed? Or you can't remember if you left dirty clothes on the floor? I know, you've got a girl stashed in your closet." Oh wait, except for the girl in the closet sounded more like my bedroom.

"None of the above," he answered. His fingers flexed and gripped the handle of my suitcase as he glanced from one end of the hall to the other. "I'm not sure what to do with you."

What did that mean? "You know, if you didn't want me to stay here, you shouldn't have extended the invitation." Okay, so it wasn't so much extended as it was expected. I wrestled the suitcase away from him. I didn't need a house to fall on me to know I wasn't welcome. I was so out of there.

"I don't want you here," he stated, immediately adding, "Not this way. Not for these reasons." He tried to take the suitcase back, but I kept a tight grip on the handle and an even tighter grip on my unraveling emotions.

"You're not here by choice, Jen, you're here by circumstance. Just last night you told me you weren't ready for any of this, yet here we are. So you make the call... my room or the spare room?"

"Is that what this is all about? I'm not ready to move in on a permanent basis, so you don't want me here on a temporary one?"

Shit, I was tearing up again. What was wrong with me?

And to make matters a thousand times worse, I was having a hard time controlling my bottom lip. It seemed to have a mind of its own, and it was determined to tremble. I chomped down hard on the offender to let it know I wasn't giving in to its tantrum.

The suitcase slipped from my fingers and landed with a thud as a dull thrumming behind my eyes made me rub my forehead and grimace. Wonderful, I was getting a headache on top of everything else. I didn't want to deal with this right now. I didn't want to deal with this ever, but *right now* was definitely my first choice.

"I'll sleep in your old room." I snatched up my suitcase and headed for the spare bedroom at the opposite end of the hall. "Problem solved."

"Whoa," I said as I stepped into Dan's old room, feeling like I'd passed through the portal of a time machine. I was suddenly fifteen again. "Has this room been registered with the historical society?"

Danny breathed a heavy sigh behind me. "Mom was so proud that she'd kept it just as I'd left it, I didn't have the heart to change it when I moved back."

I was so touched by his consideration for his mom's feelings if I had been an easy crier I would have, but I'm not so I didn't. Even if I were, I couldn't because I'd maxed out my tear quota the other night. I wasn't about to tap into next year's allowance.

So I swallowed the lump in my throat and turned my attention to a collection of trinkets and pictures arranged on the maple dresser.

My gaze settled on a framed picture of me sitting on the bright red moped he'd gotten for his fifteenth birthday. I was zooming down memory lane faster than we zipped around town on that thing.

"Oh my God," I said, picking up the photo. "I

forgot all about this picture."

"There's a lot about this house you forgot," he stated. "Like how to find your way here."

What he said rang painfully true. I couldn't remember the last time I'd been to his house since his parents died. Avoiding the place had been easier than facing the reality of their absence from it. Then I realized Danny never had that luxury. I'm sure he could have used some moral support. Even from a thoughtless, selfish bitch like me.

"I'm sorry, Dan." My words, though heartfelt, sounded hollow and grossly inadequate.

Without another word, he carried my suitcase down the hall and into the master bedroom.

I followed so I could take it right back.

"You'll be more comfortable in here."

Before I could comment on his thoughtfulness, his cell rang. He pulled it from his belt and left the room.

I wasn't sure what to do first. The bed looked too inviting not to at least give it a try before I left. I sat and bounced a couple of times to test the mattress. Nice. Next, I scooted and leaned against the pillows. Very nice.

It was the last thing I remember.

Chapter Twenty-Four

Something disturbed my dreams. I tensed and burrowed deeper as I fought against the intrusion. Just as I felt myself drifting back to sleep, it started again. That's when I finally recognized the bothersome racket for what it was.

I pushed the comforter away from my face and looked around. This wasn't my bedroom. Whenever we spent the night together, Danny always stayed at my place. That mini revelation caused me to wonder why exactly that was as I fumbled for my cell.

"Yeah," I grumbled. I was not the most pleasant person upon waking. Not that I was Miss Congeniality the rest of my waking hours, but first thing in the morning, or afternoon in this instance, was the worst for anyone who had the misfortune of being around me.

"Jenny honey, is that you?"

Like who else would be answering my cell phone?

"Hi, Daddy," I answered, adjusting my snarly tone to one with enough sugar to frost a couple dozen cupcakes *and* a triple tier wedding cake. I could be a miserable person to every other member of my family, but never my dad. He brought out a charming sweetness I reserved for only him. And don't think my brothers and sisters haven't noticed what they all refer to as my *daditude*. There's a very good reason for this sudden switch in my disposition.

"How are you?" I inquired.

"Shouldn't I be asking you that?"

"Why do you say that?" Ed Flagg had been a good detective in his day—make that a great one. He had a real knack for making people think he knew way more than he really did, which in turn had caused criminals and his children to confess to transgressions he knew nothing about. And if I was standing face to face with the man, I'd be tempted to fall on my sword just to get this interrogation over and done. But since he sat clear across town, I wasn't volunteering any information over the phone until I found out what he knew.

"Don't be peeing down my back and telling me it's raining, young lady."

I grinned at that. My daddy was born way south of the Mason-Dixon and had colorful expressions for just about every occasion. He always boasted he was American by birth, but Southern by the grace of God. You have to love a man who maintained his southern roots even though he'd been transplanted into Yankee soil more than fifty years ago.

"I don't know what you're talking about, Daddy." That came out a lot easier than it should have. Maybe I was finally getting the hang of this.

"Eddie's here," was all he said. It was enough. I knew the rest, but somehow still managed to resist the urge to fess up. You see, I've learned from first-hand experience. With this daditude of mine there come certain fringe benefits. I can't be cranky if I project sweetness and nice, now can I? And if I'm not cranky, I'm not as likely to blurt stuff I shouldn't. Trust me.

I've learned the hard way.

"That's nice," I replied. "Tell him I said hi. Are Edie and the kids with him?" I heard the typical ruckus of kid sounds and carrying on in the background. The peace and quiet surrounding me here at Danny's was practically paradise. I stretched and scooted to the end of the bed.

"Jennifer Elaine…"

Uh oh. It was never a good thing for anyone concerned when my father used middle names. Not even when the one he used wasn't mine.

"Try again," I said as I hunted for my shoes.

"Susannah?"

"Nope."

"Lynnette?"

"Bingo."

"I've had enough of this nonsense, young lady," he growled. "Eddie told me *what* happened. Now I want you to tell me *why* you've got people shooting at you."

"I don't know!" And that was the God's honest truth. Did he really think I went around antagonizing people enough to make them want to kill me? Besides my immediate family, that is.

"It has to do with that thing you do with dead people, isn't it?"

I rolled my eyes. Why did people keep calling it that? Again I answered, "I don't know, Daddy."

And I really didn't know for sure. Dad's conclusion was a reasonable one, a logical one and, in all probability, the right one, but until I heard it straight from the shooter's mouth, there was still an outside chance of it being a random, no connection whatsoever drive-by. We Flaggs were nothing if not a bunch of cock-eyed optimists. Dad was our fearless leader and the cockiest optimist of us all. He of all people should understand my hesitance in jumping to unsubstantiated conclusions.

"I want you and Dan to come for dinner tonight."

"Doesn't Lena have enough to do this week?" I was looking for an easy out. Thoughtful consideration for my stepmom sounded like an excellent place to start.

"We already got a houseful. Two more at the table won't make much difference," he countered.

That was true enough. When only assorted members of my family got together there were lots of us. The Flagg formal dining room, otherwise known as the finished basement, looked like a boarding school mess hall and seated almost as many people.

"I think Danny's already made plans for tonight." I didn't know any such thing, but it sounded like an excellent excuse. Dad's southern roots wouldn't want me to be an ungracious houseguest.

"He can change them," my father said in his most determined, not-to-be-argued-with tone. "We'll see you at six." He disconnected before I could counter-respond. That's my dad. Did I also mention he was an expert at having the last word? Believe me, we've all tried through the years and *never* succeeded. I've come the closest, I might add. I am my father's daughter.

I snapped my phone closed and went in search of Danny to inform him of our dinner plans. Not that dinner at my dad's was all that much of a hardship. My stepmom was the best cook on the face of this planet. In my expert opinion, that's as an eater not a cook, the Food Network chefs had nothing on Lena.

Dan wasn't alone when I found him in the living room having a low-toned conversation with a man I didn't recognize. First impression told me the guy was a Fed, from the tip of his polished black oxfords to the top of his neatly styled short-cropped black hair. He was a stereotypical, photo-ready example of all things government issue. Didn't these guys know their attempt to look inconspicuous is precisely what made them stand out like a cheap toupee? Now I've been known to be wrong in my snap assumptions, but I doubted this was one of those times. Just because I wasn't psychic didn't mean I didn't have excellent instincts.

Both men stopped talking and stood when I entered—the tall, dark stranger got to his feet first with Danny a couple of lazy heartbeats behind. That Dan stood at all took me by surprise. We didn't stand on formalities. For that matter, we didn't stand on informalities, either.

My gaze shifted between them before I settled my sights on the stranger and smiled as I extended my hand. "Hello, I'm Dan's girlfriend, Jennifer." The pleased grin on Dan's face wasn't lost on me. We'd never resorted to defining our relationship with titles, and I didn't understand the urge to do so now, but I felt obligated to establish boundaries from the get go.

The stranger's gaze held me and my outstretched hand in silent perusal, and he appeared almost hesitant before taking my hand.

And those eyes, so dark it was hard to tell where the pupils ended and the irises began, made me wonder if the color was real or contact-lens enhanced to create the mysterious, forbidding stare. They were disturbing eyes, shuttered and unfathomable, and they made my blood run a little colder regardless of their origin.

"Cole Kingsley," he said with a hint of a genuine smile as our hands met, tempting me to return the facial greeting. Then the curtain dropped. Every possible emotion that made us human was gone in an instant and my smile died on my lips. His face was a blank canvas, and I was startled by the glaring starkness of his disassociated stare.

I sucked a startled breath and jerked out of his grasp. My reaction caught me as much by surprise as the odd prickles crawling up my arm. Not exactly sure what it was I experienced from the brief connection, I redirected my attention to Dan as I flexed my fingers to dispel the lingering tingle. Some crazy emotions were stirring inside me, and I wasn't sure what to do with them.

"Am I interrupting?" I stammered.

"Actually, I was just leaving," said Cole as he reached for his overcoat. His suit coat fell open, exposing the holstered weapon on his hip. The gun dispelled any doubts I had about him. He was a Fed, all right. My guess was FBI.

"Please don't leave on my account," I told him. "I was on my way to the kitchen to get myself something to drink. Can I get you anything, Special Agent Kingsley?" I was taking a huge chance in my assumption, but I figured even a shot in the dark managed to hit its intended target once in a while.

"Thank you, no." His politeness was frosty and final, and if I expected any visible reaction to my address, I was disappointed.

Then he turned to Dan. "Is there a reason you chose not to mention she was psychic, detective?" His tone was downright accusing and a tad reprimanding, neither of which Dan deserved, but both of which made me take immediate offense.

Although his question was aimed at Dan, I didn't find any reason not to answer for him. "The reason Dan didn't mention it is because I'm not." Hostility poured out of me like an artery had been opened and left to freely bleed.

I touched my fingertips to my temple and fluttered my eyes dramatically. "Do the letters F—B—I mean anything to you?"

"I didn't mention she was a smartass, either," Dan interjected as he grabbed my arm and yanked me to stand beside him. "But as you can see, it didn't take her long to reveal that *charming* quality all on her own."

Again, I watched for any sign of a reaction, but Cole Kingsley displayed all the emotions of the wall behind him. His face remained stoic, his gaze dark and distant. The term poker-face leaped to mind. He was probably very good at whatever he did for the government.

That dark gaze shifted to Danny. "We'll talk more tomorrow."

Danny nodded and cast me a dark glance of his own. His I understood loud and clear.

The room still held the traces of cold air Cole allowed in when he'd left. I rubbed my arms to chase away the chill the weather and the man left behind and said, "What's with that guy?"

"That guy…" Danny mimicked. "…is the section chief of his department and a leading authority in his field."

"And what field might that be?" I asked. "Wait, let

me guess—he heads the department of dark and brooding?"

Danny hesitated, as if he wasn't sure he should tell me, but in the end he relented and said on a sigh, "Paranormal events and investigation."

Although it didn't take me by complete surprise, that bit of information did manage to get my undivided attention. "The FBI has a paranormal division?"

"It's not common knowledge, as you can well imagine why, but yes, they do. Cole informed me about his involvement this afternoon."

I was getting a bad feeling about this, and it had nothing to do with whether I was psychic or not. It was my long-term relationship with the man standing in front of me that led to the suspicions bouncing around in my head like a handful of Mexican jumping beans. He wasn't mentioning the paranormal angle just to make pleasant conversation.

"This isn't your first contact with him, is it?"

He shook his head. "I met Cole a couple of years ago at a law enforcement seminar the FBI was hosting for local level detectives. Cole was one of the speakers. We had dinner and drinks together the night before I left."

Ka-thunk went the sound of it all falling into place. "That's when you told him about me, isn't it?"

"I might have mentioned that I had a close friend who talked to dead people."

"You might have? Either you did or you didn't, Danny. Which is it?"

"My memory of that evening after dinner is kind of fuzzy."

His memory of that night a couple of years ago

might be fuzzy, but mine had total recall about certain incidents from a lot farther back than that.

"Tequila wouldn't have anything to do with this memory loss of yours, now would it?" Neither one of us were big drinkers. A few beers with pizza or a cocktail or two before dinner was about the extent of our consumption habits. So when either of us overindulged, the recollection of specific actions had been known to blur.

A sheepish grin came over him. "It would have everything to do with it, I'm sorry to say."

Since my own history with tequila, margaritas in my case, wasn't exactly one I wanted pointed out for comparison, I prudently decided to forgive and forget. Forgetting was the easy part. Forgiving took a little more effort.

"What exactly did you tell him about me?"

"Just what I said—that you occasionally spoke to a recently departed."

"And he didn't find that odd?"

"I guess what you do isn't so odd to someone who deals with paranormal oddities on a regular basis."

"But you said he just told you about his involvement with that aspect today."

Danny stopped to think about that for a couple of long seconds, and his brow creased. "That's right, he did." He gave a one shoulder shrug. "There probably isn't much the FBI finds odd anymore."

I'm sure that was true since odd and unusual were probably the better aspects of what the Bureau had to deal with on a daily basis. I didn't feel like dwelling on it more than I already had. It wasn't worth getting into an argument over, that's for sure.

"We've been summoned to Flagg manor for dinner tonight," I said, hoping to change the subject. There was something about Cole Kingsley I found disturbing to the point of distraction. I felt a desperate need to find my equilibrium and plant my feet on solid ground again. Talking about my family was a good start.

"It sounds like your dad wants to see for himself that you're okay."

"I told him you had other plans for us tonight."

He dropped onto the couch and looked at me like he knew what I was thinking. "You are not using me as an excuse to get out of having dinner with your family."

Yep, he knew exactly what I was thinking, all right.

Danny was big on family. I was sure it was because after his parents died he didn't have any left of his own. My dad had welcomed him into the Flagg fold like another son, and Danny had gone all too willingly. He was a permanent member of my family whether we wound up together or not.

I parked my butt next to him, rested my chin on his shoulder, and gave him one of my most pitiful pouts as I played with a button on his shirt. "But Danny," I whined with enough nasal intonations to make even me cringe. "You don't really want to subject us to the family inquisition twice in one week, do you? Thanksgiving Day will be bad enough. It'll be New Year's before we recover."

I loved my family, every last one of them—except for Andy Ramos, of course—but they were a pushy, nosy bunch who didn't have the slightest qualms about badgering me and Danny with personal, downright embarrassing questions about the status of our relationship. My father was the worst of the bunch. I personally wasn't ready to face the Flagg probing and prodding. Our personal lives were nobody's business but our own, and I was feeling ornery enough today to tell them all to bite me. Getting shot at in the middle of the night will do that to a person.

"Jen…" he said. "About Thanksgiving…"

"What about it?"

"I don't think it's a good idea for me to go with you this year. Christmas either."

I was stunned into speechlessness for about thirty seconds. "Cut it out, Dan," I said, giving him a playful smack on the knee. "You had me going there for a second until I remembered you'd never pass on a chance to graze on one of Lena's gut-buster holiday feasts."

As much as I wanted to believe he was teasing, I couldn't ignore the sick knot swelling to the size of a baseball in the pit of my stomach telling me just maybe he wasn't.

He wouldn't look at me. That was never a good sign. The knot in my stomach grew to size of a softball. I had to say something before it reached mush ball proportions.

"You have to go," I said softly.

"Why?"

"Because you have no choice in the matter, that's why. Like it or not, once you've been sucked into the Flagg family vortex, there's no escaping."

He breathed a little laugh. I took that as a better sign. "That's true enough," he agreed. "But what if you do find someone else in the next couple of years? Do you think Jenny's ex lover would be as welcome into the fold?"

He posed a question I'd never thought about before. Yes, it's true, I'd given in to the occasional *without Danny* scenario, but I'd never given any thought as to how his not being around would affect my overall family dynamics. Then an even bigger thought struck me.

"Hey, wait a minute. This sounds suspiciously like the opening line to a kiss-off speech. Are you breaking up with me?" Was breaking up even possible when we weren't officially a couple in the first place?

"No, nothing like that," he said as he shook his head, only not as vigorously as I might have hoped from a man wanting to convince me otherwise. It was way too slow and deliberate, not the least spontaneous, and the smile he flashed never reached his beautiful baby blues.

"Our not being a couple has never been a problem for you in the past," I pointed out. "Even that gas jockey you were dating a couple of years ago didn't keep you from coming to Christmas dinner."

"Tara was the station manager, and we'd only gone out a couple of times. It was never serious enough for us to consider spending a holiday together."

His gaze settled on my lips, and he had that look in his eyes that suggested he was going to kiss me, which was more than fine with me because he was a great kisser. I breathed a sigh of relief. It looked like our mini crisis had passed.

A lazy smile came to his lips; I moistened mine in anticipation. Here it comes...

Then without so much as a peck on the cheek, he patted me on the knee and stood as he announced,

"Well, we'd better get moving then. We don't want to be late for the Flagg family Q. & A."

Thunk went the sound of my jaw hitting the floor. My disappointment at being left kissless quickly joined it.

Chapter Twenty-Five

We arrived exactly thirteen minutes under the designated deadline. I'd perfected my timing over the years and knew exactly when to show my face for these family things. Get there too early and you're stuck doing grunt work in the kitchen. Get there late and you're relegated to the kiddy table. Thirteen minutes allowed me enough time for the mandatory meet and greet, and not much else before we marched downstairs.

"Aunt Jenny!" My five-year-old nephew squirmed off his mother's lap the second I came through the door and barreled toward me with a full head of steam.

"Hiya, Zak," I said, holding him at arm's length and side-stepping his attempt to wrap his grubby little paws around me. A full head of steam wasn't the only thing he had going. There was greenish yellow snot smeared across his cheek and something purple and sticky-looking clinging to and around his lips. Yuck.

"Hey Maddy, you want to come get your kid?" I held him away from me by his shirt collar. He twisted and wriggled under my grip as he tried to escape. "There's stuff coming out of his nose."

My sister never failed to amaze me. She's a nurse, for crying out loud—a geriatric one, but snot was snot regardless of the vintage. You'd think she'd have a better handle on keeping green and purple stuff like this off her kid, or at the very least under control. Double yuck.

"There's a box of tissues right behind you," said Maddy, never bothering to move, or even look at me for that matter.

I snatched a tissue from the box and handed it to Zak. "Here you go." He grabbed it, stuffed the whole thing into his mouth, and started chewing.

"Uh, Maddy. Your kid's eating the tissue."

"Before or after you wiped his nose?"

"Before," I answered. "I gave him the tissue so he could do it." There weren't enough tissues in all of Costco for me to take on kids' snot.

With a dramatic sigh that was probably heard clear in Milwaukee, Maddy pushed off the couch and collected her son. She cast me a piteous glance, like I was the one who had the problem. Let's just say it hadn't escaped my family's notice that me and little kids don't mix.

She swiped a tissue under Zak's nose, folded it, and wiped the smeared excess with the clean side. As far as snot removal goes, her technique was flawless.

"Shouldn't he be doing that for himself by now?"

"He's only five, Jennifer. I still wiped your nose when you were that age, too—and your butt."

That brought a chuckle from every male in the room. It was those kinds of comments that kept me from ever growing up in the eyes of my family. I was and will forever be the baby. This was the youngest child syndrome at its worst, and more than likely the main reason why I wasn't fond of kids now. Who wanted to be reminded I was still considered one of them?

It's true, I have issues relating to children—my seventeen nieces and nephews notwithstanding. It's a different story when they're teenagers. I enjoyed my own teenage years, probably because of the irresponsible freedom I'd perfected during that period of my life. I have a ball with Eddie's fifteen-year-old twin daughters, whenever I'm allowed to spend any quality time with them, that is. I'm the bad influence according to their mother, remember? Sheesh. The tattoos were only temporary. And the second Edie regained consciousness we told her so.

Zak was back, sans snot. His mouth, however, appeared permanently stained. This time, however, he ignored me and went straight for Danny, which was more than fine with me.

"Hey, Dan," Zak said. "Did ya bring your gun?"

"Sure did," said Danny, sweeping aside his jacket to show the boy his sidearm.

"Wow." The child's eyes grew wide as he touched the butt of Dan's holstered Glock.

What I didn't understand was the big deal Zak was making about Dan's gun. Between the cops and inherent southern breeding in this family, a good percentage of the adult males there today were packing. I wouldn't be a bit surprised if a few of the ladies had a piece tucked in their purses, as well. What can I say? We're a family who loved their firearms, and we'll fight to the death for our Second Amendment right to bear them.

"Uncle Eddie let me hold his gun once," the boy informed us. "It didn't have no bullets in it, but I was very careful anyway cuz I want to be a policeman when

I grow up."

Danny crouched to Zak's level and looked the child straight in the eye. "We can always use another good man on the force. I'll see that your name gets added to the top of our future recruit list." The child beamed from Danny's encouragement, and they slapped high fives to seal the deal.

I rolled my eyes and wandered away. Male bonding, regardless of their size disparity, made me do that.

Speaking of male bonding...Crowded around a folding card table at one end of the living room, sat my father, uncle, Maddy's husband, and both brothers playing penny ante five card stud. I would have loved to join them, but I already knew no invitation would be forthcoming. No woman had ever breached the sanctity of any poker game in this house. Neanderthal thinking, I know, but I wasn't about to be the one to fight a time-honored family tradition. Let the next generation of females try. Danny knew how I felt, and promised to never stop me from playing poker in his house. I appreciated the sentiment, regardless of the fact he'd never held a poker game even once at his place. Not that I knew about, anyway.

I followed my nose and gravitated toward the kitchen where I found my stepmom and Andy's wife, Judy, bustling around doing what I knew were the kind of activities people did in kitchens when they had a clue as to the room's true purpose and design. Like I might have mentioned before, my genetic code did not include culinary acumen. Nor had I by osmosis gleaned much of anything useful from Lena over the years. I just never saw the purpose of cooking when there were professionals who perfected the art of carryout and delivery.

I eyed Judy Ramos and said, "Nice outfit," as I snatched a slice of cucumber from the salad bowl. "Is it part of the June Cleaver Home for the Holidays retro collection?" How else could the belted shirtwaist, pearls and heeled pumps be described? She was straight out of a fifties sitcom. The amazing part was she looked fabulous in it.

"Ha, ha..." She grinned, displaying two of the cutest damn dimples I'd ever seen on a female of any age. "Good thing I know y'all are only teasing me, Jennifuh."

Judy's a south to north transplant like my daddy. Only she's from one of those states that produces peaches, pecans, and southern belles whereas my dad's from one of those places that boasted the best coon dogs, fishing holes, and good ol' boys than much of anything else.

Judy was all things perky and ultra-feminine, a perfect example of sugar and spice and all that other fricking jazz. In spite of all that sweetness and fluff she was also a surprisingly successful businesswoman, selling Avon, Tupperware, and my personal favorite, assorted lingerie and adult toys for a company called Coming Attractions. Her products fulfilled a lot of needs. Because I did their taxes, I know firsthand she grossed triple what Andy earned last year. I derived a certain level of satisfaction from that piece of confidential information.

"Congratulations, I heard you've recently taken up cohabitating," she said with an enigmatic smile. "I've got some great new products to help make the transition into coupledom more interesting."

I knew she wasn't referring to Avon or Tupperware. I was a good customer with the lingerie and Avon. The Tupperware not so much. I didn't cook enough to invest in quality food storage containers. In order to keep leftovers fresh, there was the little detail that first involved food preparation. I figured being a regular consumer of two out of three of her product lines wasn't so bad.

"I wouldn't call what we're doing cohabitating, exactly." To tell the truth, I wasn't sure what I'd call what Danny and I were doing. Like I've said before, there's nothing more complicated than whatever it was between us, but until I had it figured out, sexy lingerie and/or other sexual paraphernalia would only add to the confusion. "It's only temporary—until my door gets fixed."

"Well, whatever you're calling it, sugah, you're still living with a man."

No wonder she did so well as a saleswoman. Her sweet southern drawl made everything sound so much more appealing.

"There's no reason why you shouldn't make the most of the situation for however long it takes to *fix your little problem.*"

I had no response for that because she was right. Sex had never been the problem with me and Dan. Between the sheets, we were as compatible as peanut butter and jelly, and I'm sure we'd be making a lot of sandwiches while I was living there. It was all the other relationship stuff that turned to stale crackers and old liverwurst.

I snitched another slice of cuke and laughed at

Judy's assessment of my current living arrangement. I leaned in closer so no one else could hear and told her, "Yeah, well, Dan's been hinting at making it a permanent arrangement."

The corners of her mouth turned upward, as if she knew this day would arrive. "Looks like congratulations really are in order."

"No," I said. "No congratulations. Not just yet."

"Why? What did you tell him?"

"I told him no, of course. You know I'm not ready for anything like that."

"You sure about that? I'm thinking the only thing y'all aren't ready for is admitting you are."

I shoved a tomato wedge into my mouth to keep from commenting on her observation one way or the other. Judy could be amazingly perceptive, for someone lacking the street smarts of us northerners, that is.

Most people wouldn't guess Judy and I are friends, good ones in fact, but we are. She knows I've got a problem with her husband, and that's okay with her even though she adores every last chubby square inch of him. And I can live with that even though I can't begin to fathom why. That still doesn't stop me from marveling at how Andy managed to attract, let alone marry, a woman like her. It's one of life's little mysteries, I guess. Better make that one of life's bigger mysteries. I mean it doesn't rank with contemplating the meaning of life or anything like that, but its right up there on my list.

My attention was drawn to the oven where my stepmom pulled a huge, blue speckled-ware roaster from the oven. When she lifted the lid, the rising steam filled the air with its heavenly aroma. And to me, heaven would have to smell a lot like Lena's pork roast. I reached around her and sneaked a chunk of potato from the pan. It was steaming hot, and burned my fingers and mouth, but it was so worth it. What's a blistered finger or two for a little taste of heaven? Gandhi himself couldn't have resisted Lena's cooking.

"Jenny!" Lena exclaimed as she replaced the roaster lid. Her face was flushed from the heat, and her eyes danced with genuine pleasure at seeing me. "Come here, child." Still wearing her elbow-length oven mitts, Lena took me into her arms and hugged me with all the gusto I'd come to expect and eventually learned to accept.

Magdalena Ramos Flagg was the antithesis of my biological mother. She was the mother I never had the first eight years of my life, although I fought against her attempts to love me for a long time. Over the years, I'd learned to resist the urge to pull away and accept her unconditional affection. I don't think I ever thanked my dad for marrying this woman and making her a part of our family. I made a mental note to correct that oversight. It was long overdue.

I relaxed into her embrace and let her mother me the way I refused to let her when I was little. She smelled like all things motherly—sweet and warm and comforting. Although I never knew why at the time, I never liked the way my real mother smelled. It wasn't until I got a lot older and wiser, and she was long gone, did I realize it was the lingering scent of men who weren't my father that made my nose wrinkle every time she came near. Because of her infidelities, I could describe what a cheating woman smelled like to this day.

"How are you, Lena?" I mumbled against her sweet-smelling, rosy cheek.

"Shouldn't we be asking y'all that," Judy interjected, poking me in the ribs. "We heard about the unfortunate incident at your apartment last night, you poor thing." She touched my arm in a way that told me she was doing it to be consoling but also in part because it was the right and kind thing to do under the circumstance. Judy was all about doing the right thing. Lowering her voice to a whisper, she said, "It has to do with that thing you do with dead people, doesn't it?"

See, this was a big part of the reason why I didn't want to come here tonight. I sighed and replied, "It's not the dead people that give me trouble, Judy."

All the adults in my family and a few of the older kids know about this thing I do with dead people. It's not a secret. It is not, however, a frequent topic of discussion around the dinner table. It's like that six-hundred pound pink gorilla sitting in the corner. Everybody knows it's there, but nobody wants to be the first to mention it. It's easier for everyone to pretend this thing I do with dead people doesn't exist. Until something like my *unfortunate incident* pushes the gorilla into the middle of the room thereby forcing one and all to acknowledge its presence. I guess that's what I get for being the only gorilla in my immediate family, pink or otherwise.

The next thing I reached for was an oatmeal cookie from a plate on the counter. I couldn't believe it when Judy smacked the back of my hand with a wooden spoon.

"Those cookies are for my Andy," she said.

I eyed the cookies as I rubbed my stinging

knuckles. "How come he gets a whole plate of cookies just for him?"

"This is his third day of phase two," she went on to explain. "I made these special to reward him for getting through phase one."

"Phase one? Phase two?" I had absolutely no idea as to what she was talking about and told her so.

"He's been eating South Beach," she drawled, as if that explained everything.

Well, it explained a lot. "So, what beach does he plan on eating when he's finished with that one?"

For that, I got another swat with the spoon.

Chapter Twenty-Six

The clock on the dresser showed it was a little after two. It felt like I'd been sleeping longer than a few hours. I get like that when I've slipped into a pork roast and chocolate nut torte induced coma. My mouth was parched and my tongue felt like a dried apricot, all sweet and soft but lacking any useful moisture. In case I hadn't mentioned it before, my stepmom is the best cook ever and, to put it mildly, I tend to over-indulge, mainly because I'm never sure when or where my next good meal is coming from.

When Danny and I'd returned from dinner with my family, we'd flopped into bed like a pair of bloated slugs and fell asleep before either of us could think about much less suggest burning off the excess calories with a vigorous round of celebrating. Our first night of unofficially living together, and all we did was fall sleep. How pathetic was that? And if Dan was conscious I'm sure he'd agree with me.

I reached for the water bottle I always kept on the nightstand. It wasn't there. Why would it be? This wasn't my bedroom or my nightstand.

I sighed as I laid there debating whether my state of dehydration was serious enough to climb out of a warm, snuggly bed and go to the trouble of traipsing down the hall for a couple sips of water. With all that thinking about water, my bladder made the decision for me.

I peed, flushed, and headed for the kitchen. I know, I know, the bathroom sink plumbing isn't connected to the toilet or anything gross like that, but I've always had a thing about drinking bathroom water. Hey, I'm not the only person out there who prefers water from the kitchen tap. Heck, I'm almost practically positive I'm not the only one in my family who thinks that way. And, although Danny refuses to discuss it, I've suspected for some time he prefers kitchen water, too. Why else would he have gotten a refrigerator with a built-in water dispenser? Fred and Ethel, however, have no reservations whatsoever about indulging in the waters from the porcelain pond. Different standards for different species, I guess.

Without bothering to turn on a light, I shuffled barefoot down the dark hall. I knew my way around this house as well as I knew my own place. Besides, how hard was it to follow a hallway to the end? I could do it with my eyes closed, and took a few steps with my eyes shut to prove it. When I opened them, I found a man standing in front of the refrigerator.

"Tony!" I screeched as I clutched my chest to certify my heart was still beating. The rapid palpitations reassured me it was. Where in the hell was Fred? He was supposed to warn me about these unannounced visits. I blew out a calming breath as I snatched a glass from the cabinet and filled it from that dandy refrigerator dispenser.

Just then, Fred moseyed into the room. He stopped in his tracks, took one look at Tony, bared his fangs and hissed, then continued on his way to the litter box. I was glad to see he was still there for me despite the fact his timing could use a little fine-tuning.

"I got a problem."

"You're dead. Your problems are over."

"I really need you to help me with something," Tony said.

"Let me guess," I said as I took a sip of water. "There's another apartment you want me to break into?"

"You didn't break into the first one," Tony was quick to remind me. "I let you in, remember."

"Yeah, well, I don't think the police would see it quite the same way," I pointed out. "Especially since they can't see or hear my alibi." Tony was new territory for me. Everything he did was stronger and more unpredictable, and he was a lot less helpless then my previous contacts. It was both frightening and exhilarating to be part of this man's afterlife.

"I really need your help, Jen."

Okay, so even Tony had his limitations. "What is it?"

"I need you to help me find Mia. She's disappeared."

"Define disappeared."

"She's vanished. I can't zone in on her whereabouts anymore."

"That's going to happen," I explained. "It's part of the "moving on" process."

"I don't want to move on!" he exclaimed. "And I can't, I won't, until I find Mia and know she's okay."

I blew out a slow breath. Guiding my dead friends into the next world, getting them to let go, wasn't always easy, especially when they fought against the process. I had a feeling this guy would not go gently into that good night.

"You don't really have a choice, Tony," I told him. "It's going to happen whether you want it to or not."

I could see he wasn't ready to hear what I was telling him because he pretended he didn't and said, "Something's happened to Mia. I know it. I can feel it."

"Maybe she got scared and ran off," I suggested. I know that's what I would have done under the circumstances.

"No, no," he said. "She wouldn't do that." He shook his head against the possibility. "Not without telling someone."

"Does she have family or friends in the area?"

"No, I don't think so," he murmured. "Vander Poole kept her on a pretty short leash."

"Then who would she tell?"

"She had a job to do. She wouldn't walk away from it." He seemed pretty adamant about that, although I couldn't for the life of me figure out why.

"Oh, yeah, who could turn their back on that fabulous career opportunity? Cleaning up after rich folks has always been one of my secret ambitions."

I've said it before, and I'll say it again. I am not a nice person. Oh, I have my moments. Ask anyone who knows me, and they should be able to recall at least one incident when I was nice. But this would not be one of those memorable times. So sue me or cut me some slack, okay? It was the middle of the night, and this wasn't my father I was talking to here. I didn't have to be nice.

"Mia was more than a domestic. She was my

confidential informant."

"Then what does that make you?" I was promptly struck with one of those amazing *duh* moments, although I congratulated myself for resisting the urge to thump my forehead as I finished, "You're a cop."

He turned away as he answered, "Not exactly."

"Fed?"

"All I can say is I'm with a government agency. I've been working undercover for the last six months. I didn't want to say anything until I was convinced you weren't connected with my investigation."

"Why would you think that?"

"You showed up just as they were moving my body from the house."

"So Danny was right. There was someone still in house."

"Yes there was, and as soon as you left, they tried to get me out of there before the cops showed up. What they didn't count on was the security guy showing up as quick as he did."

Well, well, chalk one up for Andy. "Do the local authorities know this about you?"

"I've been working with several departments in the area," he answered.

Since he seemed more willing than usual to offer information, I wanted to get as much out of him before he clammed up again. "What about the Roths?"

"They've been involved from the beginning."

"So the engagement was a ruse?"

"Briar Cliff Estates is a pretty tight community. It was the only way we could guarantee my immediate acceptance into their social circle. Angie was the one who initially approached us."

"Approached you about what?"

"Let's just say there were things going on in their neighborhood she didn't think were on the up and up."

"You're investigating some of the most influential people in the region. What for? Tax evasion?"

He breathed a little laugh. "I'm not with the IRS. And it's only a small group of Briar Cliff's finest under investigation."

Then Danny's words to me at the crime scene played in my head. *Stay out of this, Jennifer.* "Danny knows, doesn't he?"

"This has been hard on him. He's concerned for your safety, as am I."

"That didn't answer my question."

"The less you know the better."

"How do you figure?" If I could have jabbed him in the shoulder for emphasis, I would have. Instead, I tossed my hands in the air, figuring if anyone could appreciate hand gestures, a man who spoke fluent Brooklyn Italian would. The problem was I forgot I still had the glass of water in my hand and it sloshed all over me and the floor.

"My ignorance didn't keep me from getting shot at the other night," I snapped as I ripped a paper towel off the roll hanging near the sink.

"They weren't technically shooting at you."

"Would you care to tell me what they were doing?"

"Sending you a message." He responded without a moment's hesitation, which led me to believe he knew exactly what they were doing.

"Well that makes me feel ever so much better. Thanks for sharing." I tossed back the remaining water, wishing it was a shot of Jack. A little liquid courage wouldn't hurt right about now. And maybe some pretzels. It never hurt to have alcohol and food around at times like these.

"So tell me, Tony. How do you know so much about these guys and their motives?"

"I may not be directly involved in this anymore, but it's still an ongoing investigation. These people are afraid you can identify them. I can't let you get any more involved than you already are. "

"It's a little late for that, don't you think? I've been pretty involved since I discovered your dead body."

"An unfortunate coincidence," he said.

Unfortunate coincidence. Those were the same words Danny had used. I never put a lot of faith in coincidences, unfortunate or otherwise. Things happened for a reason.

"You trusted me to help you recover that stuff from your apartment, how can you expect me to help you find Mia if you won't tell me what I'm up against?"

The indecision that crossed his face was subtle but apparent. "I'll tell you everything as soon as I know Mia's safe."

I gnawed on my lower lip and figured it was just as well. "I understand," I said. "In fact, it's probably better if you don't tell me. I'm already way past my secret limit with you. If I happen to slip and say something pertinent to the case, and believe me the odds are I will, people will assume I got the information from Danny. I wouldn't want this coming back on him."

"I appreciate your thoughtfulness."

My heart gave a thumping jump at the disembodied voice coming from the hall. Danny stepped out of the shadows and held me in his sights. Gulp.

Chapter Twenty-Seven

"I—uh—was talking to Tony," I explained as I glanced around, noting the aforementioned subject was nowhere to be found. This disappearing act of his was beginning to annoy the crap out of me.

Danny tossed me one of his looks and said, "Yeah, I gathered that." He padded across the laminate floor and opened the refrigerator.

He wore only a pair of low-riding flannel boxers, and I couldn't help but watch the way his back muscles flexed and rippled as he reached into the crisper and pulled out an apple.

I could tell he was upset with me. So what else is new? But instead of wondering what I'd done to deserve it this time, all my mind could process were each and every thing I'd rather be doing with the sexy, practically naked man standing in front of me. Isn't it funny how the mind, and body, worked at stressful times like this? Needless to say, I think about sex a lot.

He flipped the golden delicious in the air and caught it in its downward spiral then brought it to his mouth in one quick, flawless motion. I heard the crisp snap as his teeth broke the peel. Bite by deliberate bite, he worked his way around the apple until there was nothing left but the stem and core. I admired his self-

191

control as much as I wished he'd say what was on his mind and get it over with. His silence was making me squirm, and not in a good way, I might add.

"Talk to me, Danny," I prompted as he pitched the core into the garbage disposal and flipped the switch.

"What do you want me to say?" His tone was unemotional and his expression was hard. An icy sliver sliced through me. I didn't recognize the man standing in front of me.

"Who are you?" I breathed. "You're not the Danny Prince I've known for most of my life." This guy was scaring me. "I want him back and I want him back right now."

"Look, Jennifer," he started.

I didn't think I was going to like what he was about to say. Nothing good ever started with the words, *Look, Jennifer*. My father started a conversation like that the day my mother left.

Feeling like the floor was about to be yanked out from under me, I let gravity suck me into the nearest chair. I hated hearing bad news on my feet.

"I can't be the Danny you want right now." Then poof, just like that he was gone.

I deserved better than that from Danny. What I deserved was an explanation.

"That's it?" I said, leaping to my feet to go after him. A second ago I'd been prepared to hear something bad, but now after hearing… Shit! I wasn't sure what I'd just heard, or what it meant. What in the hell was "*I can't be the Danny you want right now*" supposed to mean, anyway?

I came up behind him and caught him by the arm. "Don't believe for a single second you can drop something like that on me and think it's finished."

He turned on me so fast I had to step back to get out of his way. "Why can't you leave this alone?"

Danny didn't stand all that much taller than me, five inches tops since we were both bare-footed, but now he seemed a lot bigger, broader, and angrier as he loomed over me, making me feel small, and worse, insignificant.

But not for long.

Intimidation didn't work on me. Growing up in a house with seven older siblings—four until I was eight and three more when my dad remarried—I'd learned to get out of the way or give it back in spades. After a few years of fading into the background to keep from being noticed, I evolved into a spades-giving gal all the way.

I placed a single fingertip against his breastbone and said, "Back off," as I applied increasing pressure. He did as I requested. It's amazing how one little finger can move a two-hundred pound man with very little effort.

"I'm sorry," he said, rubbing the back of his neck.

"What's going on, Danny?"

He stared at me as if he couldn't believe I had to ask. "I hate that you're putting yourself in harm's way and there's nothing I can do to protect you," he said as he hung his head and heaved a disturbed sigh. "I don't suppose it'd do me any good to ask you to stay out of this Barrera business?"

"Probably not," I answered truthfully.

"And if I insisted?"

"You know better than that," I replied with a tempered sigh of my own.

"That's what I figured. Then I guess there's

nothing more for me to say." He started for the bedroom then stopped and braced his hands on the doorframe as he looked at me over his shoulder. "There is one more thing—please be careful, Jen. How would it look if something happened to you while living under my roof?"

I thumped the side of my fist against his back. "Your concern for my welfare overwhelms me."

"And your lack of concern for it scares the hell out of me," he whispered. I couldn't be certain if he'd meant for me to hear what he'd said or not. It was one of those things I couldn't ask him to repeat.

"I'll be extra careful," I promised. Although I was clueless as to how I'd go about doing that. I knew I'd have to figure it out without Danny's help.

Chapter Twenty-Eight

Danny's side of the bed was empty when the alarm jarred me awake. Judging from the coldness of the sheets and pillow my guess was he'd been up for some time. He might even have left for work by now, which might not be such a bad thing considering the minor difference of opinion we'd had the last time we spoke. Now that I thought about it, I'd prefer it if he wasn't around.

I sat up and caught a glimpse of myself in the dresser mirror. If Danny could be compared to Redford and Newman, I guess the most appropriate points of reference for me were Lucille Ball and Little Orphan Annie—light on the Ball and heavy on the Little Orphan. I held no illusions about which direction the scales tipped that morning.

A sharp rap came at the bedroom door. "Bathroom's free and coffee's on."

Well, so much for hoping he'd already left for work.

"I'll be right out," I said with a resigned shrug.

Danny's house was laid out like every other bungalow I'd ever been in. Front to back, the living room, dining room, and kitchen were arranged in typical shotgun fashion, one room leading directly into the next. Off the dining room and kitchen archways there ran a parallel hall that led to three bedrooms and a bathroom.

I made a quick dash, muttering a hasty, "G'morning," as I slipped into the bathroom and shut the door.

I did all the usual things people did first thing in the morning and managed to lasso my wild curls into a scrunchie I'd found stuffed in the back of a vanity drawer. It had never belonged to me. That much I knew. Never in a million years would I have bought that shade of pumpkin orange to go with my shade of copper red.

I cast one last glance in the mirror and eyed the riot of spiral curls shooting from the top of my head, and wondered why I bothered. Danny knew what I looked like first thing in the morning. So why was I so worried about him seeing me like this one more time?

Whatever the reason, I felt like this was somehow different. Maybe it was because I was on his turf this time. Or maybe it was because he wasn't all that happy about my being there in the first place and I felt obligated to being the perfect houseguest. Then again, maybe I was blowing this way, way out of proportion, which I've been known to do on occasion.

I shoved my reservations aside, patted the scrunchie, and headed for the kitchen.

The second I yanked open the bathroom door I heard Danny's voice and realized he was on the phone. I retreated and shut the door, leaving it cracked enough to listen. I know eavesdropping is wrong. I tell myself that every time I do it, but sometimes it was the only way to hear anything worthwhile.

"I'm interviewing the rest of the neighbors later today," he said. "I hope to finish up with Vander Poole and her maid between three and four."

I grinned at that bit of news. Danny had just handed me a free pass to the main event. Well maybe not free exactly. Danny would see that I paid in one way or another. I wasn't so much worried about the *one way*. It was the *another* that kept me awake at nights but not enough to keep me from joining him this afternoon. It's funny how things like that work out.

A tenacious curl sprang out of its tether and flopped across my forehead. A silly nursery rhyme my grandma used to recite to me sprang to mind as well, like a taunting premonition.

There was a little girl
Who had a little curl
Right in the middle of her forehead
When she was good
She was very, very good
But when she was bad
She was horrid.

That pretty much summed me up in a nutshell. If that curl was telling me I had to make a choice this morning—horrid would win hands down. In the bigger picture I figured helping dead folks move on to their final reward was about as good as it was ever going to get for me in this lifetime. It was my calling, and I took it seriously. If doing an occasional questionably bad thing to accomplish that was part of the deal, then so be it.

Danny was cramming his arms into his leather blazer when I finally made my appearance.

"You're out of here already?" I slid into the nearest

kitchen chair and eyed him with a full dose of blatant admiration and a side order of desire. He looked quite dashing this morning in a deep blue shirt and matching print tie that deepened his eyes to glittering sapphires. When he looked at me, I felt myself turn all mushy under his gaze. As much as I didn't want to admit it, this whole domestic scene was kind of nice. I could get used to sending him off to work like this every morning.

Whoa. Did that C-word actually pop into my head? Commitment wasn't a word I bandied about lightly. I shifted my interest from Danny to the ceiling and studied a cobweb forming in the corner.

"Already?" he said, taking one last gulp from his favorite blue and white Indy Colts mug. "I was supposed to meet Jeri half an hour ago." He dumped the dregs from his cup into the sink and loaded it into the dishwasher, placing it right next to his favorite blue and orange Chicago Bears mug. That was another major point in his favor. He was loyal to a fault to whatever he deemed loyal-worthy and, from what I've been seeing, pretty much housebroken. A lot of men would find Dan a hard act to follow, and a lot of women wouldn't mind being in my place.

"I left a house key for you on the counter."

"I still have a key," I told him.

"No, you don't. I changed all the locks a year ago. If you'd bothered to use it once in a while, you would have known that. Call me if you need anything else." He came toward me, and I raised my face for a goodbye kiss.

He snatched his keys from the table, patted me on the top of the head, and was out the door before I could question this display of...of what exactly? Who the hell knew what he meant by it. But I sure didn't like it.

I felt cheated, ripped off, denied what was almost practically rightfully mine. I wanted a kiss goodbye, damn it. A pat on the head was not by any stretch a suitable substitution. Where did he get off treating me like...like...like an Irish setter?

The scrunchie sprang loose and spilled curls everywhere. Talk about a portent of things to come. All I needed was Wendell to make an appearance to make my day complete.

Chapter Twenty-Nine

The one and only bathroom in Danny's house was on the small side, but he'd managed to outfit it with some really nice upgrades when he'd remodeled. I was thrilled to discover the whole house wired for sound and connected to the satellite radio receiver in the living room. This was quite an improvement over the battery-operated, piece-of-crap radio hanging on my shower curtain rod.

We both liked noise when we showered, but that's where the similarities ended. For me it had to be something loud and rowdy enough to get my blood pumping. For him it was the news and weather, dismal and dull by my definition. When I wanted to know what the weather was like, I used my head. I stuck it out the window and dressed according to how my hair responded.

Since I needed something to rock my soul this morning not rock me back to sleep, I dialed into a classic oldies station and cranked up the volume. As usual, I scared the daylights out of Fred and Ethel. They scampered away in search of a quiet corner to curl up and wait out my morning madness.

I stripped and stepped into the steamy spray, testing each setting on the great, new showerhead before settling on a combination somewhere between eye-opening and personal satisfaction. I rocked through my head to toe routine in a matter of minutes and after slathering my head with conditioner, I used the recommended two-minute wait to admire the wide wallpaper border circling the walls near the ceiling.

I'd always thought of borders as girly additions to a bathroom since most were floral motifs, but Dan had managed to find a geometric design that suited him, filled with sharp angles and textured planes in strong colors of navy, camel and turquoise.

I did one final, stimulating rinse and reached for a towel. Clouds of steam billowed around me as I swept back the shower curtain and stepped out. I cracked the bathroom door to release the excess. I didn't want to be the one to explain to Danny why his handsome new border was on the floor when he got home tonight, and examined the edges to make certain I hadn't caused any permanent damage.

Some people marched to the beat of a different drummer. Me? I boogied to it. And my favorite time to strut my stuff was right out of the shower, naked and free, jiggling whatever and wiggling everything else. Yes, I admit it, I was a closet exhibitionist and proud of it. The music set me free.

With the towel as my only prop, I shimmied and swayed to the beat with every part of me as I dried. When a classic Bee Gees tune fired up, I started movin' and a groovin' like Travolta on one of his finest Saturday night fevers.

Stepping up my dirty dancing moves, I wrapped the towel around me and strutted my way down the hall. When I reached the bedroom, I stripped off the towel in a move worthy of the late, great Gypsy Rose for my finale. What I didn't expect was applause and wolf whistles for my solo performance.

My eyes flew open at the same time my heart plummeted when I saw my audience. Danny *and* Tony were leering at me like a couple of schoolboys at their first peep show.

"I've got a pocket full of singles, but I'm not sure where to stick them."

"I'd be happy to tell you," I said as I scrambled for the discarded towel. He was quicker than me and snatched it out from under my grasp, leaving me stepping frantically around the room searching for cover.

Now this shouldn't be that big of a deal, right? Danny and I knew each other intimately. He knew about the freckles on my butt, and I knew about the tiny mole on the tip of his…well, it's there, trust me.

What was different about this time from all the others? Well, for one, I was the only one naked in the room. And two, it was broad daylight. Exposed in the harsh light of day was a whole lot different from feeling your way under the softer glow of mood lighting. Three, Danny wasn't the only one getting an eyeful. Need I go on?

From the way he looked at me I didn't have to guess what was going through his mind—and damned if Tony wasn't wearing the same shameless expression.

I scrambled for the closet and grabbed one of Danny's polo shirts. They were longer than any of mine and would hopefully cover more, or at the very least enough.

"What, no encore?" Danny asked with a

disappointed pout. He leaned back on his elbows and tossed a dirty smirk in my direction.

"Yeah," said Tony. "What he said."

"What are you doing here?" I asked as I dragged the shirt over my wet head and down my body. "I thought you'd left for work." Lucky for Tony he was already dead because the glance I cast him would have melted the flesh off a live recipient.

"I did, but when I tried to call and you didn't answer, I got worried and came back. And I have to tell you, Bunny Fur, I'm real glad I did."

"Bunny Fur?" Tony chuckled. "I can't wait to hear why he calls you that."

"Get out," I said, tugging at the hem of the shirt to keep my butt covered as I crouched to pull a pair of panties from a zippered pocket of my suitcase. "This might be your house and your bedroom, but I'd appreciate a little privacy, if you don't mind—from both of you," I blurted.

Danny propelled off the bed like he'd been shot from a cannon. "Did Barrera see you do that?"

"Geez, Dan, it's not like he can do anything else but look."

"I don't care. Get him out!" he demanded.

"Get out," I said to Tony.

"No, I don't want to go. This is the most fun I've had since I died."

I shrugged and turned to Danny. "He doesn't want to leave."

"Can't you make him? Don't you have any control over sending these… these… spooks to another place?"

"Who's he calling a spook?" Tony sounded genuinely insulted. He sure as hell looked offended.

203

I'd never seen this side of Danny. He was usually such an unflappable guy, my grounding force who kept me from flying into the kingdom of irrationality. Oh, man, were we ever in trouble if he expected me to be the voice of reason.

"No, Danny, I'm his spiritual connection not his travel agent. If I don't have any control over these people appearing to me, what makes you think I have any more influence over making them go away?"

"Are you telling me he can pop in and out whenever he feels like it and you don't have any way of controlling his comings or goings?"

"That about sums it up."

Danny's expression took an immediate turn for the worse. "Has he watched us do it?"

Mortified at the very idea, I turned a shade of red slightly lighter than my hair. Don't ask me why, but the thought of that happening had never crossed my mind until Danny presented the possibility. Sex had never been an issue with my elderly deceased. A greater interest for them was wondering if their teeth were going to be real on the other side or if they still needed their glasses when they got there. I knew with Tony that wasn't the case.

Wide-eyed, I turned a questioning glance in Tony's direction. "Have you?"

He shook his head but never managed to meet my gaze as he vanished in the blink of my eye. His reaction pretty much answered my question.

One gone, one to go. I returned my attention to Dan.

"Well, what did he say?"

"He said no." Why should both of us be self-conscious the next time we celebrate?

I grabbed my clothes and got dressed in front of God and anybody else who wanted to watch. At this point, I had nothing left to hide.

"So why did you come back?" I looked around for my shoes then remembered I'd left them at the back door.

He reached into his closet and pulled down a gray metal gun safe. He thumbed the electronic lock and lifted the lid. Inside was a snub-nosed revolver and a box of ammunition. "I wanted to give you this."

It was a sweet little .38 Special. I lifted it out and turned it over in my hand. Guns didn't scare me. I grew up around them. What self-respecting southern man didn't own at least one rifle, pistol, or shotgun? My daddy owned multiples of all of them, and Danny knew I could hold my own with any of them. I was a pretty good shot actually, especially with a handgun. Of course, hitting a hanging paper target or a flying clay pigeon was a whole lot different from taking aim and pulling the trigger on a flesh and blood predator. I wasn't particularly keen on that idea.

"I appreciate the offer, but I have my .22 if I need it." Well, not exactly with me, as on my person, but it was in my car.

"That thing's a peashooter. I'd feel better if you had something with a little more stopping power."

"Do you really think I need it?" Shooting had always been for fun. I'd never been faced with the prospect of needing a gun for protection. I'd always had a father and big brothers for that.

"I want you to have it because I don't know if you'll need it," he said as he encompassed my hand and the weapon between his hands. "You still have a permit to carry, right?"

I'd applied for the lifetime permit the second Indiana issued them. I nodded and slipped the pistol and the box of ammo into my purse. I didn't want to think about the reality of needing it.

"When was the last time you've been at the range?"

"It's been a while." I had to give it some thought. "Six months, maybe a little longer."

"Try to get over to Lawson's this afternoon. I'd feel better knowing you had some practice with that gun."

Hmmm. Although Lawson's Pistol & Rifle Range was the biggest and used by many of the local law enforcement personnel, it was the farthest away from Briar Cliff Estates. There were two closer ranges in the area, and if all Dan wanted was for me to get some practice, I didn't see why I had to go two towns away to do it.

Now why did I get the feeling he was trying to get me out of the way by sending me clear in the other direction from where he was planning to be? It made me wonder if he knew I knew where he was going this afternoon, and that I intended on joining him. If this were anyone else but Danny I'd pass it off as a nothing more than a freaky coincidence, but with him I could never be certain.

"You want me to call Craig and make an appointment? Three o'clock good for you?"

"Uh, yeah, that's fine," I said, already knowing where I was going to be at three, and it wasn't anywhere near Craig Lawson's Gun Range.

"Are you sure? I can make it a little earlier if you prefer." He came a little closer and ran a tender finger around the neckline of the shirt I'd snatched from his closet.

I hated it when he was overly considerate like this. It filled me with second thoughts about what I was planning to do this afternoon.

"Three sounds good," I said. "I should be done with my errands."

"Do you think you can stay out of trouble?"

Then he went and said something like that, and my second thoughts flew right out the window.

Chapter Thirty

Once Danny left for the second time that morning, I finished dressing and tamed my hair with a generous palmful of mousse. It didn't look too bad when I was finished fussing. I skipped the full make-up part of my morning routine and settled for some tinted moisturizer and mascara. All I planned on doing was running a few errands. Let the freckles prevail. Maybe I'd add a little blush and lip gloss before it was time to rendezvous with Danny at the Vander Poole house in Briar Cliff later that afternoon. One must keep up appearances in that neighborhood, after all.

I found the morning paper on the counter along with the house key Dan left for me. The *Lake County Times* was still neatly folded in its protective blue plastic bag. Danny had obviously been running too late this morning to look at it.

I poured a cup of coffee, grabbed a yogurt from the fridge, and dropped the paper out of its wrapper onto the table. As it flopped open, the headline jumped off the front page—Psychic Threatened After Assisting Police. Bug-eyed, I scanned the article. Relief washed over me when I realized my name had been withheld. And what a surprise, the press managed to get it wrong—again. I'm not a psychic. I'm a medium, and not the most reliable one at that. I had half a mind to call the paper and straighten them out on the differences. But the other half ruled out and convinced me it wasn't such a good idea. It was better if I remained anonymous.

A couple of pictures accompanied the article. There was one of me escorted by Dan from the Roth house and another of my boarded-up second story balcony. The photo of me showed mostly a head of wind-tossed red curls and a nose. Danny on the other hand looked handsome and commanding. The good thing was nobody would recognize me from the photo. The picture of my condo, however, was an entirely different issue. It wasn't a huge problem now because I wasn't living there, but it could cause problems later. Guess I'd have to deal with that when I moved back.

The phone rang and I answered on the first ring. It had to be Danny calling again. No one else besides Eddie knew I was there, and there wasn't any reason for him to be calling unless it was a family emergency, in which case I'd want to answer. I was a whiz at circular logic.

"Are you scared yet?" said a raspy, digitally disguised voice that sounded a lot like Darth Vader with a head cold.

"Who is this?" I demanded, immediately rolling my eyes at my stupid assumption the caller would tell me simply because I asked.

"Be afraid. Be very afraid."

"Oh, that's original." I drawled with a humorless chuckle. "You don't really expect me to take you seriously with a corny line like that?"

Click.

Huh. Guess he did.

I heard a rapid series of loud pops and raced to the front window.

A smoky haze hovered three feet in the air, and dark blue SUV squealed from curb in a billowing swirl of exhaust. It was the same vehicle from the other night. I knew it. What's more, I felt it. Now all I had to do was prove it. Sure. No problem.

Then I noticed something tacked to the tree nearest to the road. Even from where I stood I could tell it was the front page of today's paper, with a knife jabbed through my unrecognizable photo to hold it in place.

I dialed Danny's cell.

"Prince," he answered.

I tried to speak. Nothing.

When I didn't respond, he said, "Jen? You there?" It was a common enough question these days when no response was forthcoming. No matter how many cell towers were erected, or how advanced cell phone technology had come, or how many commercials say differently, there were still a substantial number of dropped calls.

"Jen?"

I took a deep breath and let the air in my lungs push the words out, "They found me."

"What do you mean? Who found you?"

"Whoever shot out my balcony door, that's who, and they were shooting again."

"I'm on my way," he said. "Check the doors and windows and—"

The line went dead. And? And what?

I punched the redial button. Nothing. Danny was as bad as I was about not returning his portable phone to the base. The convenience of a cordless was indisputable. The drawbacks were just as obvious. Note to self: Stop at Wal-Mart and buy a phone with cords attached—long ones so I could drag it with me all over the house. I couldn't get a dial tone, so I reached for my cell.

I dialed Dan's cell, and it went immediately to voice mail. I tried three more times before my cell crapped out. I hadn't charged it the night before and couldn't do it now because the only charger I had with me was the one in my car. It didn't take a genius to figure out I wasn't about to go outside to use it.

I checked the charger Danny kept plugged in on the counter. Our phones were similar, maybe I could use his. "Shit," I muttered as I realized the connections weren't even close to compatible. How hard would it be for cell phone companies to get their acts together and come up with a charger that worked with every brand or model? Yeah, like that was ever going to happen. Not in this lifetime.

The back doorknob rattled. It couldn't be Danny. It was too soon. I wanted it to be Danny. I even prayed for it to be Danny. But I was convinced it was the bad guy coming to finish what he started. I ran and hid in the front hall closet.

Now any other idiot would have run for the room where I had the gun stashed in my purse. But I wasn't your average, everyday idiot as anyone who knew me would attest.

I pressed deeper between the clothes, shifting my feet around stuff cluttering the floor, and groped around. As I wondered how much damage I could do with a wire coat hanger—it'd worked for Mommy

Dearest—my fingers touched on what felt like the bentwood handle of a walking cane. I vaguely remembered Danny's dad using one shortly before he died. That would have to do. It had to be better than a hanger.

My heart pounded like thunder when it dawned on me I was hearing more than one set of footsteps coming from the kitchen. Doors opened and closed as they made their way toward the front of the house. The footsteps drew nearer. I gripped my weapon and prepared myself to jab and thrust, hoping to get in at least one good blow before they shot me dead.

The most curious thought skittered through my mind as I readied myself for the inevitable confrontation. I couldn't help but wonder if Tony or any of my other dead friends that'd passed before him would be waiting for me when I crossed over. I didn't have much time to ponder the mystery as I heard the footsteps stop.

Glancing at the floor, I saw the shifting of shadows in the strip of light coming under the door. The hinges creaked as the light grew into a pie-shaped wedge. I adjusted my grip on the cane handle and held my breath as the door swung open.

I screamed and lunged.

My feet tangled in something I later identified as a pair of rubber galoshes, and I tumbled head first from the closet.

My weapon unfurled with a *fwoomp* as I landed in a twirl of pink tulips and yellow daffodils. The cane had somehow turned into what I recognized as one of Virginia Prince's favorite umbrellas.

I must have looked like a deranged Mary Poppins

coming in for a not so charming crash landing.

"Are you sure this is normal behavior?" Jeri Novak questioned.

"It is for her," Danny replied.

Chapter Thirty-One

"You want to give me a minute, Jer?" said Danny.

Novak nodded and left out the back, the way they'd entered, leaving us alone.

"Why were you hiding in the closet?" Danny questioned as he relieved me of my weapon and helped me to my feet.

Hiding was such a gutless word. I didn't like it, and I wasn't about to admit to doing it. "I wasn't hiding," I said. "I thought I heard gunfire so I took cover."

"No one else on the block called to report the disturbance. Don't you find that odd?"

Yes, I suppose it was odd, but not so unusual that it was worth pointing out, and it sure wasn't a valid argument as far as I was concerned. "What's your point? Half your neighbors are working couples already gone for the day, and the other half are so old they probably never heard it."

"I can assure you there's nothing wrong with any of my neighbors' hearing. The folks on this block call dispatch when a radio is played too loud. They would have called if they'd heard gunfire, guaranteed."

"It might have been a string of firecrackers," I conceded. But that was all I was conceding. I know what I heard, and nobody was going to convince me otherwise.

"We thought of that, but firecrackers would have left debris."

"What about the newspaper?"

"What newspaper?"

"The one stuck to the tree with a butcher knife. Surely one of you brilliant detectives noticed that."

"There's no evidence of it."

"Evidence, schmevidence," I sputtered. "That's all you cops ever think about."

"That's because it's how I do my job," he said on a much too tolerant note. "Which, by the way, I can't do when you've got me running to your rescue every time you imagine you're being threatened."

I gasped, shrilly and offended. He stood there and waited for me to let him have it. I had to give the man credit for that. Then of course, he had a gun and all I had was my indignation and a pretty floral umbrella.

I was so angry I couldn't see straight. Anything I said to him at that moment would come out sounding a lot worse than I intended, so I struggled to keep my mouth shut and my thoughts in check until my initial anger subsided. No easy feat for this redhead, I might add. There was only one thing left for me to do.

I had to get out of there. It would be better for both of us.

Since I was standing right there anyway, I snatched my down jacket from the closet. As I swung it around to put it on, something fell out of the pocket. It was the smaller black pouch I'd picked up from Tony's apartment. I reached for it.

Danny got to it first and pulled it open. A twist-tied baggie of what I could only guess was an illegal substance or Italian seasoning fell out as he picked it up. I had to go with the former since it was accompanied by a packet of rolling papers.

He opened the bag and held it to his nose. "I could arrest you for this."

"That's not mine," I said, outraged that he'd even suggested it was. "You know I don't use that stuff."

He gave me that look. It's not easy having friends who know Jennifer Flagg, the early years. "Oh, come on. You are not going to use that against me. That was a contact buzz, and you know it."

"If it's not yours, then whose is it?"

"It's not mine," I repeated. If Tony wasn't already dead, I swear I'd hunt him down and kill him myself. I couldn't' believe it—marijuana in a cop's apartment. Imagine that.

"Let me guess. You're just holding it for a friend, right?"

That much sarcasm was uncalled for in my opinion, even if he was spot on in his observation. "That's right, I am," I insisted. In order to get myself out of this mess I might have to give up Tony and the Griffith apartment. I weighed my options—a dead man who had nothing to lose or me? It wasn't a choice I was thrilled about making, but the scales on who to save were tilting heavily in my favor.

"It's Tony's." The decision was much more difficult than my immediate response indicated.

The look that crossed Danny's face was a priceless mixture of surprise, bemusement, and disbelief. "Is this the same Tony who's been making my life miserable since the day you found his body where you should never have been in the first place? Is that the Tony we're talking about? "

I nodded. "Yep, that's the guy."

"Still doesn't explain how the stuff wound up in your coat pocket?" He held it out as a visual reminder.

"I picked it up by mistake."

"Where?"

He wasn't going to relent until he dragged every detail out of me, that much was clear. "His apartment."

"So you lied to me about being at his place on Saturday?"

"Not technically," I said. "I was never at the Lake Shore apartment complex."

"Damn it. There's a second apartment." This wasn't presented as a question any more than he expected an answer from me to confirm it. "Where is it, Jen?" He was already reaching for his cell.

I was momentarily struck by a flash of moral conscience—even mediocre mediums were expected to follow a certain code of ethics—which might have caused me to hesitate for a fraction of a second longer than I should have with my response. If this were anyone else they wouldn't have even noticed my reluctance. But like I've said before, Danny knows me better than my own family. He knew I was struggling with a no-win dilemma.

"I'll try to make this easy for you, Jennifer," he said.

I breathed a sigh of relief at that bit of good news. I knew Danny wouldn't let me down.

"Either you tell me where the apartment is located or I bust you for possession." He flipped open his phone. ''What's it going to be?"

"That's your idea of making this easy for me?" I

gasped. "That's blackmail," I sputtered. "That's what it is. You should be ashamed of yourself for resorting to such underhanded tactics."

"Actually, it's extortion, but if that's what it takes to get your cooperation, so be it."

I studied his rigid stance, the set of his clenched jaw, and I knew he wasn't bluffing. "I'm not happy about this, Danny."

"Duly noted," he said.

"I'm doing this under protest," I added.

"Also noted."

"Griffith," I told him as I gathered my jacket, purse and shoes, said goodbye to my cats, and got out of there before Danny could *extort* any more information out of me. It was only a matter of time before it dawned on him that I'd lifted more than the weed from Tony's place. I didn't want to be around when he did. Later would be soon enough for that conversation. Much later would be even better.

I was only a couple blocks from Danny's house heading for the first stop on my to-do list when Tony decided to join me en route to my apartment to take care of a few things. There were bills that needed paying and plants that needed watering. I was also curious to see the damage in the light of day.

"That was intense," he said.

"You saw what happened?"

"Sure did."

"I'm sorry," I said. "I let you down."

"Hey, you did what you had to do."

"You're taking this better than I expected."

"I've got no problems with what you did. You wouldn't be much help to me if you were sitting in jail."

"I don't think Danny would have gone that far," I told him, although I wouldn't swear to it. Danny had been wearing that hard, clenched expression I knew could be trouble—especially for me.

"I wouldn't be too sure about that if I were you. He didn't sound like he was bluffing to me. Besides, let them do what they have to do. There's nothing important left for them to find."

"Which reminds me…" My curiosity got the best of me. "You want to explain what a bag of marijuana was doing in your place?" I turned into the drive-thru lane of the first Starbucks that came onto my radar. I needed a dose of caffeine.

"When you work undercover you have to do things that aren't always on the up and up, or even legal. I had to fit in to gain the trust of some people."

"You do realize Danny's going to put two and two together and reach the conclusion that I took more than a bag of pot from your place."

"Tell him there wasn't anything else to take, that the place was already trashed when we got there."

"You want me to lie. I'm not sure I can do that."

"It's the truth. The place was trashed when we got there."

"But not the part about not taking anything else."

"If he pressures you, give him the book of poetry. Tell him I wanted it for sentimental reasons, that it was Mia's favorite, and I wanted you to give it to her."

"You're good. That actually sounds plausible."

"That's because it's the truth."

I placed my order—a grande mocha latte with an extra shot of espresso—and pulled forward.

"Is Antonio Barrera even your real name?"

"It is as far as you're concerned."

There was such a level of finality in his tone, it smothered any further thought I might have had about pursuing that particular line of questioning, so I pulled a one-eighty and asked, "And what about the other stuff?"

"It's information that'll implicate a lot of people in a very sordid business. We have to find Mia before the authorities can move on it."

"Great. Just what I need," I muttered as I cast a nasty sideward glance in Tony's direction, "...more provisional, testosterone-driven incentive." It was a toss-up as to which man in my life was being more difficult—the dead one sitting next to me or the living, breathing pain-in-my-butt I'd just left.

"Make that espresso a double shot," I said to the barista as she opened the window to take my money.

"The trip to my condo is going to have to wait," I said as I turned my car around and steered it in the opposite direction from where I'd originally been heading. So would the rest of my errands. I needed a woman's perspective, someone who understood my dilemma, and I needed it now.

"So where are we going?"

"We're going to visit a friend of mine. I think you'll find Olivia interesting." To say the very least. Every visit with Olivia was an adventure.

Chapter Thirty-Two

Located off Route 30 south of Broadway in a rough-chiseled gray stone and rose-tinted glass building, Olivia's second floor office sat nestled between a dental laboratory and the law partnership of Frampton, Lindberg, and Stern. The only thing distinguishing her office from the others was a discreet brass plate not much bigger than a playing card engraved with Olivia Ryan, Ph.D.

Monday through Friday, Olivia was a practicing psychologist. She was also a frequently sought after, well respected parapsychologist. Rumor has it that law enforcement agencies from around the world had her number on speed dial. She'd never confirmed or denied the scuttlebutt, but hard facts don't lie. She'd been instrumental in solving more than a dozen cold cases and several more current high profile missing persons investigations. Even Danny, although he's tried, couldn't find a way to refute her astounding record.

On weekends, however, for the sheer fun of it, Olivia transformed herself into Madame Orion, a free-spirited alter-ego who delved into reading palms and tarot, and communicating with folks' dead relatives. But I'm happy to say that every day of the week she is my dear friend and mentor in all things paranormal.

Olivia is also the past president of our local chapter of Psychics and Mediums Society. I can't help but snicker every time I think about it—a group full of psychics, for Pete's sake, and not one of them had the foresight to predict what our organization's name would look like as an acronym until we ordered T-shirts. In my closet hang several rarely worn purple and black shirts proudly boasting my membership in P.M.S. Of course, now that I think about it, nobody's ever tried to mess with me when I wore one. There is something to be said for the power of suggestion.

I pushed on the polished mahogany door and stepped into the softly lit outer chamber decorated in soothing shades of tans, blues and greens. The delicate scent of sandalwood tinged the air as the hushed whisper of ocean waves cycled through the recessed ceiling speakers. Everything in the room created an atmosphere of peace and serenity. I felt relaxed and instantly better about my little corner of the world, including everyone who shared it with me.

"Nice digs," Tony commented as he made himself comfortable on a suede love seat the color of wet sandstone. Taking in the tasteful amenities, he stretched his arms across the back cushions and crossed his legs, ankle to knee. Tony appeared to be enjoying our little field trip. Perhaps Olivia's calming influence had spilled over to him.

I sat across from him on a matching club chair and focused on the watercolor seascape hanging on the wall above his head. It was a new addition since the last time I'd been there, and it intrigued me with its soft colors and subtle detail. A solitary woman dressed in a gauzy long dress stood at the edge of the water, the foamy waves lapping at her bare toes as the sheer white fabric whipped around her calves.

The crashing surf roared in my head as I felt myself drawn deeper into the painting. Something weird was happening to me, and there was nothing I could do as I moved further and further into the beckoning scene. My breathing and heart rate slowed dramatically as my eyes drifted shut.

The grit of wet sand shifted beneath my bare feet as gulls swooped and squawked overhead, and the briny bite of the sea assaulted my nose. With the sun on my face, I waded deeper into the beckoning surf.

Then it all turned to a raging, bloody whirlpool. The tranquility vanished as panic ensued. Red waves, thick and sticky, engulfed me and sucked me into its swirling eddy. Kicking and flailing, I fought for the surface, but the redness fought harder. It pulled and clawed at my struggling limbs, taking me deeper and deeper until I had no other option but to succumb.

"Jennifer."

Gasping and heart hammering, I opened my eyes. Olivia sat in the chair beside me. Her hand rested on my shoulder as she softly repeated my name.

"What happened?" I looked around and took a deep, calming breath. I shivered from the terror lingering on the fringes of ragged memories. I couldn't put a name to what just happened, and it frightened me more than I wanted to admit to anyone, including myself.

"I'd say you've made a significant psychic breakthrough."

Not what I wanted to hear. I sat back and stared at her. Olivia had been telling me for as long as I've known her that I'd only tapped a tiny part of my extrasensory abilities. I'd always pooh-poohed her in-depth observations, telling her—insisting actually—that I was psychically challenged. My one and only ability started and ended with an occasional chat with a dearly departed. End of story. I'd accepted my limitations. I wished she would.

I chose to put what happened into my own perspective. "I fell asleep and had a nightmare, Liv," I told her. "There's nothing mystical or supernatural about dozing off." I breathed a little laugh. "Is it any wonder? Everything in this room is designed for deep relaxation." It was then I noticed that Tony wasn't where I'd last seen him.

"Your friend had to leave," she explained before I could ask about his absence.

"I *really* hate when you do that," I told her. "You could at least pretend not to know what I'm thinking."

She gave a soft chuckle. "It's not so much your thoughts but your expressions that are transparent, Jennifer."

I knew it was easier to redirect my thoughts than debate the issue. "Did Tony say when or if he'd be back? I really wanted him to meet you."

"We spoke briefly, but your vision was too disturbing for him to stay. He asked me to tell you not to wait for him and that he'd catch up with you later."

"I did not have a vision," I insisted, although I felt similarly confused and scared when I'd had my very first encounter. I'd been in total denial back then, too, when my mentor had been my Grandma Flagg who'd also had the ability to talk to the dead. That's something I'm still bitter about. If anyone could reach out to me from the other side it should have been her. She's been gone a couple of years now. I'm not holding my breath, but I'm still hopeful.

"You must know by now she's with you every day."

"Will you stop that?" I jumped up and paced, as if moving around would prevent Olivia from zoning in on my thoughts.

"I'm sorry, Jennifer, but I can't help it. The energy you're projecting at the moment is too powerful for me to ignore. We've never been so strongly linked."

"Then break it, sever it, do whatever it is you have to do to make it go away."

"Those feelings you're having won't go away until you recognize them for what they are and accept them. You must embrace the vision, interpret its meaning, before you can let it go."

I shook my head against the idea. Not much differently, I imagined, than from the way I'd behaved when my grandma sat me down and explained to me about my *gift*. And like that day so many years ago, I knew Olivia was right. This wouldn't go away just because I wanted it to, either. So I took a deep breath, resituated myself in the seat beside her and came clean as I told her what I could remember.

"I'm sure the reason Tony had to leave is because I was seeing the last bloody moments of his life."

"Yes, I know," she said. "I saw it too."

"What I don't understand is why this is happening to me now..." I said. "...after all these years?"

"I suspect Tony's death was the catalyst. He's the first contact you've ever had that hasn't died of natural causes, isn't he?"

Upon my thoughtful nod, she continued. "Birth and death are the most traumatic events in a person's lifespan. When a life is cut short through a violent act, it leaves behind a powerful energy signature that disrupts everything around it. His death was like opening a door and releasing your repressed abilities."

"Why didn't you warn me something like this could happen?"

Her laughter was husky and indulgent. "My dear Jenny, I can guide you, I can advise you, but there's no way in this world or any other I could have predicted what you've just experienced, much less prepared you for it. Your abilities are as unique to you as your fingerprints. I'll do whatever I can to help you discover and develop them, but I can't tell you what they are or how they will manifest themselves. That's for you to discover. This is your personal journey."

She patted my hand like that of a beloved aunt and rose to stand in the center of the room. "I envy the discoveries in store for you."

I wasn't nearly as optimistic.

Olivia was only seven years older than me, but she'd always seemed wise beyond her years. She'd told me it was because she'd been born with an experienced soul. If that was the case then my soul must have been brand spanking, right-off-the-showroom new when I got it because I didn't understand shit from shineola when it came to this stuff. I was more of a fly-by-the-seat-of-my-pants paranormal. Actually, that pretty much described my philosophy of life in general.

The muted lighting glimmered off the delicate strand of pink opals and amethyst crystals she fingered at her throat as she closed her eyes and appeared to enter into a trance-like state.

I could never be certain if this behavior of hers was in fact real or just for effect. Not that it mattered to me. I loved watching her work. Whether she was Olivia Ryan, PhD, or Madame Orion, paranormal extraordinaire, she had a flair for the dramatic. I was in awe of her amazing abilities regardless of how she chose to project them. To have her envy me in any way was a compliment I couldn't easily ignore in spite of my reservations to the contrary.

"Tony's connection to you and his afterlife abilities are more powerful than any of your past contacts," she stated without hesitation. Then she opened her startling amber eyes and smiled at me. "But you already know this one is different from the others, don't you?"

"Oh, yeah," I drawled. "This one's different all right."

She slipped into her inner office and when she returned, she pressed a tumbled smooth green stone and a rough crystal into my palm. "The green tourmaline will help you with the emotional changes you're experiencing and bring you balance. The quartz will bring spiritual clarity and focus."

A little balance, clarity, and focus in my life might be a nice for a change, though I doubted if a couple of little pebbles had enough mystical power to do it for me. The way I had it figured, I needed nothing less than rocks the size of Mt. Everest with powers proportionally equivalent.

Chapter Thirty-Three

Tony didn't rejoin me until after I'd arranged to meet a contractor at my condo for an estimate on replacing my sliding balcony door. Because of the approaching holiday, they couldn't guarantee when exactly, but they promised they'd call when they could fit me into their schedule. I won't hold my breath.

"You okay?" I asked before I realized what I was asking. Of course, he wasn't okay. He was dead, and the dead didn't have the same set of troubles as those of us still in the land of the living.

Like I've said before, these people were real to me in every way. They might have lost every physical aspect of what made them who they were on this plane, but they still had their feelings, emotions, and memories. It was sad really, and the biggest reason why I didn't want to let any of them down. As their last connection to this earth, I felt obligated to help them in any way I could. If that meant treading into dangerous territory once in a while, then that's what I'd do.

"I stand corrected," he said. "That business between you and Dan this morning was nothing on the intensity meter compared to what I experienced back there at Olivia's. I had to get out of there. I couldn't stand to be in the same room with you."

"It was pretty intense for me, too," I admitted. "I've never experienced anything like it before."

"What do you mean?"

"Olivia believes your death awakened a dormant level of my psychic abilities."

I turned right on Route 41 and headed north. There was a Dunkin' Donuts right around the corner, and I needed large quantities of caffeine to help me process Olivia's theory. What I really wanted was a Mocha Cappuccino Blast, the one made with ice cream, but since Tony was with me that wasn't a practical option. Just because he didn't react adversely to the donuts might have been a fluke. I didn't want to take any chances after what I'd put him through earlier.

I settled for an iced coffee, which was yummy too. People who knew me thought it was strange I enjoyed cold drinks when I hate cold weather, but I didn't find it all that odd. I drink hot coffee in the middle of summer. It's whatever strikes my fancy at the moment.

He watched me suck down my first chilling swallows. I cranked up my car heater a couple of notches and sipped again. "Hey," I said. "It's all about balance."

You know, Jennifer," he commented. "It's probably a good thing it's sugar and not caffeine that causes the rage in us."

"Excellent point," I said as I settled the cup in the center console and pulled into traffic. "Because it's safe to say that without caffeine I'd be the one going into uncontrollable fits of rage."

"The amount of caffeine you consume every day can't be all that healthy, you know. Maybe you ought to think about cutting back a little."

I was startled by his candid observation. Cut back on caffeine? The concept had never crossed my mind and never would if I had anything to say about it. "Don't even go down that road," I said to him, taking another gulp of liquid bliss in defiance of his suggestion. "Caffeine is what kick starts my mornings and keeps me running on all cylinders the rest of the day."

"But—" was all he managed before I cut him off at the confrontational pass.

"No buts," I snapped. "My giving up coffee, even in small doses, isn't going to happen any time soon. So eighty-six the anti-caffeine campaign right now. Capeesh?"

"Irritability is a sign of addiction, you know."

"I'm not addicted," I snapped as I cut him a sideward glance that would have, at the very least, mortally wounded a man with blood running through his veins. He never flinched, which irked me even more.

"I'm just sayin'…" he added with a palm-open wave as he turned away and stared out the passenger side window.

I cast another quick glance at Tony. Because there was something so incredibly disturbing about a pouting dead man, I found it impossible not to feel bad about the way I acted. He was pushing buttons I didn't even know I possessed, and I wracked my brain with a million questions as to why his opinion mattered so much.

I knew what I had to do to make it right between us again. The problem was apologizing didn't come easy for me. I'd sooner bite off my tongue and swallow it whole than admit I was wrong. And just for the record, I've come dangerously close to de-tonguing myself many, many times.

"I'm sorry," I said, surprised by how effortlessly the words came out this time. "I didn't mean to snap at you like that."

"That's okay," he said with a dead-even tone that didn't leave much room for further discussion, which was okay by me. I did my part. No sense in belaboring the issue.

"Where're we going now?" he wanted to know.

"Police station," I told him. "I need to find out if Danny's still doing those interviews in Briar Cliff this afternoon."

"And you think he's going to just hand you that information?"

"Of course not. But I have ways of finding out. My brother's the chief, remember? I have inside sources."

I felt my car hesitate and do a little sputter. "Did you hear that?" I asked as I let my foot off the gas and coast for a second.

"Hear what?" he asked, which told me he hadn't.

I was only a mile away from the stationhouse so I accelerated and hoped it was nothing more than a dirty injector. It did it again and I panicked. I didn't need the hassle of an uncooperative vehicle today. I turned down the first side street and pulled over, wondering why nothing in my life could ever go smoothly. I shifted the Malibu into park and gave it some gas.

"Car trouble?" Tony questioned.

"Shhh," I said, shutting off the radio and heater to have a better listen. I gunned the engine again. Everything sounded fine to me. Of course, I didn't have my daddy's keen sense of hearing when it came to motors and the funny noises they make. He was going to have to do the final diagnostic to be certain. I dismissed the noise with an uneasy shrug, put the car into drive, and pulled a U-turn. I didn't hear anything out of the ordinary for the remainder of the trip. Weird, huh?

The police department shared a building with the fire department and municipal offices. It was an impressive four-story, ultra-modern glass and steel structure that rose in the center of our otherwise quaint Capraesque downtown like Gulliver standing up in the middle of Lilliput.

"Hey, Molly." I greeted the receptionist with a couple knuckle raps on the thick protective bullet-proof glass that separated her from the general public. When she turned to my greeting, I saw she was on the phone. I acknowledged her I'll-be-with-you-in-a-minute finger gesture and took a seat in the lobby.

I've known Molly Mueller since high school, only she was Molly Garber back then. We weren't hang-out-with-each-other friends or anything like that, but we were friendly acquaintances. We'd been in homeroom and a couple of classes together, and our lockers had been right next to each other all four years.

One week after graduation, Molly ran off and married the first guy she'd slept with, a smooth-talking sleazoid by the name of Willie Mueller. Seven years, two kids, a couple black eyes, and one broken jaw later, Molly finally discovered her backbone under all the abrasions and bruises and left the abusive bastard.

Since she got the receptionist job with the police department, Willie's made himself pretty scarce. I was glad to see she was getting her life back on track.

I catapulted out of the chair when I spotted Tony standing in front of Molly's desk. I gave him one of my really annoyed looks and did a jerky gesture for him to get out of there. He grinned, danced around like a mischievous leprechaun, then headed down the hall.

His arrogance made me wonder if he'd overheard some of what Olivia and I had discussed at her office—that his extraordinary strength comes from me. The closer my proximity, the stronger he was and the greater his abilities. It also made me wonder how far the spectral umbilical cord would stretch before it snapped and he moved on.

"What can I do for you, Jen?" Molly's voice was tempered by the thick glass. Not even the speaker plate and opening created by the pass-through tray prevented her from sounding like she was speaking from the bottom of a barrel.

"Dan around?" I asked as I stood and shouldered my purse. The extra weight reminded me of the gun and bullets Danny had given me that morning.

I glanced at the "No Weapons Beyond This Point," sign hanging near the door leading to the back offices. It looked like I was restricted to the lobby, although I doubted if anyone would bother with a purse search of the chief's sister if I decided to take the chance.

"Detective Prince is in a meeting…" she hesitated and cast a nervous glance over her shoulder toward his office before adding, "…with someone."

"Yeah, well," I said, wondering what was making her act so peculiar. "Meetings are usually more productive that way."

"Do you want to leave him a message?"

"Is Kari in her office?" Eddie's secretary and I were good buddies. We bowled on the same Thursday night league, and we tried to get together for a girls night out at least a couple of times a month. She's nine years older than me, but we clicked from the first day she was hired. She, too, is single and loving it, a fact that gives Eddie's wife all the more reason to dislike Kari, which in turn is just an added bonus for me as far as I'm concerned. Kari was also on occasion my police department source, a fact I'd deny to my dying day. She managed to keep me in the departmental loop whenever Eddie or Danny stonewalled me.

"She's out to lunch."

I glanced at my watch. Well what do you know? It was lunchtime. Where did the morning go? "I really need to talk to Dan. Do you have any idea how much longer he's going to be?" I knew he had plans to interview Franklin Roth's neighbors this afternoon. Information Olivia shared with me about one of Madame Orion's regular clients, one Eleanor Vander Poole to be specific, might be of interest to him. I certainly found the woman's attempt to contact her dead husbands fascinating.

"Can you let him know I'm here?"

Molly shook her head and cast another glance in the direction of Danny's closed office door. "He asked not to be disturbed."

Molly's behavior grew odder by the minute. "Who is he in conference with?"

Danny's door opened, saving her from answering what she was obviously reluctant to share. I heard voices, Danny's and a woman's, before I saw them exit his office.

"Oh, no," I groaned. Danny'd been in conference with Tawny Turner.

High school would have been a much more pleasant experience for me had it not been for that woman. The ink had barely dried on her doctorate when she managed to secure the job as school psychologist, thanks to the strings her father, the senator, had pulled with the school board.

From the day she'd entered those hallowed halls Of Lake Ridge High, Ms. Turner had plagued my every step. For my entire high school career, I was her pet project. It wasn't easy explaining to my friends why she'd call me down to her office at least three times a week where she'd grill me about my latest contact or how I was handling my *special gift*, as she called it. She had a file on me as thick as a Chicago phone book by the time graduation rolled around.

Last thing I'd heard about her was she'd left the school system to work for the county sheriff's department, but I'd never had the misfortune of crossing paths with her until today. As anyone can imagine, Tawny was still the proverbial pain in my rump, and I wasn't exactly thrilled about the prospect of seeing her now.

I tensed as they neared. There had also been a number of unsubstantiated rumors flying around about her and Danny when they worked on a case together shortly after her career change. The brilliant and beautiful blonde was one of those subjects that fell into the "don't ask, don't tell" category with me and Dan.

I never put much stock in the gossip. Not until now, that is. I don't know what it was about the look she gave him or the one he gave her in return, but it made me feel like a voyeur.

I didn't know whose jugular I wanted to go for first. Just because we had an understanding about these occasional extracurricular liaisons, didn't mean I have to like the fact one of them had been with a woman he knew I despised. I expected a certain level of loyalty, especially now after those commitment noises he'd made at me the other night.

I turned to high tail it out of there. No way did I want anything to do with that woman for all the obvious reasons and a few of the lesser ones. Whatever I wanted to tell Danny could wait. Then again, maybe I wouldn't tell Danny a damn thing. Maybe I'd follow-up on the information myself. Yeah, who needed him anyway?

"Jennifer Flagg! Is that you?"

The sound of her voice nailed me where I stood. Somebody give me a shot of Novocain to numb the pain shooting down my spine. She always did have that effect on me, proving yet again how some things never change.

They wended their way down the hall and into the main foyer. "You remember Tawny, don't you, Jennifer?" Dan raised an eyebrow and gave me one of those behave-yourself looks.

I crossed my arms to keep from shaking her extended hand. "Yes, I remember Doctor Turner."

"There's no need to stand on formalities, Jennifer. Please, call me Tawny. We're all adults now."

I shot Danny a withering look. "Some of us more than others," I intoned. That's when I noticed a cheek-sized splotch of what looked suspiciously like foundation on Danny's blue shirt, not, I might add, on the collar or shoulder, but just above his belt. Upon closer inspection, I detected another spot of the peachy-colored substance below the equator. Now I suppose there could be a logical explanation for this—like she was picking the lint off his fly with her teeth, for instance—but for some inexplicable reason I wasn't feeling very logical at the moment, or forgiving.

I glared at Danny. He was so going to pay for having anything to do with this lint-picker.

"Dan tells me you've made contact with his murder victim," said Tawny as she handed Danny her coat to help her on with it. It was such an easy, intimate gesture between them, I noted. He'd never helped me on with my coat. Not that I ever expected it. I couldn't play the helpless female if I tried. "I'm pleased to hear your abilities haven't diminished."

If stares were bullets, Danny would be dead at my feet. "On the contrary," I said, smiling benignly. "I'm getting stronger with every encounter. Now if you'll excuse me. I really have somewhere else I need to be." Anywhere but here would be a good place to start. Tony would just have to catch up.

"Jen, wait a minute." Danny was quicker than me and caught me by the arm as I was about to exit the building.

"What?" I hugged my purse a little tighter and refused to look him in the eye. Even when I knew we weren't exclusive, he'd always had a way of looking at me like I was special. I didn't want to see it. Or worse, not see it.

"You couldn't wait to tell her about my talking to Tony, could you?"

"That's not why she showed up today."

"Why *was* she here then?"

"I—I can't say."

"Why not?"

"I can't discuss it. It's personal."

"Personal?" I said.

"All I can say is it's not what you think."

"You have no idea what I'm thinking."

"I think I do." He seemed pretty sure of himself, smug in fact, and that's when I lost it.

"If you think for one minute I'm the least bit jealous of that... that..." I couldn't think of a noun nasty enough to call her. "Well, you've got another guess coming." I wrenched my arm out of his grasp.

"Oh, you might want to pre-spot those pants and shirt before you toss them in the wash or that makeup stain might not come out."

His jaw dropped a split second before his gaze. "Shit."

"I'm pretty sure it's only makeup, but then again considering the source, you never know."

I was gone before he had a chance to recover from his laundry dilemma.

I drove only as far as the municipal lot across the street from the police department and watched Danny walk Tawny to her car then climb into his own dark blue Crown Vic and drive away. He turned west and headed in the direction of Briar Cliff Estates.

I smiled and followed. He owed me.

Chapter Thirty-Four

I needed a plan. I couldn't very well follow Danny into Briar Cliff Estates. When he turned into the gated community and stopped at the guardhouse, I kept going and went around to the back entrance where all deliveries and service vehicles were directed. I pulled up to the smaller, less impressive guardhouse and was immediately greeted by none other than Andy Ramos.

Crap. First Tawny, now Andy. Could my day get any worse?

I lowered my window and smiled. "I'm supposed to meet Danny here. He wanted to go over my statement at the scene."

"Is that right?" Andy drawled as he approached my car with his hand resting on the butt of his service revolver. His fingers twitched like he was daring me to give him a reason to draw. I really didn't think he'd shoot me, but I didn't make any sudden movements just the same.

"Every man on the security force, including your buddy Bill, has been given strict instructions by the police not to let you in under any circumstances. You are, as we say in the business, Flagg, persona non grata around here."

Those were pretty big words for a man who was

eating Florida beaches with his wife's permission. There was nothing left for me to do. I backed up and left.

It's important to understand I wasn't giving up. I was just retreating to regroup and come up with a new and improved game plan.

I kept on driving as an idea formed in my head. Who else would a girl turn to when she needed help? Her daddy, of course.

My dad's business was situated on twenty-five acres south of town on an unincorporated chunk of land he bought for practically nothing forty-five years ago. After putting in his twenty years with the same police force Dan and my brother worked for now, Ed Flagg retired and started his second and more lucrative career.

There now stands a six bay modern garage on the front part of the property, and an auto salvage yard hidden behind a high privacy fence at the rear. Another building off to one side held Dad's vintage car collection. My personal favorites were a mint '57 baby blue Chevy convertible, a cherry Shelby Mustang, and a DMC-12, better known as the *Back to the Future* car, minus the flux capacitor and time travel capabilities, darn it. Who, after all, wouldn't like to go back in time and right a few wrongs or fix a few wagons?

I drove around back and parked next to one of the Flagg's fleet of fire engine red tow trucks. Before I had both feet inside the door, I was greeted by Dad's second-in-command and long-time employee, Ray Lacy.

"Well butter my butt and call me a biscuit, if it ain't my little Jenny Penny come for a visit."

I grinned at his greeting. Who needed a DeLorian

time machine? Ray always made me feel perpetually twelve years old.

Now Ray was an interesting story waiting to be told. Somewhere around my sixteenth birthday, my oldest sister Lani told me that one of our mother's one night stands had been with Ray. He wasn't the one who left the greasy fingerprints. Those came a little later, long after Ray was nothing more than a notch on my mother's garter belt.

When I confronted my father bearing all the insolence only an outraged teenager could pull off and asked him why he'd kept this man around after what he'd done, Dad had told me that getting rid of the best body man in the business for that one indiscretion was tantamount to shooting a horse because it threw a shoe. Daddy sure did have a way with words. Personally, I would have shot the horse *and* the rider.

"Jenny, honey, you're a sight for these tired old eyes." Ray came around the counter and gave me a big hug. Beneath a pungent layer of Old Spice there lingered the ever present scent of a man who'd worked around cars all his life. My dad smelled pretty much the same, only his secondary scent was Stetson, and would be for a very long time if the supply of bottles he collected every Christmas from his grandkids was any indication.

Ray's hug was as familiar as my dad's, too. From as far back as I can remember the man had never been anything but super nice to me, which made it next to impossible to hate him for a mistake he made before I was born. Now how would it look if I persisted in holding a grudge against someone who never missed my birthday or any other gift-giving holidays?

And no, he's not my biological father. Although the possibility had crossed my mind on more than one occasion until I realized I'd inherited this thing I do with dead people from my father's side of the family. Today's DNA tests couldn't confirm my paternity with any better accuracy.

I hugged Ray back and asked, "Is Dad around?"

"Ed should be back any minute now." He gave a little wink. "Course, he did go home for lunch today so he's more'n likely having more than a baloney sandwich, if you know what I mean."

Eeewww. Yes, I did know what he meant, and the thought of my father catching a nooner was not an image I wanted in my brain. Ever.

"He sometimes loses track of the time when he and Lena—"

"Whoa," I interrupted. "Will you look at the time?"

He clicked his cheek and winked. "Course who can blame him with that hot little number he married?"

"Yep, it sure is getting late," I said, trying hard to delete the picture he'd planted in my mind. My stepmom was a lot of wonderful things. A loving mother, an excellent cook, a faithful wife—*hot, little number* was nowhere on that list.

"Is there anything I can help you with, Baby Girl?" To my dad and Ray, I would be perpetually their baby girl. Now that I think about it, there were a few other friends of my father who called me that. I guess my paternity crossed through more than just Ray's mind.

As I'd gradually learned over the years, my mother fooled around with most of my dad's buddies at one time or another and a few of her friends' husbands, as well. My father, sensible man that he was, must have decided it was easier in the long run to get rid of her than look for all new friends.

I glanced at the clock on the wall. The big sparkplug was on the four and the little plug was on the one. "My car started making funny noises," I said. "I wanted Dad to take a look at it for me." I also wanted one of the loaners he kept for his customers, preferably something that wouldn't raise a red flag with the guards at Briar Cliff.

"Shoot, Jenny girl, gimme them keys," he said, snatching the key ring from my hand. "There's no need to wait around for your daddy with something like this. I'll take it for a spin and see what I can hear."

"I'm in kind of a hurry this afternoon, Ray. I'm supposed to meet someone within the hour. I was kind of hoping I could leave my car here and take one of the loaners out back."

"We gave out our last loaner this morning." He reached over the counter and grabbed a set of keys from the desk. "Here, take mine. You can bring it back in the morning."

As it turned out, Ray's car wasn't just any car. It wasn't even really a car. I wasn't sure how exactly it would be classified. It was a Hummer. Not one of the scaled down models, either. Oh no. This was the mother Hummer of them all—the really, really big one with a winch on the front and a towing hitch on the back. I could pull stuff from both ends if I was so inclined.

"Uh, what happened to your Silverado?" I asked. He'd owned a Chevy truck of one kind or another for as long as I'd known the difference.

Ray stroked the Hummer's tubular chrome bumper. "I got a real sweetheart of a deal from a woman who was selling off all her husband's toys after she caught him having a private session with their marriage counselor. She gave me a good price on his fishing boat and trailer, too."

I eyed the Hummer and gulped a couple of times as I walked around the vehicle. Sheesh! It was almost practically school bus yellow, for crying out loud, and from my perspective just as big. How could I be inconspicuous behind the wheel of something this size and color? The thought of driving Ray's full-size pickup had already caused me considerable worry. I wasn't too sure I could drive something this intimidating.

Coming around the driver's side, I noticed something that changed my mind and made me smile at the irony. Guess what Ray or the previous owner never got around to removing from the lower left hand corner of the windshield. That's right, a Briar Cliff Estates residents' medallion. When things work out like this, I have no other choice but to take it as a sign it was meant to be.

I grabbed the keys from Ray, thanked him profusely, and hoisted myself into the vehicle.

Infused with an over-abundance of confidence, I cruised through the Briar Cliff front gate without a hitch. Neither of the guards gave me or the vehicle more than a passing glance. The tinted windows might have something to do with the former. I know the medallion had everything to do with the latter. My confidence level raised another healthy notch. I was on a roll.

Now, let the record show I'd been tempted to return to the back gatehouse to see if I could put one over on Ramos since putting anything over on Ramos was right at the top of my favorite things. But, let the record also show I decided against the blatant move on the slim chance he was having an even better afternoon than me. Confidence was one thing. Sheer stupidity was quite another.

I parked around the corner from the Roth house, which was still cordoned off with crime scene tape and probably would be for a while, and studied the Vander Poole house and surrounding property from a safe, inconspicuous distance. Danny's unmarked squad was nowhere to be seen, which made me wonder where he'd gone. I sure hoped I hadn't missed him. That would really suck considering all the extra trouble I'd gone through to get there.

Figuring I had a little time to waste, I turned my attention to the dashboard of gizmos and gadgets. After fiddling with the heater adjustments, I found a comfortable level to keep my feet as well as the rest of me warm without turning me into a sweat ball under my down jacket. Then I discovered something really wonderful—the heated seats. Oh man, there was no describing the bliss of having a toasty warm butt.

I played with the radio next. I was practically positive I could find something a little more modern and a lot less tranquilizing. There had to be some rule or regulation against using an audio system of this quality for listening to a local AM station that played the mellow, and I do mean m-e-l-l-o-w, tunes of the 40s and 50s. Sinatra, Martin, Boone, Bennett, and Clooney were this station's stock-in-trade. I know this because it's the same station my dad had on in the garage and his own personal vehicle.

I was debating between country and alternative when I was startled out of my decision by a hard rap at the driver's side window. It was Detective Dan looking more perturbed than I'd seen him since, oh, I don't know, when I left him this morning maybe.

I rolled down the tinted window just enough to peer out and said, "How'd you know this was me?"

"Andy called me. We figured you'd try something so I had you followed. What are you doing here, Jennifer?"

I rolled the window down a teensy bit further. "Same thing you're doing here. I need to talk to Mrs. Vander Poole and her maid. I figured it'd be easier if we did it together."

"This is official police business, Jennifer. You can't tag along just to satisfy your morbid curiosity with this case."

I lowered the window completely. "I've got a legitimate reason for being here. I've been officially asked by the deceased to locate Mia Ruiz and give her a message." Yeah, that sounded good. And it wasn't even a lie. Even better. Not that I ever expected Danny to fall for it.

I did leave him speechless momentarily, as he stammered over his response. I don't believe I'd ever done that before. He recovered much quicker than I would have liked, however.

"What you've got is a whole lot of bubkes and the request of a dead guy, neither of which will get you one toe inside that door if I have anything to say about it."

I decided I needed some real face-to-face with him so I opened the door. "C'mon, Danny," I said as I dangled one leg outside of the vehicle. I couldn't quite bring myself to totally leave the comfort of the bun warmer. "You know I have to do this for Tony. At least let me listen to what she has to say. Tell you what—you can do all the talking. How's that? I won't say a word. I promise."

That's when he laughed at me. He actually opened his beautiful, kissable lips and laughed in my face.

"Give me one good reason why I can't accompany you," I challenged.

"Let me count the ways," he sighed. "One, you don't know how to keep quiet. Two, your mouth has a real nasty habit of engaging way before your brain, and three, I'm not stupid enough to jeopardize this case, my career, or your safety by bringing a civilian into an investigative interview. How's that for starters?"

Then he pushed his jacket away from his hip and reached around his waist. I was momentarily distracted by the fact that he'd changed clothes seconds before it crossed my mind he was planning on forcing me to leave at gunpoint. I scooted back into the car and tried to shut the door. His response time was a hair's breath quicker than mine.

Before I could stop him he clamped one handcuff around my left wrist and snapped the other on the steering wheel. I'd been so intent on arguing my case I hadn't thought about any other options he had at his disposal. Damn. I was usually quicker than that, and more than likely a quart low on caffeine.

I struggled against the restraint and squealed like a banshee. "All right, all right," I said. "Point taken, now let me go."

"You might as well make yourself comfortable, sweetheart," he said as he thumbed the door lock,

"...because you're here for the duration." Then he slammed the door against my further protests and walked away.

Without so much as a backward glance, he crossed the street and followed the curved flagstone walkway to the white stone façade of the Vander Poole mansion. The second he was ushered in, I dug through my purse and produced a key ring which held not one but a pair of little silver cuff keys.

My daddy didn't raise no dummy. No siree. Not when it came to stuff like this, anyway. Handcuff keys, I'd discovered, were pretty much universal, and I wasn't about to let any man, not even Danny whom I trusted beyond completely, use them on me without having a backup plan. I had another set in my nightstand drawer. Just never knew when they'd come in handy.

Chapter Thirty-Five

No matter how much a house cost or how original an architect thought he made his design—a house was still a house. It might have a few more amenities, a few more bathrooms, a couple of thousand more square feet, and be built with higher end materials, but the basic layout was usually similar to that of a house costing one-tenth the price. I decided to play a hunch and followed my gut instinct, which was all I had left to go on.

I jumped out of the Hummer and set the alarm. I wasn't taking any chances on this one disappearing like my Malibu. If anybody so much as breathed too close to the Hummer, I'd be the first to know about it.

I scurried past Danny's unmarked squad, made my way up the driveway, and around the side of the garage toward the rear of the house. There was a six-foot cedar and stone privacy fence blocking access to the back half of the house and yard.

I tried the gate latch. Well what do you know, it lifted without so much as a *clickety snick,* and swung open just as soundlessly. Now this was undoubtedly considered trespassing, I reminded myself as I slipped into the back yard and shut the gate behind me. But I wasn't doing it with malicious intent, so that made it okay, right? I was rationalizing again. Oh well.

Just as I suspected. I could see Mia in the kitchen through a rear window, and she was talking to someone who looked remarkably like what's his face from Tony's apartment building. Ramon, yeah, that was his name. How did he fit into this picture? Things were getting more confusing by the minute.

I couldn't hear what they were saying—not that it mattered because in all likelihood it was in Spanish anyway—but judging from their expressions and excited gestures, it was an intense exchange in any language. He waved his hands in wild, expressive mannerisms, and she returned the gestures with equal enthusiasm.

I wished Tony was here to see for himself that Mia was alive and well. I closed my eyes for a moment and focused all my energies on sending him a message. Since we were supposed to be so strongly linked according to Olivia, I figured it was worth a shot.

When I opened my eyes, I glanced around, expectant and hopeful. No Tony, only what was there when I'd closed them. I shook off the disappointment that had sugar-coated my skepticism and refocused my attention on the reality right in front of me.

In the light of day, Mia looked so incredibly young, a slip of a girl really with soulful, dark eyes and a permanent sadness stamped across her delicate features. Even the smile she bestowed on Ramon was heartbreaking as he prepared to leave.

Leave? Oh my gosh! Ramon was leaving. He was zipping his hoodie, pulling up the hood. I couldn't let them find me there. He'd never fall for that Health Department Inspector ruse a second time. I was surprised he fell for it the first.

I looked around for a place to hide. The gardener's shed sitting off to the side looked promising. I scurried behind it, pressing my back to the wall, seconds before I heard the back door open.

Their voices were low, and I didn't understand much of what they said, but *adios, mi amor,* I understood loud and clear. Goodbye, my love—now wasn't that an interesting development. I was getting dizzy trying to keep all the players straight in this unfolding telenovela. Although, the way things were going, I wouldn't have been at all surprised if Franklin Roth himself made a guest appearance for a little game of hide the tamale with this chick.

Their goodbyes went on and on. They weren't kissing and hugging as much as communicating, vigorously again I might add. The Spanish language can be so intense when spoken with the passion these two expressed, but since I couldn't understand more than an occasional word or two, I glanced at my watch. They'd been at this goodbye thing for almost twenty minutes. I was tempted to jump out from my hiding place and scream, "Enough already!"

The cold seeped through my jacket and jeans and settled deep into my joints. I ached all over, and my feet had lost all sense of feeling. I jogged in place to ease the stiffness in my back and hips, and a painful tingling replaced the numbness. Terrific. In an effort to alleviate my miserable state, I'd managed to make myself feel worse. To keep from feeling sorry for myself, I turned my attention to my surroundings.

Old Man Winter obviously didn't discriminate between the classes. A yard in November, even one in this upscale neighborhood, was as dead and desolate as a middle class one across town. Except for the stately row of tall pines lining the rear of the property, this one was no exception. Dismal grays and bleak browns were the landscape's predominant colors. Even the evergreens didn't look happy to be there. They shivered in the wind, and I swear the rustling of their branches expressed their displeasure loud and clear. Is it any wonder why I hate this time of year? It was downright depressing.

I shifted my stance and peered through the shed window behind me, wondering if rich people kept anything different in their sheds than people did in my dad's neighborhood. There was enough natural light left for me to see inside. Assorted yard tools hug in a neat row against the back wall along with a wheelbarrow and fertilizer spreader. There was a potting bench stretched along the adjacent wall, scattered across the top lay assorted clay pots, hand tools, and bags of fertilizer and potting soil. Taking up most of the center, there stood what I assumed to be a riding mower or maybe a small snowplow tucked under a tarp. There was nothing interesting in there either, unless I was maybe Martha Stewart or Bob Vila.

I sighed and pressed my forehead against the cold, dirty glass, and wondered if this dude was ever going to finish his goodbyes and leave. The corner of something sticking out from under the mower cover caught my wandering attention.

Wait a minute. Wait a minute! Could it be? I turned away telling myself it wasn't possible, but the minute Mia's visitor finally took his leave I intended on finding out.

As I tried the door, I wondered if it was it too much to expect it to be unlocked. Yep, apparently it was. Was it also too much to think there would be a key hidden under the rubber doormat? Nope. There it was, leaving its distinctive outline in the dirt when I picked it up, just like in the movies. Once again, the line blurred between reality and fiction.

I let myself into the shed and tore back the tarp. Eureka! It was my open house sign.

Well, in all fairness, I suppose I had to lean toward the realistic side of this discovery. Maybe it wasn't my sign, but it was one that looked exactly like it. I couldn't prove it was the same sign that lured me into the Roth house, but really, what were the chances it wasn't?

I dropped the tarp, letting it settle into its original position, and looked around for other clues as I thought about the implication behind this discovery and how I could connect it to Tony's murder.

The first thing I'd noticed was how new the tarp looked. I knew how tarps usually looked, because my dad used them to cover pretty much everything that didn't move. They were practically indestructible, and he kept them for a long time. The ones he had were stained and smelled bad compared to this one that smelled like…well, nothing but new canvas. Even the packing creases hadn't had time to relax. Nope, it didn't take a genius to figure out this one hadn't been there very long. A couple of days was my guess. At the very least, long enough to hide an open house sign I concluded with a satisfied nod.

I locked the shed, replaced the key under the mat, and knocked on the back door. When Mia answered, I fast flashed my Costco membership photo ID to look official and said, "Hello, Mia, my name is Jennifer Flagg. You don't know me but I have a message for you from Tony."

"I don't know a Tony," she said in stilted English as she lowered her gaze and shook her head to emphasize her denial.

"He knows you," I returned. "Quite well, from what I've been told. He knows your friend Ramon, too."

Her olive complexion blanched. "I don't know what you're talking about."

"I understand you're scared," I told her. "But you've got to trust me. Tony's concerned for your safety."

"I told you. I don't know anybody named Tony." She shook her head more vigorously and tried to close the door.

I wedged the toe of my sneaker against the brass kick plate and held it open. "Mia, please listen to me. I can help you."

"No one can help me now," she said as she shoved me out of the way and slammed the door.

I stumbled down the stoop like a drunk at closing time and hit the pavement hard. Damn. That was the second time in less than an hour I'd let someone catch me off guard. I was going to have to work on quicker response times.

Annoyed, I picked myself up and did a cursory inspection of my person. I flexed my arms and jumped up and down. Everything appeared to be in working order. I couldn't say the same for my best pair of jeans, now sporting a quarter-sized hole in both knees. Well, I guess they weren't my best pair of jeans any longer. The only thing they'd be good for now was a nice pair of Daisy Dukes come summer.

"If Mia won't to talk to me," I grumbled as I checked for any other apparent apparel damage as I brushed myself off, "how am I supposed to help her?"

"That's not Mia," said Tony.

I whirled to face him. "Sure it is," I retorted. "She said so."

"No, she didn't," he countered. "She never said she wasn't, but she never said she was, either."

I thought about what he said. "No, I guess she didn't, did she?" How had I missed something that basic?

"No, and it's not her."

"Are you sure?" I questioned. As much as I wanted to believe him, Tony's word in this matter could not be taken at face value. I needed to be certain he was drawing from reality and not distorted memories. "She sure looks like the woman I saw the other night."

"She bears a striking resemblance, I'll give you that, but it's not Mia."

"Then who is it?"

"Her name is Cara, no Carmen—Carmen Schwartz."

My eyebrows rose significantly. "Schwartz?" I took a wild stab in the dark. "Let me guess, she's married to an American citizen?" I'd heard about these immigration scams.

"Only on paper. You'll find a lot of illegals working around here with surnames that don't fit their ethnic profile. They're brought here through underground labor markets and given new names. After they get here, they're informed they're expected to work to pay for their transportation and the papers to prove their new identity. The lucky ones, or maybe I should say the smart ones, manage to get out with or without the promised documentation."

"And the dumb and unlucky ones? What happens to them?"

"That's what I was trying to find out when I was murdered."

"Are you talking about human trafficking here?"

"That's part of it."

"Why are you telling me this now?"

"Because I need you to believe me when I say that's not Mia. I need you to believe me when I say I've got a really bad feeling about her disappearance."

What was it about this guy that made me forget everything I've learned from past experiences and trust his instincts over my own? "What do you want me to do next?"

Tony briefly explained and I reluctantly agreed. Danny was so not going to like what I was about to do.

Never mind Danny. *I* didn't like what I was about to do.

Chapter Thirty-Six

With Tony urging me every step of the way, I went around to the more impressive double-wide front door and rang the bell.

"I need to speak to Detective Prince," I said when Mia answered without as much as a flicker of recognition when seeing me standing there. I dispensed with the pseudo ID. I figured why bother. She hadn't paid attention to it the first time.

She stepped aside and I stepped inside. Whoa. I was snow-blinded, and it took a few seconds for my eyes to adjust to the glare.

The Vander Poole residence was in serious need of color therapy. The whole foyer was white. There were pale-veined white marble floors, textured white walls, and the plush, velvety white carpeting spilling down the grand staircase. Even the woodwork and banisters were stained a creamy shade of antique white. White was okay as an accent, but this was way over the top.

"Who is it, Mia?" A woman I assumed was the widow Vander Poole appeared from a room off the entry. She strutted—there was no other word to describe it—toward me with her head high as she approached. I'd love to know where she learned to move like that because I wouldn't mind taking a few lessons. A walk like that could come in handy. I'm sure the view from behind was equally magnificent. I wondered if Danny had the good sense to appreciate it.

For someone referred to as the Widow Vander Poole, she was way younger than I'd expected. My guess was she wasn't all that much older than me—forty max—but a very well preserved forty. Actually, I'd consider myself lucky to look that good ten years from now. Aw hell, who was I kidding? I should be so lucky to look that good now. She was a stunner. Except for her icy blue eyes, the cool practically platinum blonde was as pale as her colorless surroundings, right down to the winter white wool slacks and matching silk jacquard blouse.

Aside from everything else, the really weird thing about meeting her was I felt like it wasn't for the first time. My annoying memory for photographs was kicking in again. I was positive I'd seen that flawless face somewhere before, and it was going to drive me nuts until I figured it out.

I forced a smile and held out my hand. "Hello, you must be Eleanor Vander Poole. My name is Jennifer Flagg." Her handshake was limp and perfunctory; just what I'd expect from someone who thought I wasn't worth the effort.

"Jennifer?" I heard exclaimed from a room directly to my left. Danny appeared in the doorway with eyes the size of half dollars and an expression that told me he wasn't happy to see me. Huh, and here I thought he'd be thrilled.

I just smiled. "Hello, Detective Prince," I said. "I would have been here sooner but I was unavoidably detained." I reached into the side pocket of my purse and handed him his cuffs. "You forgot these in the car."

"Is this your partner, Detective?" Eleanor Vander Poole's question was delivered with a dubious raise of her delicately arched brows. This superior attitude of hers was really beginning to bug me.

Before Danny could answer, I jumped in, "Actually I'm here to speak to Miss Ruiz. I have a message for her from a client of mine."

Danny groaned.

"Client?" Eleanor Vander Poole reiterated. "Are you a lawyer?"

Tony jabbed me in the ribs before I could reply. I arched and flinched in surprise and took a step away. Since I couldn't return the favor, I wasn't used to them touching me with such mastered, overwhelming enthusiasm. Even the few who had gotten the hang of it had never been so presumptuous to think it was okay to take these kinds of liberties in front of the living.

"Are you all right?" Eleanor Vander Poole asked.

I couldn't answer because Tony chose that moment to poke me harder. I grunted and jumped.

She directed her next query toward Danny. "Is she having some kind of a fit?"

"No, I don't believe so," Dan answered as he leaned in close to me and whispered, "But I'm about to have one if you don't knock it off."

"I can't help it," I returned as I jerked and twisted out of Tony's reach.

"Tell her you need to talk to Mia," Tony all but shouted in my ear as he pushed me, hard enough to lose my footing, and I stumbled forward.

"I need to talk to Mia!" I exclaimed as I took a couple of steadying steps.

Mrs. Vander Poole stepped back to place some distance between us. "What business could you possibly have with my maid?"

"Tell her," Tony encouraged, nudging me and causing me to jerk and jump yet again.

I looked straight at the young woman and asked, "Are you Mia Ruiz?"

"Of course she is," her employer interjected as the young woman nodded obediently.

Tony poked me again, and I blurted, "Is she a legal immigrant?"

"Jennifer…" Danny warned.

"Of course she is," Eleanor Vander Poole exclaimed. "What on earth would make you think otherwise?"

I ignored them both and addressed Mia. "I suppose you have papers to prove that."

"Si," Mia murmured, casting a hasty glance in Mrs. Vander Poole's direction. "Senora keeps them for me."

"That's right," the lady of the house confirmed. "I keep them in my safe."

"Ask to see them," Tony prompted. He pressed his palm against my back. The ventriloquist and his dummy take their show on the road.

"I'd like to see them," I said as courteously as possible. Damn, he was good. I'll bet nobody saw his lips move.

At the same time Danny jumped in with, "That won't be necessary, Mrs. Vander Poole. Thank you for your time. We'll be leaving now." He grabbed me by the arm and steered me toward the door quicker than I could say green card.

This time it was Tony's groan I heard.

"Oh, there's one more thing," I said, glancing over my shoulder as I dragged my feet to slow Dan down, "…are you a Realtor, Mrs. Vander Poole?"

"Certainly not." She didn't appear pleased that I asked. "Whatever gave you that idea?"

Danny continued to urge me away, but I managed to get in one more question. "You aren't planning on selling this place any time soon, are you?"

"No, I'm not," she said as she slammed the door on our backsides the second we cleared the threshold.

"That woman doesn't have any immigration papers in her safe," I said as Dan hustled me down the walk. Even my long legs were having trouble keeping up with his determined strides. "And if she does, dollars to donuts they're as phony as her double-Ds."

"Shut up, Jen," he growled.

"You're not listening to me," I said, wrenching free from his grip. I was really getting fed up with his pushing me around. "Tony insists that's not Mia. I have to believe him and find out."

"And you're not listening to me," he said. "I told you to shut up."

Nothing he said was going to keep me quiet. I was determined to have my say. "And what about the open house sign she has hidden under a tarp in the gardener's shed out back, huh? What about that?" I felt pretty smug about making that discovery.

When we reached the Hummer, he whirled me around. There was a fury in his eyes I'd never seen before. I just might have pushed him farther than I'd ever pushed before. Then again maybe not, but it sure seemed like it at the moment.

"You've been snooping around her backyard?" At

my nod, he added, "You've really gone too far this time, Jennifer."

"That's the beauty of it, Danny," I told him. "Because I'm not a cop, I don't need a warrant to snoop around somebody's backyard." From the astounded look on his face, I realized I was going to need a lot more fairy dust on that line of logic to make it fly.

"And if you had snooped and left without bringing me into it, whatever you found *might*, just might, be admissible as evidence. Just the fact you're the chief's sister will bring your actions into question."

"But you heard her. If she isn't a Realtor or planning on selling her house, why is she hiding an open house sign in her shed? Which, I might add, is identical to the one I saw in front of the Roth's the other night."

Danny dragged his hand down his face and sighed. "I don't know and I don't care. If it isn't legally obtained, it doesn't exist as far as I'm concerned."

"But—"

"End of discussion."

"There's something very wrong in that house, Danny. I can feel it."

"Oooo," he expressed with bug-eyes and a wave of his hands. "It's probably the widow's dead husband trying to get in touch with you."

I glared at him. "If you don't want to understand why I do what I do, fine, I get it. But don't you dare start making fun of it."

I thought his watching poker on TV was weird, but I'd never ridiculed him about doing it. "I've been given an opportunity to help these people. I'm all they've got left, and not you or anyone else is going to stop me from doing whatever they need me to do. You got that?" I pushed him away.

Because it felt so good, and because I suddenly remembered he had one coming for the Tawny thing, I pushed him again. It didn't take much to make me happy. A little violence, a little retaliation, a little hostility, and I was good to go, which was exactly what I planned on doing next.

I tugged the Hummer key from my pocket and hit the keyless remote. The monster vehicle made the most hellacious noise. Shit. I forgot about the alarm system. I fumbled with the key ring and finally found the right button combination to silence the cacophony.

"I got to hand it to you, Jennifer. Nobody makes an exit quite like you do."

Now it was my turn. "Shut up, Danny," I said as I reached for the car door handle.

He grabbed me by the arm and pulled me toward him. I squirmed and struggled as he held me in an embrace I wasn't sure I wanted from him at the moment. I wasn't happy with him and he knew it. He was peeved with me and I knew it. He was going to kiss me and I was going to let him, damn it. It didn't change our current status, but it sure helped temper them for a few blissful moments. And since my mind wouldn't let me kiss a man I was mad at, I stuffed the Tawny incident in my "future reference" bank, keeping it close to the front for easy access. Trust me, it wasn't over 'til I said it was over.

He gathered me tighter into his arms. Danny's kisses were always demanding and downright melting, but this was the kind of tongue kiss that left no mistake for what it represented.

My knees went weak, my legs turned to jelly, and I moaned into his mouth to let him know I approved of whatever it was he was doing and his reasons for doing it. I wrapped my arms around his neck and held on. Oh, man, if this wasn't a loaner I'd be willing to give a whole new definition to the term sport utility vehicle. We wouldn't even need those heated seats.

When he broke the contact, I grinned like a freaking idiot as my eyes tried to focus on his face. "More," I said.

He grinned and gave me one of those I-can-get-Jennifer-to-do-anything looks.

That kick-started my befuddled brain into functioning again, and I frowned when his motives became all too apparent. I wriggled out of his arms to break the spell he'd cast over me.

"Don't make me choose, Danny," I said as I climbed into the Hummer. "Because you won't like my answer."

Chapter Thirty-Seven

I left Danny standing in the middle of the street with his very kissable mouth hanging open as I gave the Hummer a little extra gas and lumbered away.

He had a lot of nerve thinking he could kiss his way into getting me to stop what I was doing for Tony. And what really galled me was his ploy almost worked. A couple more unbelievable kisses like that might have done the trick. Jeez O'Pete! Just when you think you know a guy, he does something like that.

From now on, I was going to have to be on red alert around Danny because he didn't like losing any more than I did. Rest assured, he wasn't going to take this lying down. Well, actually, now that I think about it, lying down was exactly what he had in mind—with me on the bottom.

Right then and there, I decided to keep the appointment he'd made for me at Lawson's Gun Range. I harbored a lot of pent up hostility. I needed a way to expend it. I'd never found anything more satisfying than pulling a trigger and making a lot of noise in the process. Trust me, I'm not a psycho kook looking to take out a theater full of people or anything like that. It's never crossed my mind to use a gun on anything but a paper target. But I won't deny the rush I get from hitting the bull's eye. Believe me, this was a lot healthier and safer than drinking or drugs.

It was already dark by the time I arrived at the innocuous concrete block building sitting in an industrial complex west of the interstate. I maneuvered the Hummer into the middle of two parking spots near the back of the lot and walked the extra distance to the entrance.

The second I stepped across the threshold, I heard the muffled report of gunfire coming from the range located in the basement.

The owner, Craig Lawson, peered at me from his chair behind the counter. "Hey, Jenny, I was beginning to think you'd stood me up."

Craig was two years older than me. He'd joined the Marines right out of high school and six months before his twenty-first birthday he'd joined the ranks of disabled veterans. A sniper had severed his spinal cord and left him paralyzed from the waist down.

With a warm grin, he wheeled around a glass display case of revolvers and semi-automatics and took my hands. "It's so good to see you."

I tried not to flinch from the pressure his two-fisted handshake exerted. He had a grip like King Kong. Of course, I knew there was good reason for all that amazing upper body strength. Craig was a power-lifting gold medalist on the U.S. Paralympics Team. The wall behind him was covered with framed photos and newspaper clippings touting his amazing accomplishments.

"It's good to see you too, Craig," I said as I gave him a lingering peck on the cheek. There was a really big tender spot in my heart for this guy. Not because of what happened to him, although there was that, but because he'd been my first serious crush when I was fifteen. We'd dated for a while. He even took me to his senior prom. But the relationship had never developed beyond the good friends we are now.

He scrutinized my left hand. "Still no ring from Prince, I see."

I breathed an uneasy laugh and tugged my hands out of his grasp. "You know that's not what we're about." I wasn't comfortable talking about the state of my relationship with Danny, especially now when my feelings about the man weren't very nice.

"Yeah, yeah, I know all about the pact the two of you made. I thought it was dumb when you made it, and I think it's even dumber you're actually sticking to it."

It was time to change the subject. "What's the biggest handgun you've got?" I asked as I settled my gaze on the display case of rentals behind him.

Pointing to the weapon lying all by its lonesome on the top shelf, he answered, "Fifty caliber Desert Eagle."

I eyed the monster pistol. The recoil would undoubtedly knock me on my ass the first time I pulled the trigger and more than likely the second, third, and fourth times as well. "Let me have it. And two boxes of ammo."

He eyed me with all the skepticism I expected. "Dan said you were coming in to practice with a .38. What'd he do to piss you off this time?"

I laughed at that, but after giving it further thought, I realized Craig was right. The only time I came into Lawson's lately was when I was madder than hell at somebody. Nine point nine times out of ten it was

Danny, which was one of the things I loved most about him. He was the only man in my life who didn't put up with my crap and gave it back when he thought I deserved it. Be it anger or passion, Danny had a way of taking my emotions to the extreme.

"You don't want to know," I finally said as I reached into my purse. The gun Danny gave me would suffice. I wasn't fifty caliber mad any more.

If I expected two boxes of ammo and a .38 revolver to ease the annoying bug up my ass, I was sorely mistaken. Stopping every six shots to dump the spent cartridges was frustrating me more than helping. A revolver was a real pain when all I wanted to do was get off as many shots as possible in the shortest amount of time. Since I was forced to stop and dump the cylinder and reload, the unproductive time I wasted gave me pause to think about why I was there in the first place.

I still couldn't believe the way I'd let Danny get to me today. I should've been ready for counter measures like that. Hell, he'd probably learned those distraction tactics from me in the first place. That he'd used them when he did made me wonder what else he had up his shirtsleeves—his recently changed shirtsleeves, I reminded myself.

The second I remembered the reason for his middle-of-the-day wardrobe change, my anger escalated like a roller coaster. I flip-wristed the cylinder closed, took aim, and fired, and fired, and fired. That poor paper bastard never had a chance.

By the time I'd finished decimating several targets, I knew I'd stayed past closing time. There was nobody left in the range but me. Craig only stayed open late one night a week, and if I remembered correctly, tonight wasn't it. But I also knew he wouldn't kick me out until I was good and ready to leave.

As I reached the top of the stairs, I heard a pair of familiar voices. I found Dan and Craig chewing the fat over a large cheese and sausage pizza and a two liter bottle of Coke. Monday night football was on the flat panel hanging on the back wall, but neither one of them seemed too interested in the game, probably because neither of the teams playing were the Bears or the Colts. Team loyalties ran deep in these parts.

I slapped the shredded targets on the counter and snatched a gooey piece of pizza from the middle.

Craig scooted one of the targets across the glass toward him, leaving a couple of tomatoey fingerprint smudges in the process, and gave a low, appreciative whistle.

"Nice groupings," he said. "I'd say she got the hang of that revolver." Craig twisted the paper silhouette so Dan could better see my handiwork. "What do you think?"

"Yep, I'd say so," Danny agreed.

I was certain it was all the below the belt shots that held their rapt interest. Crotch shots always got a man's attention. Go figure.

"I was inspired," I told them, throwing a greasy-lipped grin in Danny's direction.

"Obviously," Dan returned.

"You're the last person I expected to see," I told Danny as I eyeballed him. "What *are* you doing here?"

He mumbled his answer in what sounded to me like, "Orders from headquarters."

I wasn't sure I'd heard him correctly. "Excuse me?"

"I drew the short straw," he said a little louder.

I still didn't understand. "What's that supposed to mean?"

"Eddie thinks you need a keeper... a bodyguard. And I'm afraid I can't say that I blame him."

"Yeah, right," I half-laughed as I peeled a string of mozzarella from my chin.

Craig snagged two paper napkins from the stack on the counter. "I don't think he's joking, Jen," he said as he wiped his mouth with one and handed me the other.

He missed a splotch of sauce on his cheek, prompting me to lean across the counter to swipe it away. He winked and blew me a kiss. "Thanks, babe."

I winked back. "You bet, C.B." Now everyone assumed when I called him that the initials stood for Craig Bryan, which in fact they do, but only Craig and I knew when I used them they stood for something else entirely. It was our personal little secret, and would remain so forever.

Craig hitched a thumb in Danny's direction. "How about we ditch this guy and run away to the Bahamas together."

I tapped Craig's nose with the tip of my finger, not much differently, I supposed, then when I was trying to make a point with one of my cats. "It's tempting, but you think we're being fair to Sandy? She's invested an awful lot of time and effort on you, after all."

"Yeah," he sighed. "You got a point." Then he brightened and said, "She might be up for a weekend threesome."

"Still in the Bahamas, right?"

"Of course."

"It's a deal. Check with her on a date and get back

to me."

"It'll be a good six months before we can go, you understand. Cause that'll be how long it'll take for my neck to heal after Sandy breaks it for even suggesting it."

"I was counting on that," I told him with a grin.

"So was I," said Dan, without the grin.

I snarfed down a second hunk of pizza and washed it back with a swig from Danny's pop cup. "Thanks for dinner, guys. I'm out of here." I shouldered my purse and tossed them an over-the-shoulder wave.

Chapter Thirty-Eight

Danny caught up with me before I reached the exit.

"What now?" I snapped as he grabbed me by the arm. I tried to wrench it out from under his grip, but he held tight. This was getting old, and I sighed the fed-up, intolerant sigh of a woman who'd maxed out on her limit of manhandling, regardless of the man doing it.

"This isn't funny anymore, Danny. Let go of me."

He was just enough bigger and stronger for his bullying tactics to work as he spun me around and pinned me against the wall. "I'm not joking, Jen. You're not going anywhere without me."

He was crowding my space big time, but it was his dead serious expression that grabbed my attention. I glanced to Craig. He didn't look like he was in on the joke, either.

"What's going on?" I finally asked.

Dan cast a quick glance at Craig then resettled his baby blues on me. "Something's happened at your condo building this afternoon. Your neighbor Mrs. Fogarty's car sort of caught fire."

"Oh my gosh, is she all right?" Annabelle Fogarty was one of the saner ones living in the building. Her I liked. I might not have been as eager to inquire about some of the others as I was about Annabelle. Not nice, I know, but true.

He shook his head. "She wasn't anywhere near the car when it went up."

"Was anyone else hurt?"

"No. The only casualty was her car."

"Thank goodness. Do you know how it happened?"

"That's going to take some time to figure out. There isn't much left of her *white Malibu*."

My eyes widened as an icy knot settled in the pit of my gut. "Oh, no," was all I managed to say as it all dropped into perspective. I swallowed hard to keep down the pizza I'd just devoured.

After the initial shock passed, I asked, "You're going to find out who's doing this, aren't you?"

"We're working on that, Bunn." He rubbed my shoulder in a way, I guess, to let me know he understood my fear and frustration. It wasn't working. It was going to take a lot more touching and rubbing to calm me down—like full body contact, preferably sweaty and naked.

I know, I know, sex shouldn't be the first thing I think about when my life could be on the line. But whenever I get stressed my mind tends to wander. Sex, even thinking about it, is a great distraction for me. It calms me down and helps me to focus. Call it a safety valve of sorts. The problem is I once made the mistake of confessing my escape mechanism to Danny. Now every time he catches me *zoning out* as he calls it, he thinks I want to have sex. Sure, I'll admit I've faked a few staring spells over the years. But I figure if doing that prevented me from faking anything else, there's got to be some merit to it, right?

"In the meantime," Danny added, eyeing me

suspiciously. "Eddie's instructed me to stick with you no matter what."

Things were looking up. Sticking to me no matter what wouldn't be so bad with it being Danny and all.

We waited for Craig to lock up and the three of us left the building together. The Hummer and Craig's full-sized, specially equipped van were the only vehicles left in the lot.

"Where'd you park?" I asked as I looked around for either the unmarked or the Mustang. Danny had a knack for parking in inconspicuous places. He was good. This time he was exceptionally good. I couldn't spot his car anywhere.

"Jeri dropped me off so I could ride shotgun with you."

Then I had an even better question. "How'd you know I'd be here?"

"Where else would you go when you were pissed off at me the way you were earlier?"

He had a point.

He tried to take the keys away from me, but I held tight, adamantly. No way was he going to take me out of the driver's seat. I needed to hang on to something, anything, I could still control. For now, driving that big ass Hummer was it. He climbed reluctantly into the passenger seat and cast me one of those looks as he drew the shoulder harness across his chest and snapped it closed.

I pulled the Hummer onto Kennedy Avenue and headed south.

"This thing I do with dead people—" I started to say then stopped abruptly when I realized my phrasing. "I mean this connection I have with the dearly departed…" Yeah, I liked the sound of that a whole lot better. "…can't possibly be the reason people are trying to scare me, can it?" I couldn't bring myself to use any more definitive terminology than that. *Scare* worked for me. There were far uglier words I could substitute for *scare*, but I didn't think I could deal with any of them at the moment.

What I needed was a professional's perspective, and Danny was the closest thing I had to one at my disposal. I had every confidence he'd be able to fill in the blanks. What I was really hoping was for Dan to tell me I was being paranoid, or at the very least just plain ridiculous in my assumption.

"I think scaring you is the least of your problems," he said as he settled into the cushy, warm leather seat. He could have at least pretended to be more concerned with my situation than the heated padding under his exceptionally fine butt.

That wasn't what I wanted to hear. I expelled a loud, annoyed snort as I turned right off Kennedy onto Main. I intentionally cut the wheel a little too sharply and barreled over the curb. I could only imagine how close the telephone pole looked from Danny's passenger seat perspective.

He didn't waste any time letting me know. "Jesus, Jen, how about taking the next turn with all four wheels on the asphalt, okay?"

"I'm sorry, Dan. Did that *scare* you?"

"A little," he admitted, albeit reluctantly. Admitting to any level of fear was not something he took lightly.

"It's not a good feeling, is it?"

"It never is."

"Try to keep that in mind," was all I said without emotion as I took the next turn with deliberate caution.

"You're angry." Lucky for him this was not posed as a question. If he couldn't tell by now, then there was something more wrong with this relationship than my reluctance to commit.

"A little," I mimicked.

"You want to give me a hint as to why? Or are you going to make me guess?" He sounded as frustrated as I'd expected.

I blew out an equally frustrated sigh. "I'm just a little spooked right now, that's all." I wasn't willing to concede to anything more than that.

"Are you spooked enough to take these incidents seriously and stop this Barrera nonsense?" He sounded hopeful if nothing else.

"I can't do that." Telling Danny anything else would be a lie. And like I've said before, I've got a teensy problem with out-and-out lying to him. He and my dad are the only ones I've got issues with about that.

"Damn it, Jennifer." He pummeled his gloved fist against the seat. "Why the hell not?"

"I'm committed to seeing this through."

"What exactly do you have to see through? You're doing this for someone who's already dead, and more than likely so is the maid. You're the only one who's in mortal danger."

"I need to keep looking for Mia until I know for sure one way or the other. I can't explain it. It's just something I'm compelled to do."

He let loose with a deep, growling sigh that sounded like it originated in his feet, gaining momentum until his frustration rolled off him in giant waves. He'd been doing that a lot lately—a lot more than usual, anyway—but I didn't want to deal with it right now so I chose to focus my full attention on maneuvering the Hummer through the side streets of a residential shortcut. Sometimes ignoring the problem was easier than dealing with it, at least until I could sort through this mess and make some sense out of it.

He shot me a sideward glance that told me, in no uncertain terms, he knew what I was doing. I never doubted he wouldn't.

"For reasons I won't go into, I'm going to let you get away with this silent treatment—for now."

For now was okay. For now was enough. For now might be all I had. For now seemed like the perfect occasion for White Castles. I made a U-turn and headed for the Crossroads of America, otherwise known as the intersection of US 41 and Route 30.

Chapter Thirty-Nine

The pungent aroma of a dozen little hamburgers smothered in onions and pickles filled the Hummer's cavernous interior. Two orders of fries and a couple of chocolate shakes completed our dining pleasure. I couldn't wait to get home and dig in.

Danny's cell rang as I turned onto his street.

"Prince," he answered as I eased the Hummer to the curb in front of his house and cut the engine. I'd decided a few miles back parking on the street was easier than attempting to maneuver the oversized vehicle into the undersized, single-width driveway. I wasn't about to risk taking out part of Dan's house if I miscalculated by a foot or two. God, I missed my Malibu. There's a lot to be said for the comfort of long-term vehicle familiarity. I cast a sideward glance at Danny and smiled. The same could be said for people.

As I opened the car door, he grabbed my arm to keep me from going anywhere, all the while listening to his caller. He gestured for me to wait one minute and cut a calculating glance in my direction as he asked basic, non-revealing questions. I snitched a couple of fries and sipped on my shake as I tried to decipher Dan's cop-speak without success.

I licked the salt from my lips as my smile turned

into a frown. The very least he could do if he wanted me to wait for him was give me something interesting to listen to. What's worse, he wasn't revealing a single visual cue for me to work with, either. That damn stoic cop face was firmly set, and I was getting bored.

"What's going on?" I asked the second he snapped his phone shut.

"Let's get you inside first," was all he said as he hopped out of the Hummer and hurried around the hood to the driver's side.

I was so struck by this out of character consideration, I couldn't move. Without uttering a single a word, I let him open the car door, help me and the food out, and escort us all into the house.

We'd barely crossed the threshold when he grabbed me by the shoulders and turned me to face him. "Promise you won't leave this house unless I'm with you."

I didn't make blanket promises like that unless there were multiple orgasms involved. "What the hell is going on? Does this have anything to do with that call you got?"

He gave an imperceptible nod. If I hadn't been watching, I would have missed it. "There's been another murder in Briar Cliff, this time a young woman with curly red hair."

In spite of the obvious implication, I refused to connect the dots. The white car incident had been quite enough for one day, that a redhead was murdered was more than I wanted to think about.

His fingers dug into my shoulders as I tried to move away, and he shook me just enough to get my full and undivided attention. "Promise me."

Words escaped me, but I managed to nod once, twice, three times.

He pressed his forehead against mine and peered at me through gentle eyes. "I have to go."

"What?" I grabbed him by the lapels and glared at him. "You're leaving me?"

"It's my case, Jen. I don't have any choice."

I hated myself for behaving like some helpless, clinging vine, but I hated those responsible for causing these feelings in me more. I had to suck it up and get past it. "Then let me go with you. Who knows, if her death is connected to Tony's, the victim might talk to me."

A flicker of indecision crossed his face before he shook his head against the suggestion. "I don't think so. It's not a good idea."

"What happened to you sticking with me no matter what?"

He grinned and waggled his eyebrows. "I'll stick to you when I get back."

A few hours ago, I might have been pacified with a promise like that. But now, under these circumstances, I cast him a glance that told him I didn't appreciate his offer.

His sexy grin morphed into a gentle smile. "You'll be fine," he assured me as he pressed a kiss against my forehead. "Eddie's posted a patrol right outside."

Halfway out the door, he paused and returned. He swiped the Hummer keys off the counter and pocketed them. "Just in case you get the crazy notion to follow me," he explained.

I could only stare at him in disbelief. Did he really think taking my keys would stop me? It might slow me down a little, but stop me? I don't think so. Briar Cliff wasn't that far. I could hike in from the protected backside of the neighborhood where it butted against a wooded preserve.

His gaze narrowed as he considered my impassive expression. I saw the wheels turning as the sudden flash of inspiration crossed his face. I knew that look. I'd seen it that afternoon only a moment before he'd handcuffed me to the steering wheel.

I took a couple of cautious steps back. If he thought he was going to handcuff me to keep me here, he'd better think again. As I turned to run, he was right on my heels.

I'd barely made it to the next room before he had me pinned face down across the dining room table. No matter how hard I struggled, I couldn't break free of his stronghold. He straddled my legs and braced my hips against the edge of the table with his backside pressed against mine. His size and leverage held me down, and the next thing I knew he was tugging off my sneakers.

As suddenly as he had me pinned, he released me and stepped aside. I popped up like a punch clown and turned on him.

"My shoes?" I sputtered as I pushed my hair out of my face. "You wanted my shoes? What the hell is that all about?"

"Just a little added insurance to guarantee your cooperation in staying put," he said as he headed out the door with my keys in his pocket and my sneakers tucked under his arm.

In spite of my outrage, I had to give the man credit. It was twenty degrees outside. Taking the only pair of shoes I had with me was ingenious. Damn it.

Chapter Forty

Disgruntled, discouraged, and shoeless, I gathered the White Castle bags and shuffled to the living room. I flipped through the multitude of satellite channels and settled on watching the last hour of *Viva Las Vegas*. I fell asleep before I'd finished the fourth slider.

Groggy and disoriented, I woke up to the flickering light of a hokey Viva Viagra commercial slicing through the ghostly form of a man sitting on the arm of the couch. It wasn't Tony. Tony I would have expected. Tony I might even have predicted. But this guy was a total stranger.

The not so weird thing was I was used to waking up with strange men all the time. Now for some women that confession would generate horrified gasps and a few raised eyebrows. It's never been a problem for me because these nighttime visitors are usually dead and more or less harmless. Except for Danny, of course, but he doesn't count because he's very much alive and his presence can be extremely detrimental to my emotional well-being. But that's a whole other issue I'd just as soon not take out and examine at the moment. The unknown guy sitting near my feet was quite enough for now, thank you very much.

"Who are you?" I sat up, clicked off the TV, and

flipped on a nearby table lamp to get a better look at my late night visitor. He wasn't as young as Tony, but he wasn't anywhere near as old as my previous contacts either, that's for certain. My guess, give or take a couple years, was fortyish, and if asked by the cops to give a description of him I'd have to say he was average build, average height, and average looks—a face in a crowd—nothing special, but certainly nothing memorable, either.

Once the room was fully illuminated, I also discovered my man Tony sitting across the room quietly observing my exchange with the stranger.

"I'm Don Dunston," he answered. He paused momentarily before adding, "Or at least I used to be."

"You're still Don Dunston," I assured him. "You're just the dead-point-oh version of Don Dunston now." I reached for my milkshake—now turned to chocolate milk, but still better than nothing—and took a sip. "So, what can I do for you, Don?"

"I don't know."

I had to admit he did look a little confused. I've seen a lot of emotions expressed by my dead contacts. Confusion wasn't normally one of them. Surprise, resignation, disappointment, pissed off, those I could spot from twenty paces, but confusion was usually reserved exclusively for the living.

Don jerked his head in Tony's direction. "He brought me here. He said you could help me with my...uh…problem."

I shot Tony a baffled glance. "You're bringing me referrals?"

He shrugged and flashed me those damned dimples like that was enough of an explanation. No one had ever drummed up business for me before. I wasn't sure if I should be furious or flattered. I chose to take a conservative approach and reserved judgment, at least until I'd heard the circumstances behind Don's demise.

Tony shrugged again, like he didn't have a choice in the matter, which led me to believe otherwise because things like this didn't just happen.

I swung my feet to the floor and picked the sleep from my eyes. "Well, Don, Tony should have also told you that's not how it works. You have to tell me what I can do for you."

"Other than not being dead anymore, I can't think of anything."

He wasn't the first to make that request. "Sorry, but that one's beyond my capabilities."

I scooped up the rest of the burgers and headed for the kitchen to shove the leftovers in the fridge for Dan. Don followed, hanging on my every word as if I was the Dalai Lama and he was my most devoted follower. Looks like I had myself a Cling-on with this one.

Or maybe he just hadn't gotten the hang of motivating by means of telepathy yet. I wondered if he knew he had the ability without Tony's intervention.

Not my problem, I told myself. I was here to help him resolve an earthly dilemma and guide him into the hereafter, at the very least, point him in the right direction. That's all. Informing him about his newly acquired skills, however temporary, was not part of the job description.

That said, my problem notwithstanding, I couldn't help myself and told him anyway. "You could have just thought about coming in here, you know." Sheesh, why did I always feel personally responsible for educating these people?

Tony chose that precise moment to appear, like a spectral visual aid. "See," I said, with a sweeping hand gesture worthy of Vanna White. "Like that."

"Yeah, I know. I prefer to do things like when I was still alive."

That made as much sense as anything else so far so I nodded in deference to his choice. "So tell me, Don, how'd you die?"

"I was shot in my home office a few hours ago." There was that confused expression again. "At least, I think it was only a few hours."

"That's probably all it was," I told him. Their perspective might be out of whack on a lot of things, but their sense of timing never seemed to be affected.

"You live in Briar Cliff Estates, don't you?" Although I asked this of Don, I watched for Tony's reaction to my question. I saw nada. He'd learned to hide his emotions well, which was just another contradiction from what I'd learned to expect.

"That's right," Don answered, sounding impressed.

I'd be impressed too if I didn't already know how these two-for-one deals had worked for me in the past. The deaths were always in close proximity to one another, and they had to be somehow related. The close proximity part was an absolute. The second part was a bit trickier to nail down. The definition of related could be open to broader interpretation. I needed more information to be certain.

Although I was pretty sure of his answer, I asked anyway. "Has your body been found yet?"

He answered my question with a slow, practiced shake of his head. "Nobody's been around. My wife left with our sons to spend the holiday with her parents in Phoenix. Even our housekeeper was given the week off."

Well, that eliminated a couple of usual suspects. Not wife, check. Not kids, check. Probably not the housekeeper, either. I did think it was more than a random chance the killer took advantage of an empty house once again. There seemed to be a pattern forming, though how it fit together with Tony's death was still unclear.

"Why didn't you go with your family?" My gaze cut between Don and Tony. I think I knew what Don needed for me to do for him.

Don never hesitated with his answer, "I stayed home to catch up with some paperwork."

"You don't want your family to come home and find you like that, do you?" Finding Tony, a total stranger at the time, had been an unsettling event for me. I couldn't imagine how I'd react if it were someone I cared about. I didn't want his family coming home to find him and wonder how Don Dunston done died.

"Wow," he said, turning to Tony. "You said she was good, but I never expected this."

I chose to take my bows later. "What's your address?"

When he told me, I realized he lived less than a block away from the Roth house in a row of over-priced townhouses designed to look like New York brownstones. They stretched along the west bank of a fairly large retention pond lavishly landscaped and pretentiously called Lake of the Briar Cliff. I'd say that nailed the close proximity criteria.

"So who shot you?"

Don shrugged and said, "I don't know. I didn't get a look at the shooter."

Oh man, here we go again. "Let me guess, they shot you from behind."

He slapped his thigh, or what was the equivalent of slapping a thigh for a dead man because it was a soundless effort, and shook his head in amazement. "Damn, you are good."

"Yeah, I'm a regular mindfreak."

"That's what I was thinking," he said, laughing.

The mounting similarities were what I found freaky. "Tell me the murderer didn't leave your windows open to try and disguise the time of death."

He stopped laughing and looked at me in a way that sent a shiver down my spine. "How could you possibly know that?"

"Lucky guess," I told him. I rubbed my temples to ease the painful thrumming behind my eyes and glanced in Tony's direction. He shrugged again and tossed me another one of those damnable grins. The man was not helping.

There was really only one thing left for me to do.

Chapter Forty-One

I retrieved my cell from my purse and called Danny.

"Hey, how's it going?" I said.

"We're almost finished here." He sounded flat out exhausted. I felt awful for what I was about to do.

"Rough night, huh?"

"You have no idea," he said to me. "But I should be home soon."

"I wouldn't count on that if I were you," I told him.

"I don't like the sound of that."

There was no way of breaking the news gently, so I jumped right in without preamble. "You've got another body in Briar Cliff."

There was a lengthy pause, about a dozen heartbeats worth, before he asked, "And how in the hell would you know that?"

"I'm sitting here with the victim. Tony brought him by a little while ago."

A slow expulsion of breath was followed by, "Geez, Jen. How am I going to explain this one to Jeri? She already thinks you're a certified nutcase. Now I've got to figure out how to tell her we've got another body without bringing you into it."

"Just consider me an anonymous tip," I suggested.

"Please don't try to help. Just give me what you've got, and I'll take it from there."

I told him the address and everything else Don Dunston told me. It was Dan's response that surprised me.

"Shit. I'm standing right in front of the place."

"Is that where you found the dead woman?"

"Her body was found near the lake fifty feet away."

"You think the murders are connected?"

"I don't know what to think. I'm not making any assumptions until we find the other body." Then he disconnected, leaving me with a whole new set of questions I didn't have answers for.

"What happens now," Don wanted to know.

"We wait," I told him. If my hunch was correct, Don wouldn't have long to wait. I figured he'd vanish as suddenly as he had appeared once his body was discovered and removed from his home. I could be wrong, but I was hopeful. Very hopeful, in fact. I didn't think I could handle dealing with two dead guys demanding my attention if he didn't.

Since we had some time to waste, I sat back and made myself comfortable on one end of the sofa. "So, Don, what'd you do for a living?"

"I'm a lawyer." Don parked himself on the other end of the couch while Tony took a seat across from us.

Well that deepened the suspect pool considerably. Who, after all, hadn't thought about taking a whack or two at a member of the legal profession?

"What firm were you with?" For a lawyer, this guy wasn't much of a talker. I felt like I had to hold up both ends and the middle of our conversation. And Tony, well, he was behaving like Silent Bob.

"I worked for Frampton, Lindberg, and Stern."

Why did those names sound so familiar? They stuck in my head because I'd seen them somewhere before, of that I was certain. When the light bulb went off, it pert near blinded me. "Those are the offices off Broadway in the gray stone building with pink-tinted windows, right?"

He stared at me again with that totally amazed look on his face. How about that? Thanks to my quirky memory and a couple of strokes of sheer dumb luck, I was coming off sounding like a freaking, mindreading, psychic genius. Little did he know I was none of those things and a whole lot less. But I had to admit it felt good to know someone thought it, even if it was undeserved and came from someone whose opinion didn't count for much.

Now, if a flash of brilliant inspiration told me how Don and Tony's deaths were connected, then and only then would I consider myself truly amazing.

Don vanished about an hour after I spoke to Danny.

"I have to go now," were his last words to us. Then he was gone.

I glanced at Tony who sat slouched in the club chair looking pleased with Don's expedient departure, which got me to thinking.

I kept telling myself I should be as pleased as Tony, but I wasn't. Something about this whole Dunston situation didn't sit right. It was too perfectly executed, too cut and dried for me to believe Tony didn't have a hand in the outcome.

"So, tell me, Tony..." I tucked my feet under me,

grabbed my mug from the end table, and asked, "Was Don one of the Briar Cliff residents under your investigation?"

He laughed. Only it wasn't of the amused variety. "What gave you that idea?"

"You brought him here because you found him, and you found him only because you were at his house tonight. I don't get dead guys doubling up like this too often. The only way it works is if his death is somehow connected with yours. What I want to know is why you were at his house tonight?"

He stared at his feet, a sure fire sign of a man avoiding the issue. Men's patterns didn't change just because their blood stopped pumping.

"The way this works is when I ask a question, I expect you to respond with an answer."

"Finding Don's body will give the police plenty of answers to a lot of questions."

"That's why you brought him here, isn't it?"

He cast me a mysterious smile. "I needed his body found and found quickly. I knew you wouldn't let me down."

"You know, if you weren't dead, you'd be at the top of my list of suspects in Don's murder."

"Don't waste your pity on Dunston. He was one of the bad guys."

"Did he have anything to do with Mia's disappearance? That's why you went there tonight. You were looking for her."

He fell silent. When he finally spoke, I didn't expect what he said, "I've grown very fond of you, Jennifer."

I smiled. His declaration wasn't entirely surprising.

He wasn't the first dead guy to develop feelings for me. He was, however, the first one to tell me who wasn't grandfather material. I wasn't sure how I felt about that.

"Changing the subject with that sentimental drivel isn't going to get you out of answering my question."

"I mean it, Jen. I've been thinking about this, and I've decided Dan's right. You need to back off and let the police finish what I started."

"Why this sudden change of heart?"

"Dunston was a major player in the people-trafficking operation. The police will have plenty to investigate once they find his body."

"With your help," I stated.

"With *your* help," he corrected. "I couldn't have done this without you, but I don't need you anymore."

That hurt.

"This is getting too dangerous."

"So, that's it? You're giving up looking for Mia?"

"No, I intend to keep looking for her, but I don't need you for that." He stood and smiled, and snapped me a sharp salute as he faded. "Thanks for everything, doll."

I headed for bed wondering if that might be the last time I'd ever see him. The thought made my heart hurt. I was going to miss him.

Chapter Forty-Two

"Grounded!" The idea was so ludicrous, I started to laugh. "You're grounding me?"

Danny was bluffing. Teasing. He had to be. I laughed again in an effort to get him to join me. Why wasn't he laughing? Or talking? He just stood there watching me with those damnable blue eyes as I processed his pronouncement. Maybe I didn't understand him correctly. Yeah, that had to be it. There was always that possibility.

"C'mon, Danny, you're joking, right?"

He shook his head as he helped himself to another cup of coffee. "Your safety is no joking matter."

I should have known something was up when he'd entered the kitchen wearing sneakers, jeans, and a button-down blue oxford with the sleeves rolled to his elbows. He rarely wore jeans to work, and then only when he was on special assignment. Why don't they call him what he really is—Jennifer's babysitter.

"I don't have time for this paranoid nonsense, yours or my brother's." I headed to the bedroom and pulled jeans and sweater from my suitcase.

I hugged the clothes to my chest and sank to the bed. I was so angry I couldn't stop shaking. Angry and admittedly a little scared.

In spite of the conclusions Eddie and Danny had reached, I refused to let a couple of random events keep me from getting on with what I had to do. I refused to be intimidated, I refused to be afraid, and what's more, I refused to be any of the things Danny or anyone else expected me to be.

"Jen."

"Go away." I rolled to my side and curled into a ball with my back to him. "I'm not happy with you." I wasn't happy with the world, but Dan was a good jumping off point.

The bed dipped and he snuggled behind me, wrapping his arm around my waist. I tried to wriggle free, but he held tight, nuzzling my neck and planting little kisses along my hairline. I still wiggled, but more to give him better access to other places to kiss.

"So, what can I do to make you happy?" His words vibrated down my spine as his fingers crept under my sleep shirt. He found a nipple and rolled it between his fingers.

Nipples were so easy. Unlike other body parts that required more concentrated effort, it didn't take much to make nipples happy. It would appear one particular part of Danny wanted in on the action, too. It was perking up and getting downright ecstatic.

A compliant purr escaped as I snuggled my bottom into the bend of his legs. I figured what the hell. Why waste a perfectly good rise in his Levis?

I couldn't move from all the happiness Danny had lavishly heaped on me. Was it possible to be paralyzed and tingling at the same time? As I pondered this physical anomaly, I heard the ringing of a distant phone. I knew from the tone it wasn't the house phone, and I was sure it wasn't Danny's cell since it was still clipped to his belt attached to his jeans presently lying in a heap on the floor. That meant it had to be mine. I reached that brilliant deduction about the same time it stopped. I hoped they left a message because I couldn't work up enough energy or interest to care at the moment. I rolled to my side and promptly went to sleep.

Two hours later I awoke to the intermittent beeping of my phone reminding me I had missed a call. I sat up with the intention of searching for the annoying offender and discovered Danny still peacefully passed out beside me. He barely stirred when I stood, which led me to the conclusion that now might be a good time for me to sneak out of the house.

I pulled on my clothes and tiptoed past the sleeping Prince. I was barely across the bedroom threshold when I heard him rise and tug on his jeans. I should have known his detective antenna was turned on high and tuned solely on my whereabouts. Scratch making a clean get-away from my to-do list.

I retrieved my phone from the living room and listened to the voicemail as I traipsed through the dining room for the kitchen to see if there was any coffee left. I needed caffeine bad.

There were three messages in all. Guess I must have missed the first two while I was getting happy.

The first call was from the window store, but all they had to say was they didn't have anyone available to come out until Friday and they'd call back when they had an exact time. No big surprise there.

The second was from Ray Lacy telling me he didn't find anything wrong with my car, not even a dirty injector, and I could pick it up any time. Again, no surprise.

The third started with what sounded like traffic noise, the steady-spaced rumbling of trucks and whooshing cars, and then the same sharp pops I'd heard out front the day before. Then there was silence until the automated female voice announced I had no more new messages.

I deleted them all—the first two because they weren't important enough to save and the last because Dan would only overreact if I told him about it. I'd decided to go with my theory because I didn't like Dan and Tony's. These were nothing more than overt scare tactics and, since I wasn't actively searching for Mia anymore, I didn't have anything to worry about, right?

I glanced at Dan, who sat at the table watching me with a dead even gaze. I could never tell what was going through that handsome head of his when he looked at me like that. It was so much easier to know what was on his mind when we were in bed, more than likely because there wasn't much going on up there when he was in a prone, on top of me position.

"Nothing important, I take it."

"Nope," I answered. "Just the door store and Ray from the garage."

"And the third?"

"The third?"

"You deleted three messages."

"Oh, that. Nothing but background noise, no talking."

He watched me, and waited, as if he expected more of an explanation.

So I added, "Must have been a wrong number."

"Do you always react like that from a wrong

number?"

I frowned. I hadn't realized I'd reacted at all, let alone *like that*. It was time to change the subject.

"I need to take the Hummer back to Ray and get my car," I told him.

"Fine, I'll go with you."

That was way too easy. I expected more of an argument out of him. Looks like the argument needed to come from my end. "I don't need a chaperone."

"Maybe not, but you've got one just the same." He stood, buttoned his shirt, tucked it into his waistband of his jeans, and re-buckled his belt. The last thing he did was clip his holstered gun to the hand-tooled belt I'd given him for his twenty-seventh birthday.

"I don't need a bodyguard, either."

"A shot out slider, a burned up white Malibu, and a dead redhead says otherwise."

"You don't know for sure any of those things are connected." I sounded a lot cockier than I felt. Fear had that effect on me. The more fearful I got, the more defiant I behaved.

He stared at me for a couple of heartbeats. "You don't actually believe that."

"I thought if I said it out loud I might."

"Did it work?"

I shrugged. "Not really."

"Didn't think so."

Now it was Dan's phone that interrupted. He answered, listened a long while, and hung up without saying more than a half dozen words.

"It seems your newest dead friend ..."

"Don," I interjected.

"That's right," he confirmed. "Don, worked with

the other victim, Janis Biggs."

"The redhead," I stated. It was important I keep the players straight.

"The redhead," he repeated. "She was a paralegal at the same law firm where he worked."

"Frampton, Lindberg, and Stern."

"Dunston told you where he worked?" I could tell Danny was still having a difficult time comprehending my afterlife conversations. He's known about this thing I do for years, but he's never actually seen it firsthand or been this involved before. I tried to look at it from his perspective and realize how disconcerting it must be. Unfortunately for him, I wasn't feeling very understanding at the moment.

"We were making conversation while we waited for his body to be discovered. Did you know those offices are in the same building as Olivia's—same floor, in fact."

Danny was thoughtful for a couple of long minutes. "Have you been to Olivia's recently?"

I nodded as I poured myself another cup of coffee. "Late yesterday morning. I wanted her to meet Tony. Why?"

"That settles it." He snatched his gun off his belt and tossed it with his keys on the counter. "We're not going anywhere today."

Chapter Forty-Three

I reached into the popcorn bowl sitting on Danny's lap and came up with nothing but a handful of greasy no-pops. Before I sucked the butter off them in a desperate fit of boredom, I scraped the kernels on the side of the bowl and wiped my hand down the leg of my sweatpants—the very pair I'd changed into the second Dan had informed me I was under house arrest.

I cast a hard glance at my warden, who appeared to have reached a meditative state of consciousness. Either that or he was simply brain dead from the hours of mindless television we'd watched all day.

He was dressed in similar fashion, sweats, tee, and gym socks, and I couldn't help wondering why he looked so much better in the uniform than I did. He looked great, in fact. Sexy and desirable and…

Uh oh, that wasn't a good sign.

Maybe now would be a good time for me to make a run for it. I might have tried, too, except I'd lost all sense of feeling from the waist down and he still had my shoes.

"My butt's numb," I said as I pushed off the couch and rubbed the aforementioned part of my anatomy. It burned and tingled as I felt the blood return to the fleshy area.

"I'd be happy to do that for you," Danny offered with a leering grin. "And then we could celebrate the return of your circulation."

I was tempted. Recreational sex had to be a better diversion than what we'd been doing. At least there'd be a better reason for being this stiff and sore.

"No," I told him. "I'm still mad at you." Not only was he holding me captive, there was still the matter of his dirty laundry that needed to be explained—one blue shirt and a pair of dark slacks to be specific.

"Come on, Jennifer," he groaned. "I already told you I can't go into details about how that make-up got on my shirt."

"And pants," I reminded him.

"By all mean, let's not forget the pants," he sighed wearily. He aimed the remote at the TV and shut it off with a quick snap of his wrist. Not much differently, I would imagine, than if he'd been holding a gun and pulling the trigger. He tossed the remote aside and pushed himself off the couch.

"What's it going to take to convince you nothing happened? All I did was offer consolation to an old friend."

"By letting her nuzzle your crotch?"

Good grief. Did that shrill, shrewish voice come out of me? I was appalled by it. I couldn't begin to imagine what Danny was thinking. Jealousy was obviously not one of my more attractive traits—that much was clear.

"I didn't *let* her do anything. I was standing, she was sitting, it was an accident, and that's the last I'm saying on the matter."

I wanted to believe him, really I did. I'd never

known Danny to lie to me before. But this was Tawny we were talking about. It was her I didn't trust. It wasn't fair I take out my mistrust of her on Danny. Cabin fever had obviously lowered my resistance because I told him, "Okay, Dan. I won't mention it again."

He breathed a sigh I couldn't decipher. Could be relief, could be surprise. Either way, he was getting off easy and he knew it.

"I need a nap," I announced. "Doing nothing all day has been exhausting."

"Want company?"

"Maybe later."

He followed me to the bedroom anyway. I was hoping he would. Maybe I could convince him to offer me some much needed consolation.

****

By the time I woke up, I was feeling a whole lot less annoyed and a whole lot more relaxed. The kind of nap I'd taken had done me a world of good. Danny had seen to it. I sighed and stretched and wondered what we were doing for dinner. I was starving. I'd worked up quite an appetite. Naps will do that sometimes.

I rolled to my back and stared at the shadows on the ceiling as I tried to make sense out of my forced confinement. I felt like a prisoner of Danny and Eddie's over-protective imaginations. If I'd lain in stasis, the day couldn't have been any less productive. Unless they weren't telling me everything. Which, of course, was a distinct possibility, but one I'd be hard pressed to prove one way or the other. I sure hoped they didn't plan on continuing this violation of my civil liberties for any length of time. Maybe it was time to question Danny about tomorrow's agenda so I could plan accordingly.

As I shuffled out of the bedroom, my cats raced to greet me. Well, to be totally fair in the assessment, I was greeted by Ethel and glared at by Fred. I gave him a double take. He looked like a drowned rat and two sizes smaller than normal.

"What happened to you?" I asked Fred as I picked him up. He was dripping wet and smelled suspiciously like my shampoo. I grabbed a towel from the hall linen closet and vigorously rubbed his wet fur.

I found Andy Ramos sitting at the kitchen table eating a ham on wheat and washing it down with a bottle of imported lite beer. I couldn't begin to explain how many ways of wrong that was. Domestic should have been good enough.

"What are you doing here?"

"Dan had to go out, so he asked me to stay with you until he gets back."

"Why is Fred all wet?" I continued to rub my cat dry against his squirming protests until his back claws laid a set of three-inch tracks across my forearm, I let him go and he hit the ground running. Fine. He could finish drip-drying.

Andy never looked up from his food. "I gave him a bath," he mumbled. It was then I noticed both his hands and forearms covered in scratch and bite marks. I recognized Fred's handiwork.

"Cats bathe themselves, Ramos." I reached into the fridge and pulled out a cold imported for myself.

"Let's just say he needed it and leave it at that, okay?"

"Did he get into something he shouldn't have?"

"He got something on him he shouldn't have."

"What?" I asked as I snatched the other half of his sandwich from his plate and took a big bite. Hmmm, it tasted better than I expected with the imported. I took another bite.

Andy raised his gaze, looked me square in the eye, and stated, "Pee."

I swallowed without chewing. "You peed on my cat?" I choked as I reached for my beer to wash down the lump of bread and processed lunchmeat.

"It was an accident."

I stared at him and said, "You *peed* on my cat."

"I didn't do it on purpose!" he exclaimed. "Damn cat followed me into the bathroom and jumped on the toilet as I started to go. I tried to stop, but it was too late."

"You—peed—on—my—cat." I thought maybe if I stressed each word it might take the hilarity factor out of the situation. Nope, not a chance. Beer spewed out my nose as I bust out laughing.

Without so much as a smirk, Ramos pushed away from the table with his shredded hands. "You own Danny a new shower curtain."

I laughed harder.

Chapter Forty-Four

I startled awake and glanced hopefully at Danny. Hey, it wouldn't be the first time he'd woke me in the middle of the night for a quickie celebration of something or other. Just having him in bed with me was enough of a reason.

I sighed. It wasn't Danny. He was dead to the world. I cringed at my choice of words. I hated that particular expression, for reasons I shouldn't have to explain, but it seemed most appropriate at that moment. A quick glance at the nightstand clock told me it was a little after three—the middle of the night.

I curled against him, practically purred at the warmth he imbued, and tried to go back to sleep, all the while telling myself I must have dreamed him calling my name. Even after months apart, it hadn't taken us long to reconnect and take up where we'd left off.

Try as I might, I couldn't fall back to sleep. Probably the naps I'd taken on and off all day.

"Jennifer—"

It would appear I wasn't dreaming after all. I was fully awake and realized the voice was coming from the living room.

I slipped out of bed and into sweat pants. Then I dug around in a dresser drawer for one of Danny's T-shirts because he had clean ones available.

The only light in the living room came from the street, but it was enough illumination to find Tony lying on the couch looking a tad more see-through than any of his previous appearances. Don't ask me how I'm able to differentiate one level of transparency from another, but I can, and Tony was definitely less visible.

Oh man, this was so not a good sign. I kneeled beside him, wanting to help without the first clue as to what I could do. Dead people, like newborns, didn't come with instructions. I'd never dealt with one this close to transitioning. They always took their leave long before this point. I was treading uncharted waters here and was afraid I was in way over my head.

"Give me your hand," he said, holding out his palm.

With a helpless shrug, I did what he asked and placed my hand where I could see his should be. Although I didn't expect it to do any good, I also figured it couldn't do any harm. Then a miraculous thing happened. We made real contact. Not only did he touch me, but this time I was able touch him in return. The whisper-soft pressure of his fingers curled around my knuckles. I gave a little squeeze that made him smile.

"I can feel your heart beating," he said.

"I wish I could tell you the same," I said with a sad, little smile. In spite of my initial impression of this guy, I'd grown attached to him in a way I'd never felt with my previous contacts, and I was going to miss him more than I could ever say. Dealing with the dead for so many years had taught me to remain objective and detached. I wasn't prepared for the rush of emotions tying me in knots over his imminent departure.

A thick lock of dark hair fell across his brow, and I couldn't resist the urge to push it from his forehead. I marveled at the whisper soft feel of him beneath my tentative fingertips.

"I feel funny."

"I'm sure you do." This was what I imagined was the equivalency of dying for the dead.

"What's happening to me?"

"I'm no expert, mind you, but my guess is you're starting to transition."

A wave of panic crossed his fading features. "I can't leave yet. Not before I know what happened to Mia. Isn't there any way to stop it?"

"I-I don't know," I stammered as an overwhelming sense of helplessness settled over me. "No one has ever tried before. When did this start?"

"I'm not sure exactly. I was roaming around the Vander Poole house searching for some clue as to what happened to Mia when I suddenly felt this uncontrollable urge to get back to you. The next thing I know I'm here calling your name."

He closed his eyes and rattled something under his breath in flawless Spanish. I could only assume he was praying, or confessing. Either way, I needed translation.

"Tony," I said to get his attention. "You probably don't have much time left. If there's anything you want to get off your chest, this might be a good time to do it." If he left now, he'd be leaving me with more questions than answers. I wanted closure as much as he did.

He opened his eyes and smiled. "You've been a good friend, Jennifer. I appreciate everything you've done."

Touching sentiment as that was, it wasn't what I wanted to hear.

He stared at the ceiling and rolled his head back and forth in slow, deliberate defiance. "No, no, I can't. Please, I need more time! Go away! Please go away. Leave me alone."

"Okay, I'll leave you alone," I replied. I understood his need for privacy and started to stand.

"Not you," he said. "The light."

With a larger than normal dose of skepticism, I questioned, "There really is a light?" I couldn't believe it. I was hearing a genuine, first-hand confirmation of that blasted, often spoken about, but never proven light.

With a heart-thumping mixture of conflicting emotions, I cast a wary glance in the same direction Tony gazed. Whew. Since only the dead or dying claimed to see it, I was more than a little relieved I didn't catch even a glimmer. In spite of my relief, I was still disappointed. Well, who wouldn't be? This was a momentous occasion, after all. I couldn't be any more thrilled if I'd discovered proof of life on Mars.

"Can you describe it for me?" Just because I couldn't see it didn't mean I didn't want to know what to look for when my time arrived—many, many, *many* years from now, I silently added in case the someone or something that made these decisions was paying attention.

"Jennifer!"

"Well, you can't blame me for being curious."

"Try to focus, huh? I need you to help me fight it."

I didn't know how to do that. I'd never been faced with a situation like this before. Nobody had ever asked me to stop their transition. They had all looked forward to the moment when they moved on, embraced it actually, and they usually left without any fanfare or fond farewells. Poof! One second they were there and the next they were gone, never to be heard from again. I always told myself it was better that way.

Then inspiration struck. "Olivia," I exclaimed. "I'll call Olivia. She might know what to do."

It was worth dragging her out of bed for something this important. It struck me funny most of her late night calls were from clients trying to get rid of ghosts and misguided spirits. Leave it to me to need her help in keeping one around.

I retrieved the portable phone from the kitchen and dialed her number from memory. She answered on the first ring. If this had been anyone else but Olivia, I'd have found that weird considering the time. The fact is it was her quirky behavior I loved most about her. I would have been disappointed had she behaved in any other way.

"Hello, Jennifer." Nope, not even her immediate greeting was particularly surprising, caller ID notwithstanding. "How can I help you tonight? Or should I make that morning?"

I experienced some serious reservations once I explained Tony's predicament and she'd told me what I needed to do. "Are you sure that's going to work, Liv?"

She chuckled at my uncertainty. "Our line of work doesn't come with guarantees, Jennifer. You know that."

"But it's worked when you've done it, right?"

"I can't say I've ever had the pleasure."

"Then how can you be so sure it'll work?" My

voice raised several octaves. Panic will do that. I didn't like going where Olivia had never ventured.

"I've been told it's a reliable, although short-term, solution to your friend's dilemma. He needs to understand this is only a stopgap. The light will not be denied forever."

With my hand cupped around the receiver, I turned my back to Tony and whispered, "I'm not sure I can do this, Liv." The process seemed both creepy and sensual, and I wasn't sure which part bothered me the most.

"Jennifer, our senses are our greatest tools. Sensuality sits at the very core of our power. You *can* do this. I have every faith in you. If you lead with your heart, your mind and body will follow."

Her astounding vote of confidence sounded a lot like Thor Rasmussen, a motivational speaker I paid an obscene amount of money to learn his secrets of empowerment when I was in college. I'd felt empowered enough after listening to the first twenty minutes of his bullshit to ask for my money back, so I guess it'd worked. At least that's what they told me when they refused to give me a refund. Live and learn.

"Keep in mind, Jennifer, if you decide to do this, for the remaining time he has left on this plane you and Tony will be inextricably linked."

No big deal, I thought. I'd dealt with Cling-ons before.

After a few more encouraging words from Olivia, I expelled a sigh of resignation and agreed to give it a try.

Chapter Forty-Five

"Tony," I said as I crouched beside him. "According to Olivia the only way to keep you from transitioning at this time is for you to use a living vessel to ground you to this plane until the portal closes."

"Huh? You lost me at 'according to Olivia.'"

"You need to join with a living soul to stick around a little longer."

"Why didn't you say so?"

"I was quoting Olivia," I explained.

"Didn't I see this in a movie once?"

"Could be—most paranormal fiction, however dramatized, is based on facts. Are you ready to give it a whirl?"

"Is this going to hurt—you I mean? Cause if it does, I won't do it."

I was touched by his concern for my welfare. "Olivia assured me it's a relatively painless event, although she did warn me it's going to feel a little weird at first for both of us." I hoped weird was the worst of it.

"How long will we have to stay joined?"

"She said it shouldn't take more than a few minutes. Once you receive the strength from me to fight the draw of the light, the portal should close. What you need to understand is this isn't a permanent solution. But it should give you a little more time to find Mia." Or at least what happened to her.

"Couldn't we find some homeless *guy* to take me in?"

With fists on my hips, I stared him down, appalled and insulted. "You've got a problem with using a woman?"

He flashed me one of his charming, dimpled grins. "Some of my fondest memories involve doing so."

I held up my palms to keep him from taking this conversation to a place I preferred not to go. "If you start with the sexual innuendos, I'm never going to be able to go through with this."

"So who gets to be on top?"

"I'm not going there…"

"Sorry," he said without a shred of remorse, I noted.

I forced myself to stay focused on the goal, not the process of getting there. "Can we get this over with, please?"

"Now you sound like a girlfriend I once had."

"Tony, please stop. I really can't take any more."

"Had one that said that, too."

"Tony!"

He pursed his lips and assumed an expression of choirboy innocence. "Okay, so tell me what we gotta do next, doll."

"We need to join chakras." I'd never held much belief in any of this chakra business, but Olivia did. Since I didn't have a better idea, I was willing to give her suggestion a try for Tony's sake.

"You lost me again."

"Sit up," I told him. I wasn't about to go through a lengthy explanation just to get to this same point in the process. "Now I'm going to sit in the same place you're occupying."

"One other thing…" he said, sounding a tad hesitant, like he wasn't sure he should interrupt but couldn't help himself.

I cast him an over-the-shoulder glance. "Now what?" I wanted to get this over and done, and his continual interruptions were keeping me from doing that.

"What's a chakra?"

"It's an energy source that exists in all of us. There are seven main chakras that run from the top of our head to the base of our spine. The only one we need to concern ourselves with is the root chakra which grounds us in the physical world."

I turned my back to him and took a couple of deep breaths to help relax. Yeah, like that was all it would take to prepare me for what I was about to do. For that to happen, I'd need a quart of Jack and a big bag of Tony's special blend tobacco. Unconscious, or the very least oblivious, would definitely be the best way to go. Talking to dead people was one thing. Physically interacting, connecting with them on this very personal level, was quite another.

I wiped sweaty palms down my thighs, but my stomach wouldn't stop churning. Acid reflux was moments away.

He took my hand and squeezed it. "Jen, you don't have to do this."

"I want to, Tony. Really…" It was at that split second in time I realized I meant what I said. For the first time since I'd developed this gift, I had a chance of doing something more for Tony than I'd ever done for any of the others—something important and meaningful.

"Okay, as long as you're sure." His hands gripped my hips and squeezed playfully. "Please be gentle."

"Only if you promise you'll still respect me in the morning."

"That goes without saying."

That said, I clenched my teeth and allowed him to pull me down. I sucked in a long, startled breath as I settled into place. A warm, tingly, not entirely unpleasant, sensation filled me as we melded.

"It's working," said Tony. "I feel stronger already, and the light isn't as bright."

"I've done some strange things for my dead friends," I murmured as I rolled my head on my shoulders. "But this is by far the strangest."

His essence wrapped around me. I had no frame of reference for comparison, but I had enough sense to know I was experiencing something quite rare and indescribably wonderful.

"I don't know if I should be telling you this, but I'm starting to feel good—real good, in fact."

I was thinking the same thing, but chose not to bring it up. It wasn't exactly sexual, but the euphoria rushing through me was pretty darn close.

My emotions were running high and tight. I moaned one of those long, soulful sighs that indicated I was at the very least enjoying the moment. I didn't think I could take much more.

"So how's it going, Tony? You think we're about finished?"

"Please tell me you're not doing what it looks like you're doing with Barrera."

"Fuck," I whispered, which was undoubtedly the worst expletive I could have chosen, and the look on Danny's face when he stepped out of the hall shadows pretty much reflected a similar sentiment.

"I believe I asked you not to tell me that."

"No, no, that's not what I meant. I said that because you caught me..." That didn't come out right either. "Not that we were doing anything I didn't want you to catch us doing. It's not like that at all." If I kept this up I might have a deep enough hole to bury myself. "Tony and I were just sitting here...talking." Among other things.

"Talking..." he reiterated, wearing an incredulous expression I detected even through the darkness. It fairly radiated with a life of its own.

"You really shouldn't jump to conclusions."

"Well, it's a little hard not to considering you're wearing that look," Dan said.

Now it was my turn to wear the look of incredulity. "I have a look?"

"You know, Jen..." Dan crossed his arms and took a controlled breath. "I'd say this pretty much ranks right up there with the recent Tawny incident, don't you think? How about we call it a draw and vow to never mention either one again."

That sounded like a real good plan to me, and one I could live with. "So, you want to shake on it, or what?"

"Shaking's good..." He held out his hand and pulled me to my feet. "...for starters."

Jennifer, wait...

That little voice inside my head sounded different

somehow. It sounded like a man's voice. It sort of sounded like Tony.

Jennifer...

I glanced behind me at the place on the couch I'd just vacated and where I expected to still find Tony.

No Tony.

I turned on a lamp and looked around the room.

No Tony.

"What's the matter?" Dan wanted to know.

"I can't find Tony. He was just here—now he isn't." I peeked around doorways and under cushions. Maybe the melding didn't work. Maybe the light took him anyway.

"So what? You said yourself he comes and goes as he pleases." He gripped me around the waist and steered me toward the bedroom. "I say good riddance."

"You don't understand—this wasn't supposed to happen after we—"

Danny's brows rose so high I swore they shook hands with his hairline.

"—did that thing we agreed not to mention," I finished, chomping down hard on my lower lip to keep from saying more.

"Come to bed," Dan urged.

"You go ahead. I'll be there in a minute." I had to find out what happened to Tony.

Clearly not happy, Dan sighed dramatically and mumbled something about "crazy" and "foolishness" and "head examined" as he turned and left. It wasn't too hard to fill in the blanks.

I headed for the kitchen where I found Fred crunching on a late night snack of kitty kibble. He lifted his head, took one look at me, and yowled at the top of his lungs as he arched into an attack position.

"What's wrong with you?" I asked.

I think it's me.

"Tony! Thank God you're still here." I glanced around, but couldn't find him anywhere. "Where are you?"

I'm right here. I seem to be stuck.

"What do you mean stuck? Stuck how? Where?"

Here, inside of you, that's how.

"What?! Stop fooling around. Get out this instant!"

Don't you think I've been trying?

"Try harder!"

I think maybe we might have melded too long.

That was undoubtedly the understatement of the century. The trick here was not to panic. I grabbed for the phone. "I'll call Olivia. She'll know what to do." God, I sure hoped she knew what to do because I didn't have a clue.

The second I heard her pick up, I jumped right in. "Dan's in the bedroom waiting to make love, but I can't let him because Tony's stuck inside of me!"

"I take it Dan has a problem with that?"

"He doesn't know! He's got issues with me talking to dead people. I'm pretty sure he's not going to be pleased to know one's taken up residence."

"So how can I help?"

"Get him out."

"Dan?"

"No, Tony!"

"I'm not sure I can do that."

"What do you mean? Why not?"

"I thought you said he wanted to stick around a little longer to find his friend."

"I did, but what does that have to do with getting him out of me?"

"I can't extract him without losing him to the light."

"Are you saying his only options are staying inside of me or leaving with the light?"

"I thought you understood that. You're all that's holding him here. That's why it's only a temporary measure. There can be devastating consequences when two souls occupy one body for any length of time."

"Why am I just hearing about this now?"

"What did you think I meant when I said you'd be 'inextricably linked'?"

Well, duh!

This wouldn't have been a problem if we'd found a homeless guy like I wanted.

This wouldn't have been a problem if I'd learn how to say no more often.

"So how long will I be stuck with him?"

Stuck with me? That's kind of cold, don't you think?

"He'll leave as soon as you find his friend."

Guess that means you're back to helping me look for Mia, huh?

Well, double duh! And the sooner the better.

Chapter Forty-Six

One of the last things Danny told me before he left for work that morning was, "Don't leave the house until I get back." To which I didn't immediately comment because I was already making plans to the contrary. I knew the rules. It didn't count if I didn't respond.

"Jen, did you hear me?" he asked as he stuffed his arms into his leather jacket and reached for his cell and car keys from the counter.

"I heard you."

There's nothing wrong with my hearing. The problem is I don't listen very well. Never did. And if the bad guys don't get to me first, Danny will undoubtedly offer to take me off their hands and do it for them when he finds out I went against his specific instructions.

"I don't need to get Andy over here again, do I?"

"No!" I exclaimed.

"I didn't think so." He grinned and kissed me on the top of the head. "Call me if you need anything."

What I needed was to get the heck out of there so I could get Tony the heck out of me. And to do that, me and Tony had things to do, places to go, people to annoy, that sort of thing. The clock was ticking.

I had this hunch. It was a big one, too strong to

ignore, and we had to follow it because the problem with hunches, particularly the big ones, was they couldn't be ignored any more than the man inside my head.

Between the hunch and Tony, I couldn't help myself. We needed to move, and since Tony couldn't go anywhere without me, we were partners again until the bitter end.

We, meaning me and the stuck-in-me Tony, spent the morning doing some in-depth investigative Internet surfing. My total recall for photographs, combined with what Olivia had told me on Monday, and the things Tony was telling me now gave me a starting point and led me to discover some very interesting things about Eleanor Vander Poole. The formerly LeAnn Winston, formerly Nora Powell, and last but not least, nee Ellie Mae Booker, which by a stroke of unbelievable coincidence happened to rhyme with the world's oldest profession, was also the one she used to hone the skills she needed to coax rich, older men out of their money and into early graves.

"How did this last husband of hers die?"

The short version is he died in a boating accident.

"And the long version?" I had a feeling this one would be a lot more interesting.

The story goes—

"The story?" I interjected.

According to the police reports, the only witness to Mr. Vander Poole's accident was Mrs. Vander Poole. The three-man crew, as well as the other couples on the charter were below deck when the accident happened.

That was convenient. "So what exactly did she say she witnessed?"

319

According to her, they were standing on the rear deck when he clutched his chest and collapsed.

"So he had a heart attack."

Not exactly. When he collapsed, he hit his head.

"So it was head trauma."

Not exactly. When he hit his head he fell overboard.

"The cause of death was drowning?"

Not exactly.

"If it wasn't exactly any of those things, how *exactly* did the man die?"

When he hit the water, he was attacked by a shark.

"So it was a shark that finally did him in?"

Not exactly. They never found enough pieces of Charles Vander Poole to determine a definitive cause of death.

"That's it, I've heard quite enough." It was time to move on. "Tell me about Franklin and Angela Roth?"

There was a long pause, enough to make me ask if he was still with me.

Why d'you do it, Jennifer?

"Do what?"

All of it, any of it.

I'd been hoping he wouldn't ask me that, even though I'd been asking myself the same question. I hemmed and hawed, hoping he'd turn his attention to something else. I fiddled with the pen and pencil cup sitting next to the monitor. I took a sip of coffee. Ugh, cold. I gnawed a thumbnail ragged.

I'm waiting.

I shrugged nonchalantly. I hated getting cornered. "I don't like unfinished business, that's all."

Riiiight...

"I like you, okay." Damn, that was hard.

You love me, admit it.

"I don't love you. I just like you—a lot." Telling anyone I loved them didn't come easy for me. It didn't come at all, actually. Even Danny had never heard me say those exact words.

I did love him. Danny, that is. I'd just never told him in so many syllables. Maybe I ought to make that my New Year's resolution. As far as Tony was concerned, what can I say? I'd developed a real fondness for the guy. Yeah, I suppose in my own way, I loved him, too. I couldn't tell him any more than I could tell Danny. I should really put some serious thought into working on that emotional shortcoming.

"About Angela and Franklin Roth," I said, hoping to guide him back to safer, way less personal territory.

You're pathetic, you know that? Why is it so hard for you to tell someone you care about them? Or that you might even miss him when he's gone?

I stalled a little more and picked at the edges of the mouse pad. "I will miss you," I murmured.

What was that? I didn't quite hear you.

"You're a pain in my ass and I hate you."

That's what I thought you said. Now, where were we?

"Angela and Franklin Roth," I reminded him.

Angie is a Realtor who handles only multi-million dollar homes like the ones in Briar Cliff Estates. She's the one who brought the domestic workers situation to the attention of the Feds, who in turn contacted the international task force I work for.

"Why the two apartments?"

I was working both sides. I had to maintain two

totally separate lives.

"But your engagement picture was in the paper. Don't undercover agents usually try to keep a low profile?"

You met one of my contacts. Do you really think Ramon or any of his friends read an English newspaper, let alone the society page?

"Good point," I said. "But if you didn't suspect Eleanor Vander Poole at that point, why were you using her maid as an informant?"

Mia was convenient. She lived right next door, and she was a documented illegal. She helped me trace the source of where they were getting their papers.

"Enter Don Dunston," I said. It was all falling into place.

Mia was able to put me in touch with dozens of others, all living and working in Briar Cliff. I was building a strong case and closing in on the person or persons behind this trafficking operation. Falling in love was never part of my plan.

His obvious vulnerability might make it easier for me to ask about the night he was killed. I hesitated, but only for a moment. Call it a need for closure, but I really wanted to understand. "What events took place the night you died?"

After Angie and Frank left for Indy, Mia snuck out after her employer went to bed. We shared a bottle of wine, we made love, and we fell asleep in each other's arms. Who knew our spending the night together would end the way it did.

I felt his anguish and the weight of his sadness.

"Okay, back to Eleanor Vander Poole," I said, hoping that by redirecting his thoughts would lessen the intensity of mine.

It's clear she isn't the grieving, helpless widow she'd led people to believe she is.

"So what do we have to do to nail this lying, manipulating black widow?"

He gave me some passwords that got me into government-restricted data bases. It was mid-afternoon by the time we'd filled in a few important blanks and put a couple of key puzzle pieces together.

The picture wasn't a pretty one, or a promising one. Eleanor Vander Poole had used so many intermediaries and middlemen, it wasn't going to be easy to finger her as the mastermind. We needed hard, firsthand evidence. We had to confront her.

I called and left a message on Dan's voice mail telling him I had to go out, but I didn't say where or for what. That I called when I knew he'd be in a meeting where he couldn't be reached had nothing to do with it. I thought telling him anything was more consideration than any man who hid my shoes in the bag of cat litter deserved.

Chapter Forty-Seven

As I pulled in front of the Vander Poole house, my cell phone went off with the tone I'd assigned exclusively to Danny—"Danny Boy." Yeah, I know it's corny, but if I had to choose a song for every emotion Danny stirred in me, I'd need more memory on my phone—a whole lot more.

I debated about answering it. He was going to yell at me, or worse not yell at me, and who needed that?

It stopped. Whew, that was a close one. I turned off the ignition and retrieved my purse from the passenger seat. The weight of the .38 boosted my confidence a couple of healthy notches. I could do this. I had to remain objective and think like a cop. A cop without a warrant or probable cause that is, which made being a civilian in this particular instance a good thing. I could get away with things they couldn't.

"Danny Boy" started up again.

He's not giving up. Maybe you ought to answer and get it over with.

Those were my thoughts exactly, but I wasn't used to them speaking to me with a Brooklyn accent.

I dug under my mass of curls and tapped the button on my Bluetooth. It was coming down to a battle of wills, and since we were both contenders for that championship title, I decided to get this round over with, hopefully with a few points in my win column.

He started in immediately. "Jennifer…" I winced at his menacing tone. It cut right through me like feedback from a faulty PA system. "Where are you?"

"Uh…" I stalled. "You don't want to know."

"Yes, I do." He tempered his tone, which usually meant he was one step closer to losing his temper. It's funny how that worked. The softer he spoke, the more I worried. There wasn't anything funny about that.

"Knowing where I am isn't going to change what I have to do," I argued. "So you're better off not knowing."

"This recent behavior of yours isn't normal, Jen…"

Don't I know it? But I was compelled to keep doing it, for Tony and for Mia. And for all the dead people down the road who'd come to me for help above and beyond the usual heartfelt farewells and final last words. Over the last couple of days, I'd reached the conclusion Tony would not be my one and only challenge in the years to come. He'd opened a Pandora's Box, so to speak. Now I was left with making the most of the things that escaped.

"…not even for you."

He just had to add that. I closed my eyes and quietly seethed.

"I have to do this, Danny." I was more determined than ever.

"Why don't you come down to the station so we can talk about it? Better yet, why don't you meet me at the Starbucks on Main?"

Even though the lure of a Grande Caramel Macchiato and a scone sounded wonderful right about now, suspicion niggled at me more, and started me wondering.

"Why'd you choose the one on Main," I questioned. "When there's a Starbucks right around the corner from the P.D.?"

"I thought the one on Main was your favorite."

His voice had reached that barely above a whisper point, and I had to concentrate to hear his last comment. Any second now, he was gonna blow.

I heard hushed mumbling and shushing in the background, like one or more persons were trying to keep me from knowing Danny wasn't alone. And doing a piss-poor job of it, I might add.

That's when Danny's real motive hit me. *Now* I remembered what GPS really stood for—*Global Positioning System*—and my phone was equipped with it. He was tracking me through it.

"You sneaky sonofabitch," I screeched. "You already know where I am."

"There you go, jumping to conclusions again."

"I didn't have to jump this time, Danny. You pushed me!"

"You didn't leave me much choice. Your irrational behavior forced me to take drastic actions."

"Oh, pulleeze." I jumped out of the Hummer and slammed the door. "You and I both know I've behaved a lot worse than this, and you've never resorted to tracking me like an escaped convict."

"If you're determined to do this, Jen, at least wait until I get there. We'll do this together."

I considered his offer.

A cop will only make Vander Poole clam up.

Tony was right. "Thanks for the offer, but I'll

pass."

"At least wear your Bluetooth and keep the phone line open."

Suspicion had become my bosom buddy. "Why?" I stretched the word like a piece of sugarless bubble gum.

"So I can at least monitor what's going on until I can get there."

"I don't need your help." I tapped off the headset, and turned my phone to vibrate only.

The headset softly toned in my ear. It wasn't "Danny Boy" but I knew who it was. "What now?" I asked.

"Don't do that again."

I hadn't thought it possible, but his voice had reached an all-time low.

I didn't have time to argue. "Fine. Have it your way." I reached the immaculate white double doors and rang the bell. "Just don't talk to me, okay? It's bad enough having dead people talking to me without another disembodied voice traipsing through my head." One was quite enough, thank you very much.

Instead of simply agreeing with my request and leaving at that, he made it worse by chuckling in my ear. It crossed my mind to flip him off, in more ways than one, but I knew it wouldn't do any good. If the man was nothing else, he was obsessively persistent.

"You're going to pay for that," I threatened.

"I've no doubt."

I was forced into submissive silence—not an easy thing for me to do, I might add—when the grand dame herself answered the door.

"Miss Flagg," she said. Surprise and contempt frosted her bored and breathless greeting. "To what do I own *this* visit?" She was dressed in the palest of pink Spandex workout clothes and spotless white cross-trainers. It didn't surprise me she worked out. It took a lot of effort to keep a body that toned and jiggle-free.

Not that I'd know from personal experience or anything like that. Anything that jiggled on me was au natural and pretty much work-out free. The only parts of me that ever got a decent workout whenever I went to the gym were my eyeballs from ogling the hunky, muscle-bound men working the free weights.

"I apologize for intruding on you like this, I know I should have called first, but there's something I really need to discuss with Miss Ruiz before I can finalize this matter for my client. Is she here?" I stepped forward with the expectation of being invited in.

She stood her ground and blocked the entry.

"This really isn't a good time," she said as she started to close the door. "Why don't you come back tomorrow?"

Don't let her put you off. We need to get into that house.

I slapped my palm against the door to stop her from slamming it in my face. "Tomorrow is Thanksgiving," I pointed out. "That wouldn't be convenient for either of us, now would it?"

She sighed the annoyed sigh of a woman not accustomed to having her demands questioned. I could see the wheels turning under all that perfect platinum hair.

"It'll only take a minute," I said, pushing on the door. In spite of the determined set to her lovely jaw, she stepped aside. I ignored Danny's whispered warning not to enter the house as I entered the lioness's den.

As casually as possible, I reached beneath my hair and turned him off. I'd deal with him later, or vice versa.

The woman gave a waving gesture toward the formal living room. "Wait in there," she stated. "I'll get Mia."

"Thank you," I said as sweetly as I could.

Watch it, Jen. That much sweetness could put me into serious sugar rage.

While I waited for the Mia double, I took a good look around.

Whoa, mama. There had to be a year's salary in pretty but useless tchotchkes sitting around. Hey, just because I grew up on the Indiana side of Chicago didn't make me a total hick. I've managed to find my way to Michigan Avenue a few times. I knew what I was looking at here: Limoges, Baccarat, and Lalique were the few I recognized at first sight.

I glanced at my watch. For someone who hadn't been eager to have me here, Eleanor Vander Poole was sure taking her sweet time getting back to me. Maybe she thought if she kept me waiting long enough I'd give up and leave. If that's what she thought, she didn't know the last kid in a line of eight learned patience *and* endurance.

I planted myself in a wing-back chair like I was settling in for the winter and leafed through a copy of Vogue. The magazine was thicker and heavier than the models featured in it.

It seemed like too much of a coincidence that the widow entered shortly thereafter. I wouldn't be surprised if she had a surveillance camera in the room.

She carried a silver tray and placed in on the inlaid coffee table between us. I also noticed she'd changed out of her workout gear and now wore a soft wool skirt in the palest shade of blue with a matching cashmere sweater set, the under shell's neckline was scooped low enough to reveal a set of perfectly matched alabaster breasts. A single strand of exquisite pearls encircled her slender throat. No doubt those babies were real—the pearls not the boobs. The latter were as phony as the pearls in my jewelry box.

She'd sure moved up in the world since her days of *Ellie the Belly*, Off-strip Vegas showgirl, which was just a respectable name for everything else she'd done offstage.

"I brought tea," she announced in a tone that clearly told me she didn't think I had enough sense or breeding to know.

"How very kind of you," I said with an equally condescending tone. "I do hope you didn't go to any trouble on my account." The frosty look she shot me suggested in no uncertain terms that I perform an act on myself I would personally prefer to do with a partner. I returned a sloe-eyed, satisfied look that suggested I'd already been there and done that, thank you very much.

I accepted the cup and saucer she offered, but no way was I going to eat or drink anything she served. I already thought she was capable of spiking the bubbly. Slipping a little something extra into my tea wasn't too far of a stretch. And those lovely little cakes and cookies on the tray were undoubtedly to die for.

"I really don't understand what's taking Mia so long," said Mrs. Vander Poole. "I asked her to join us as soon as she finished up something for me." She stood and headed for the hallway leading to the back of the house.

"Please don't go to any more trouble," I said as I placed my teacup on the silver tray and stood to leave. "I'll have to come back later. There's somewhere else I really need to be now."

What are you doing, Jennifer? You can't leave.

I didn't know what it was, but I had this compelling urge to get myself the heck out of there. My instincts were a lot like my cats. When they spoke to me, I listened and obeyed.

"Are you sure?" she asked as she took a couple of steps toward me.

There it was again—that gut-twisting sense of doom crawling through me. I may not always be able to talk to the dead when they were around, but I often felt their presence just the same. There was something dead or dying in this house, and was enough to tell me to get the hell out of there.

"Perhaps you'd like to reconsider," she said as she lifted her hand from the folds of her skirt to reveal a snub-nosed revolver gripped in her meticulously manicured fingers.

Chapter Forty-Eight

Well, there it was. That explained the icky feeling I'd been having. Oh yeah, no doubt about it, a gun in the hand of this chick would definitely do it. I took a steadying step away and gripped the back of the wingback chair I'd just vacated.

Don't do anything stupid, Jennifer, like give her reason to pull the trigger.

Excellent advice I hoped I could follow.

"I thought stilettos were your weapon of choice," I said, keeping a close eye on her trigger finger. It curved loosely near the trigger guard, but still too close to the trigger to suit my level of comfort.

"Oh," she sighed and shuddered. "Who knew how messy that would be? I ruined a beautiful pair of Jimmy Choos with that crude Latino's blood."

"That must have been awful for you, especially when a pair of rubber Wellies would have been so much more appropriate for the messy occasion."

"Shut up!" she snapped as she waved the gun.

I flinched and braced myself. "Gunshot wounds can be pretty messy too." I felt compelled to point out that fact. "You wouldn't want my blood all over this pretty rug. It looks expensive." I was walking a fine line between keeping her talking and pissing her off.

"Of course it's expensive!" she said, fairly foaming at the mouth. "It's Aubusson!"

Is that anything like the Autobahn?

I could only imagine what she would have done if I'd told her it looked like it came from Farmer John's Flea Market. I decided to keep that observation to myself.

This woman was crazy. I don't mean the kind of harmless crazy that makes a person walk naked down the middle of Route 30 waving a Union Jack and singing *Dixie*. The kind of crazy I'm talking about in connection with this woman was spelled with a capital C, and that rhymes with D, and that stands for dead.

This was that unpredictable kind of manic crazy that made a person do things that seemed perfectly normal for any average, everyday psychopath. Trust me on this one. If there's one thing I've learned over the years it's that crazy is a relative thing, mostly because I have more than my share of crazy relatives. That's the naked, flag-waving, singing variety, in case anybody's interested.

And to make matters worse, aside from the crazy part, I saw pure, unadulterated evil. She looked at me as if I was nothing more than a piece of gum stuck to the bottom of her Blahniks and all she needed to do to get rid of me was to flick me into the garbage with the blunt end of a butter knife. It didn't take too much more of a leap to determine I was going to die by this woman's hand, just like Tony, and more than likely Mia.

Considering the insurmountable odds against my getting out of this alive, I was surprised by the unnatural calm settling over me. I stared her down, figuring if she was going to shoot me, she was going to have to look me square in the eye when she did it.

As if reading my desperate thoughts, she grimaced and screeched, "Stop looking at me like that. I'm only doing what my husband would have wanted me to do." She cast the gun a loving look. "I cherish this gun. Charles gave it to me. It's a LadySmith AirLite," she said.

Was that supposed to mean something to me? A gun was a gun, as far as I was concerned. They all killed in the wrong hands.

It's nice to see she has her priorities straight.

Amen, brother.

"He told me to always keep them guessing."

"I'm really no threat to you," I pointed out. Especially since the .38 Danny had given me was at the bottom of my purse, which was sitting on the French provincial desk across the room.

"I have to kill you," she said. "And since the men I hired to do it are incompetent idiots, it looks like I'm going to have to do it myself."

"So they weren't just trying to scare me?"

"Hell, no. I wanted you dead. You're a loose end that needs to be tied up."

There goes my theory.

"Killing you is the only way to stop you."

"Stop me from doing what?" I asked.

From out of the corner of my eye I caught a glimpse of movement outside the floor to ceiling picture window. The cavalry had arrived. I hoped she was turned enough away to keep from catching the activity going on out there.

"Why'd you do it?" I asked.

That's good, Jen. Talking is good. She'll be less likely to shoot you if you keep her talking.

Or if I say the wrong thing, she'll shoot me all that much sooner.

"Kill Barrera, you mean? I didn't kill him. Not directly, anyway. All I did was incapacitate him. It was Mia who actually finished him off, with one of the heels she 'borrowed' from my closet for her midnight tryst."

"You're telling me Mia stabbed Tony?" No wonder he refused to tell me who killed him. It was as I suspected from the beginning—he was protecting someone.

No! Don't listen to her. Mia didn't do it.

"I knew what she was up to, where she was going that night. I spiked the wine and left it out, knowing she'd take it, lying little thief that she was. What I didn't count on was them not drinking enough of it to knock them out. They were woozy but still conscious when I walked in on them. When he tried to stand, he stumbled and fell flat on his face, and that's when she plunged the heel into him."

That's not how it happened. I remember now. I fell on the shoe heel. Oh God, it was nothing but a stupid accident.

"Why would she do that? Tony loved her."

"Who told you that?" She looked at me like I'd told her what color thong she had strung between her cheeks. "It's true, then? You really can talk to the dead?"

"Occasionally," I answered with a modest shrug.

I had to hand it to her. The woman recovered quicker than most did after hearing about this thing I do. But I guess if she didn't see it as something she could exploit, it wasn't worth more than a passing consideration. Such is the life of an under-appreciated medium.

"What about the other stab wound?" I questioned. No way was that one accidental.

Her lips curled into a reminiscent smile, as if she were reliving the gruesome event—with obvious pleasure, I should add. "I learned a long time ago that all men think with their dicks first and foremost. Jabbing my heel into his crotch was my way of letting him, and every other man for that matter, know he'd been outsmarted by a woman."

"Are you sure that's how it happened?" I questioned. I had no doubt about the crotch-stomping part, but I was hoping she'd tell me more about Mia. The young woman had been alive when Tony's body was found. Only this crazy woman knew what happened to her after that.

"Are you questioning my account of the events?" She waved the gun over her head like Lady Liberty flagging down the QE2.

"Well gosh, let me think about that a minute. You smuggle humans for profit. I'm not sure that makes you a real credible witness."

Instead of getting pissed, she dismissed my accusation with an offhanded shrug. "What's the big deal? Everything, including people, has a price. I sold myself for years, in one way or another. As you can plainly see it hasn't hurt me any."

Oh, yeah, how could we miss how well adjusted she is?

I was thinking the same thing.

"These people didn't have a choice. You lured them away from their homes and families with promises of a better life, and then you turned around and sold them into servitude."

"I charged for expenses. There were transportation and handling fees that needed to be paid, and those documents don't come cheap. There's a price for the chance to live in this country. Many of them were grateful for the opportunities I offered and were willing to do anything to stay."

"But not all of them, right? Some of them didn't appreciate what you were doing for them. The life expectancy of the ones who refused to cooperate wasn't very long, was it?"

"You'd be amazed at how clumsy and awkward these people are. They had accidents, tragic, but unavoidable accidents."

"Is that what happened to Mia? Did she have an unavoidable accident?"

"That stupid girl thought she could outsmart me with her duplicity. Even after I told her I'd overlook what she'd done as long as she kept quiet and resumed her duties, she went and put that open house sign in front of Roth's house so the body would be found before we could dispose of it. I taught her, though— over and over and over—until she finally understood the meaning of obedience and loyalty."

"What did you teach her?"

"Rest assured, she'll never disobey me or anyone else again."

That's what I was afraid of.

Me too.

There was a thump and a series of muffled thuds in

what sounded like someone walking across the roof. It distracted the crazy broad just long enough for me to hit the deck and scramble for cover.

She whirled and fired.

I swear the air dispersed past my cheek as the bullet whizzed by.

That was a little too close.

He could say that again.

I peered around the chair and watched her wobble and stumble when her heel caught in the carpet fringe. Using the desk to catch her balance, she righted herself, shook her hair from her face, and said calmly, "I had a nice little business going until that horrid man started snooping around, sticking his nose where it didn't belong… asking all those questions." She was frothing again, her breathing coming in short, ragged gasps.

"Is that what you call it? 'A nice little business'?" I scooted around the side of the chair and crouched between the couch and a brass-based Tiffany floor lamp.

"It's all about supply and demand. For months, all I heard at the country club was bitching and moaning about how hard it was to find reliable help. I simply saw a need and filled it."

I shoved the lamp and down it went, the stained glass shade shattered on impact along with several china trinket boxes it swept off an end table on its way down.

The noise made the widow scream and spin on her stilettos. The next thing I could reach was the tray of tea and goodies. I caught two fingers under the silver rim and flipped it off the table. The tray made a wonderful, rich *bong* as it landed bottom side up, and the china crashed and shattered into so many pieces not even all the king's men would know what to do with them.

There was a sleek crystal vase sitting on the table beside the chair. I grabbed it by its fluted top and flung it with an overhand toss, hoping to clunk her in the noggin and end it here and now. My aim sucked and I missed her by a city mile. It hit the wall behind her and splintered into a thousand pieces. Maybe that was a job for all the king's horses.

"What are you doing?" she squealed as she shot off another round in an excited fury. I was real glad to see her aim wasn't any better than mine. The bullet hit the wall behind me.

It's good that she's using a revolver.

I had to agree. Lucky me, she had only six bullets compared to what, maybe ten or twelve if she was using a semi-auto?

Give her another reason to shoot at you.

Easy for him to say.

Spotting another curio within arm's reach, I snatched it up and gave it a fling. It sailed through the air and landed with a satisfying crash. I actually grinned when I heard her fire.

She's getting wild. That one wasn't anywhere close.

"You bitch," she screamed. "You fucking, cop-sucking bitch."

Whoa. That was harsh.

True enough, but how'd she know?

It was time to move. I scrambled behind the couch, hung a left, and took a head first dive under the baby grand near the floor to ceiling bay window. I snagged the hanging fringed tail of a delicate ivory lace runner draped across the piano and gave it a hard yank. Every silver-framed photo tumbled down in domino fashion, one right after another.

The crashing noise was punctuated with another wild shot. What number was that? Round four or five? Damn it, I'd lost count. Four, I decided. It was four.

"Stop it, stop it…" she whimpered as she kneeled down not three feet away from me to salvage what she could from the shattered rubble. Oblivious to the glass shards, she reached for an eight-by-ten glamour shot of herself taken what had to be twenty years ago.

I scooted farther under the piano. From there I had an unobstructed view of the goings on outside. There were at least half-a-dozen marked and unmarked squads surrounding the house. They were parked on the grass and cordoning off the street.

"If you don't like what I'm doing in here," I said. "You should see what they're doing to your lawn."

The photo fluttered to the floor as she climbed to her feet, the gun, unfortunately, still clutched in her fist. "They can't do that. They're ruining the landscaping. Look at what they're doing to my bushes. Stop," she screamed, pounding on the window with the butt of the gun. Another shot went off. "Get off my property at once. I'll have you all towed away if you don't leave this instant."

There came a splintering crash as the front door busted open. She fired again. That was six. I was positive she'd fired all six rounds.

"Jennifer!"

"Danny…" I breathed. Profound relief washed over me as I unwound my limbs and crawled out from under the piano.

The cold barrel of the revolver pressed hard against my temple.

"That's it," I said as I grabbed her slender ankle and yanked her foot out from under her. Her other foot flew up in unison and she went down like a felled sapling.

My heart stopped when another shot rang out as she hit the floor. The bullet hit the ceiling, knocking off a chunk of plaster that landed near our heads. Guess I lost count. *That* had to be the sixth round.

I tucked and shoulder-rolled like I'd seen stunt men do a hundred times in the movies, and scrambled to my knees, doubled up my fists, and started swinging.

She flailed the gun in my direction. "Go ahead," I told her. I could be real brave when threatened with an empty revolver.

"Jennifer, stop," Danny shouted from across the room.

We both turned to the sound of his voice. He took a step toward us. "Stop," he said again. "It's over."

"Always keep 'em guessing," she said through swollen, bloody lips. Before I could stop her, she aimed the gun at Danny and pulled the trigger.

The report was deafening.

With stunned surprise written all over his face, Danny clutched his right side, staggered back, and hit the wall behind him. He went down in slow motion, his gaze locked with mine until he reached the floor and slumped forward.

I was so past the point of pissed, there hadn't been a word invented yet to describe the fury building in me. I balled my fingers into a tight fist and backhanded the bitch. There were no words to describe the satisfaction I felt from hearing her lovely, manmade aristocratic nose crunch and shift under my fisted knuckles. She gave a pitiful whimper, curled into a fetal ball, and promptly passed out.

I couldn't get to Danny fast enough. Two paramedics were already tending to him. A uniform grabbed me around the waist to prevent me from getting in their way. He pulled me aside, told me to stay put, and went to check on Eleanor Vander Poole.

"Is he going to be all right?" I asked no one in particular. "He isn't…"

"No, Jennifer, he's not dead."

I looked around and found Tony standing behind me. I'd never felt him leave.

"But Mia is," he added.

I closed my eyes against his words. "You found her?"

"Actually, she found me," he said. "Her body's in a freezer in the basement."

"I'm so sorry, Tony."

"She wants to talk to you." He pointed toward the top of stairs.

There she was, young and beautiful and radiantly translucent.

"Gracias," she said, looking at me with eyes that no longer held the deep sadness I'd seen that first day. Then she smiled and held out her hand for Tony to join her.

"She was briefly the love of my life. Now she's my beloved for all eternity," he said. He leaned toward me and pressed a kiss to my cheek. "My gracias goes double, Jen. I couldn't have finished this without you."

The paramedics had Danny strapped to the gurney

and were wheeling him out the door. "I really have to go," I said.

"Yeah, me too," Tony said as he joined Mia.

"Oh," he said as an afterthought. "Give that stuff from my apartment to the cops. They'll know what to do with it."

I nodded in understanding as they took each other's hand. "I'll see that they get all of it."

"Except for the book of sonnets," he added as they started to fade. "I'd like you to keep that as a reminder of our time together."

As if I'd ever forget.

Chapter Forty-Nine

Somber and frightened, I sat in the hospital emergency waiting room with Eddie beside me holding my hand. I glanced at the clock on the wall and realized what seemed like hours since they'd wheeled Danny into the trauma room was in reality less than thirty minutes.

I glanced around and discovered the room filled with police officers, uniformed and off duty, all waiting for the same news. I couldn't express how grateful I was for their supportive presence. My eyes filled with tears, and I blinked them away. I had to stay strong for Danny.

"Is Jennifer Flagg here?" someone asked. I looked up and found a short man dressed in green scrubs with a stethoscope hooked around his neck and white rubber clogs on his feet.

"I'm Jennifer Flagg," I said, standing. Eddie stood with me and draped a strong, supportive arm around my shoulders.

The doctor motioned for me to join him in a side room for the sake of privacy. Layers of death and sadness filled every corner of the tiny, windowless room.

I felt it the moment I stepped inside. It closed

around me, suffocating and stifling. I wanted to bolt and run for the nearest exit.

"I'm Doctor Lambert," he said as he closed the door. "Since you're listed as Daniel Prince's next of kin, there are a few things we need to discuss about his condition and course of treatment."

I blinked back more tears. Danny'd never said a word. I guess I was the closest thing to family he had since his parents died.

"Is he going to be all right?"

"The bullet caused some internal injuries. We need to operate."

I had difficulty processing the information. "How could there be internal injuries? He was wearing a vest. The bullet hit him in the shoulder."

"The bullet actually caught him under his arm," the doctor said. "It ricocheted off a rib where it punctured his lung and nicked a kidney. We need to go in and repair the damage."

"I'll sign whatever you need," I said.

As if on cue, a nurse entered and handed me a clipboard with all the pertinent forms.

"Here," she said, pointing to a highlighted line near the bottom of one form. "And here." She pointed to another place on another sheet—a yellow one this time.

I scribbled once, twice, three times. I lost count after that. When I finished the final form, I stared at my signature. Danny was right. It really did look like Bunnifur Flagg.

I swallowed hard to keep from choking on my tears and asked, "Can I see him before you take him into surgery?"

The nurse nodded and motioned for me to follow.

I entered the trauma room, unsure of what I'd find. Emergency room scenes on TV were sure a lot less messy and a lot roomier than the real thing. I worked my way around the monitoring equipment and pressed myself into a narrow space at the head of the gurney.

Danny's eyes were closed, his skin pasty white. The floor and sheet covering him was spattered with blood—his blood—and tubes ran out of both arms, his chest and his mouth.

I leaned in close and touched his bloodless cheek. He didn't respond. "Danny," I said.

I pressed my lips to his temple. He was cold and clammy to the touch.

I came in here determined not to say anything he could misconstrue as negative or hopeless. I knew the second that bullet tore into him I'd rather live with him on his terms than live without him on mine. When faced with the alternative, the decision had been an easy one to make.

"Anything you want from me when you get out of here, Danny. Anything at all."

Chapter Fifty

My family celebrated Christmas in a big, over the top way. I guess the sheer number of us involved made it that way without much real effort. It's a crazy day of off-key carols, enough food to feed a third world country, and holiday merry-making filled with all the teasing and loving a big, crazy, multi-generational family can inspire and produce. As much as I complained and groused about them, I know I wouldn't have it any other way. I couldn't imagine my life without a single one of them.

I'd even wished Andy a sincere Merry Christmas when I arrived earlier that afternoon. If you can't bury the hatchet on Christmas Day, what's the point? Peace on earth and good will toward men included Andy Ramos. What made it all worthwhile was knowing I still had three-hundred and sixty-four other days of the year to make his life miserable.

My dad was a stickler about waiting until every last member of his family was together before one gift could be opened. Few exceptions had ever been made, and fewer excuses were given. As the family grew, and in-law obligations took precedence, our tradition got pushed later and later. It was already dark by the time we gathered around the tree for our family gift exchange.

Danny and I sat smushed in a corner on the floor near the tree as we watched my nieces and nephews tear into their presents. He'd been included in my family's festivities long before his parents passed away. They had all been added to the guest list years ago. Being an only child, my dad sort of adopted Danny, in an unofficial kind of way, and treated him no differently than one of his own sons.

While I'm on the subject of Danny, I have to add that Dad's also under the impression that me and Danny will eventually settle down and get married—to each other, that is.

Marriage to Danny or anyone else is something I try not to think about. I'm happy with the way things are now. Much to everyone's surprise, we're still living together. Even though the repairs on my apartment were finished two weeks ago, I haven't gotten around to moving back to my place yet. And to my even greater surprise, I'm in no hurry to leave. I've discovered I kind of like sharing a bathroom and a bedroom with a certain sexy, blue-eyed detective, and he certainly doesn't seem to be in any hurry for me to leave.

I was under the impression Danny didn't want anything more than giving cohabitation a whirl either, until he opened his hand, revealing a small, blue velvet box wrapped with a slender gold ribbon and bow, and wished me a husky, "Merry Christmas, Bunny Fur."

My heart stopped beating as every man, woman, and child in the room stopped what they were doing. You could have heard a pine needle drop.

I wasn't ready to make a commitment beyond living together. I thought I'd gotten the message across to Danny. The velvet box cradled in his palm said differently.

His smile was tender, and he looked at me as if we were the only two people in the room. I knew that look, and I wanted nothing more than to go back to his place and have our own private holiday celebration.

"Danny," I said softly, wide-eyed and stunned beyond further expression. "Danny," I said again, more hesitant this time.

"Open it," he urged, nudging my fingers into action. "Anything I want, remember?"

I never knew until that moment he'd heard my whispered concession.

Holding my breath, I slipped off the ribbon and snapped open the lid. My heart started beating again as I gasped aloud. It was the most exquisite diamond solitaire I'd ever seen, only it dangled in a simple bezel setting from a delicate gold chain.

He leaned forward and whispered in my ear, "I'm sure glad it wasn't the ring you thought it was."

He released the chain from its mooring pins and drew it out by the clasp. It glistened with a thousand shots of color under the twinkling lights of the tree.

"Let me help you put it on."

I held up my hair as he draped the chain around my neck. He clasped it at my nape, and the diamond settled into place, falling just below the hollow notch in my throat.

"It's beautiful," I said, touching it, feeling the cool setting against my warm skin. I smiled as he kissed me on the cheek. His lips lingered, the heat of his touch shooting through me with as much fury as the guilty knot sitting in the pit of my stomach.

He leaned back and took a long look at me and his gift. "It looks nice," he said. "I knew it would." He pushed himself from the floor and stood. "I should be going."

"What's the rush," I said. "You're not scheduled to go back to work until after the first of the year." His earlier insistence that we go in separate cars suddenly made sense to me. He'd planned on an alternate escape.

"It's been a long day," he explained as he stepped around the strewn gift boxes and piles of crumpled wrapping paper and headed for the door.

I jumped to my feet and went after him.

"Nice going, Jen," my brother Rob growled as I passed.

Andy snorted his obvious contempt as he popped another butter cookie into his mouth. It looked like the world's beaches were safe from extinction.

I ignored them both, which was a whole lot easier than telling them what they could do to themselves and getting in trouble with the mothers in the room.

On my way out the door, I snatched a jacket off the nearby coat tree and flew down the concrete porch. I hit a patch of snow-crusted ice on the bottom step, and my foot twisted out from under me. I went down on one knee but managed to hang on to the porch railing to keep from landing flat on my face. I pitched myself back and landed hard on the third step instead. Tears sprang to my eyes as a jarring pain shot from my tailbone to nape.

I sat there for a second to catch my breath. The cold concrete spread its icy chill through my skirt to my thighs and sent an uncontrollable shiver through my body.

The tweet of his keyless remote echoed in the cold, silent night, and the interior light popped on as he opened the door.

"Danny!" I screamed, needing to get his attention before he climbed into his car and drove away.

He paused and peered over the roof.

He had to see me. The porch light was on. Anyone within a mile radius could see me sitting there. I knew from past experience it shed a wide arc of light over the porch and most of the front yard. Dad had installed it when his first daughter started dating. Small planes had been known to buzz our street in search of the local county airport. There had been no lingering smooching on the front porch at the end of a date for any of us.

"Don't go," I said. My voice trembled and cracked. The cold night air hurt my throat and burned my lungs as I tried to draw a deep enough breath. I needed to get this settled between us. Danny'd always been my rock, my dependable, always there for me, solid foundation. If he left like this, I was afraid it would never be the same between us again.

When he didn't move, I squeezed my eyes shut and hunched over, dropping my head into my hands. I didn't want to see him drive away.

I forced myself to keep from crying. Not only did Danny hate sniveling females, but I could easily freeze to the stoop if I broke down now.

The heat of his body radiated over me like a favorite blanket as he sat beside me. He scooted closer until our hips and shoulders touched.

He braced his heels on the bottom step, rested his forearms across his knees and clasped his gloved hands together. "Why'd you come after me, Jen?" he asked.

He sounded truly bewildered.

There were a hundred things I wanted to say to this man, but all that came out was, "I never thanked you for the necklace." Why was it so difficult for me to voice my feelings aloud?

He pulled off a glove and took my hand.

"You know I love you, don't you?" I said, leaning into him as he wove our fingers together.

"Yeah," he answered. "I know. But it's nice to hear you say it when you don't think I might be dying." He planted a lingering kiss at the sensitive place where my ear and hairline met. His breath warmed my cold flesh and set my heart pounding. Oh, those wonderful, magical lips.

I fought the urge to climb into his lap and take this kissing business to a whole new level, but I could feel a dozen or more pairs of prying eyes peering at us through the front window. There'd be more, I was sure, but the window wasn't big enough.

"I'm not ready to settle down."

"I know that, too," he said against my hairline. His hands crept inside the jacket and pulled me closer.

"You'll be the first to know when I am," I said as I snuggled into his warm and tender embrace.

"I'm counting on it."

I sighed and smiled, relieved to know we were back to status quo.

See what I mean? Danny understands me like nobody else ever will.

Well, at least until Wendell shows up with a message of impending death again.

A word about the author...Michelle Witvliet

As an only child, Michelle has made up characters and stories since she was a little girl. She didn't start documenting the exploits of her imaginary friends until she was a wife and mother with two little girls of her own. Many years and a lifetime later those imaginary friends are still bugging her to tell their stories.

Michelle's first published work, a Viking anthology, went the way of the dodo when the publisher went out of business. However brief and disappointing this first experience was for Michelle, it fueled her resolve to persevere, resulting in the contemporary romance, *Damn the Man*, a 2006 RWA Golden Hearts finalist.

Damn the Man and its sequel, *Damn Good Man*, are available in electronic and print format from The Wild Rose Press. Michelle lives in Northwest Indiana, where her Medium Rare series and both Damn books are located.

~~
Find her at:
Facebook: http://facebook.com/AuthorMichelleWitvliet
Twitter: @micwit604
email: michellewitvliet@sbcglobal.net
Her website is currently under major reconstruction.

Thank you for purchasing
this publication of The Wild Rose Press, Inc.
For other wonderful stories of romance,
please visit our on-line bookstore at
www.thewildrosepress.com.

For questions or more information
contact us at
info@thewildrosepress.com.

The Wild Rose Press, Inc.
www.thewildrosepress.com

To visit with authors of
The Wild Rose Press, Inc.
join our yahoo loop at
http://groups.yahoo.com/group/thewildrosepress/

My grandma taught me a long time ago the key to going places where you don't belong is act like you belong where you're going. As I tried the doorknob, in spite of Grandma's lesson, I kept an ear out for snarling Dobermans just the same.

Well, what do you know, it wasn't locked. No guard dogs, no audible alarms, no S.W.A.T. team rappelling from the roof...That sure seemed like an all-systems-go to me. I did one last quick glance around before I reached the point of no return.

Oh, who was I kidding? I'd reached that point the second I spotted the sign.

"Hellooo," I called as I poked my head into the foyer. I heard scraping and a couple of muffled thumps, the hurried patter of footsteps, and then nothing but silence.

"Hello?" I said again. "I'm Jen Flagg. I saw the sign out front. I've come to look at the house." More silence.

The hairs on my neck prickled a little and sent a wary, though no less disappointed, shiver down my spine. "If this is a bad time, I can come back."

"No, no, please come in," a pleasant voice invited just as I was about to retreat. "Your timing is perfect."

He sounded friendly enough, and eager, of course. I would imagine I'd sound eager and friendly too if I was the Realtor selling this place. His cheery demeanor was all it took to chase away my earlier moment of apprehension.

"I'm in the kitchen, straight down the main hall."

That sounded promising. The kitchen probably meant there'd be coffee, and maybe even cookies. The enticement of refreshments propelled me forward.

Praise for *MEDIUM RARE: DEAD MAN TALKING*

"Quirky, headstrong medium Jennifer Flagg hits the streets of Northwest Indiana in this humorous debut paranormal mystery series."

~Author Cheryl Dragon